HE L GOODNIGHT

BOOKS BY MICHAEL SCANLON

Where She Lies
The Child Before

HER LAST GOODNIGHT

MICHAEL SCANLON

Bookouture

Published by Bookouture in 2020

An imprint of Storyfire Ltd.
Carmelite House
50 Victoria Embankment
London EC4Y 0DZ

www.bookouture.com

ISBN: 978-1-83888-076-7
eBook ISBN: 978-1-83888-075-0

This book is dedicated to Terry McDonagh and the Pen and Ink Writers' Group, also to the memory of the late Louise Lawrence.

So, you leave the light on because you're scared of the dark.
I like that. Because now I can see you.

PROLOGUE

The rain plopped through the leaves, dripping down onto the old man's head, ebbing across his deeply creviced face to the tip of his chin and, finally, to the ground. But he didn't notice. He didn't notice anything, his mind too preoccupied replaying memories in crystal-sharp clarity, as if they were of yesterday. A gust of wind threw needles of cold against his skin. Old age had made his body feeble now, sensitive to chills. But he paid no notice to that either. It was the memories that tormented him. Memories of love and loss, and mostly of Emily Tuffy, the only woman he had ever loved… until now.

The older he became, the even clearer those memories seemed. Of the Lilac Ballroom, just outside Cross Beg, as real as if it were before his very eyes, its grey walls rising out of the boggy ground. Despite its pretty name, it had been an ugly building, with a high rectangular wall to the front, a long flat roof to the back and a row of small dirty windows all around. Nothing but a damp cavern, except on Saturday nights when it was transformed, when the crystal globes turned, reflecting the spotlights with cascades of twinkling orbs that shimmered across the mass of heaving, sweating bodies beneath. A thousand people or more filled the Lilac on those Saturday nights, and they travelled there by bus and car, bicycle and foot, in wind and rain, from every corner of the county.

But the Lilac Ballroom was nothing but a ruin now, the roof long since caved in, its walls covered in ivy and wild brambles.

Eddie sighed, and thought, *If only I could go back.*

He closed his eyes and imagined he saw her again. Emily Tuffy, standing on the opposite side of the hall. It was summertime, the ballroom like an oven. She wore a green summer dress, black shoes, the lights glinting on the silver buckles, and her hair held up with a single pin. He had been able to feel the heat beneath the fabric of her dress as they waltzed, his hand secure on her waist, lost in the moment he had waited for all week. It was only a matter of time before he would ask her to marry him. But Eddie was a cautious man, and first he had to be sure of his job at the meat plant, and that his father would sign over the farm as he'd promised. Then, when all was in order, and only then, would he ask.

He knew now, with the value of hindsight, he shouldn't have waited. That had been a mistake. Because he had lost her. She had gone to America, fed up with waiting. He should have asked, should have followed his heart, and trusted that everything would work out. *If only I could go back.*

But he could not go back. It was too late for that.

He shook his head, trying to untangle his jumbled-up thoughts. But now he had a second chance. Was it possible? The thought was enough to allow him a slight smile. He felt it in his pocket, reassuring himself with the touch of the small velvet-covered box. Once more he smiled. *A second chance?* Maybe. Just maybe, it was not too late.

Today he would not make the same mistake. Today he would take his chance. Today he would ask her – oh, what a beautiful creature she was – to be his wife. Yes, she was younger than he, by many years it must be said, but it could be *her* second chance too, to escape the misery of her life. No longer was he worried about getting a job in a meat plant, like he had when he'd been courting Emily. He had been prudent with money. Some even said he was rich. More than anything, he wanted to change her life, to make a difference, and he knew he could do it. He could do it, if given the chance. In return, all he wanted, for however long he had left on this earth, was an end to this terrible loneliness, to be able to share the love that was in his heart, to be able to bring happiness to another's life, and so add meaning to his own.

The wind stirred, bringing with it a memory. He and Emily had taken the bus to Clifden, eaten in the Café Continental, on the first floor of a building by the square, from where they could see the harbour and the sea beyond. They had eggs and sausages with a big pot of tea and thick slices of soda bread. Tourists were amongst the diners, the different languages spoken a reminder of the great world that existed beyond the horizon. She had told him then that he was the sweetest man in the whole wide world, the type of man any woman would want to spend her life with. 'You remember that time?' she said. 'When I was poorly and you came to see me. There was a terrible storm, but still you came. You brought leeks, carrots and mutton. You made it into a broth because I couldn't eat.'

She had leant over the table and kissed him full on the lips. He had loved her more than anything. He understood now that look on her face, her big brown eyes tender and questioning... *When?* It was the time, she was communicating to him, to ask her to marry him. He did not know it then, but he knew it now. He had made the mistake of thinking that Emily Tuffy would wait forever. She did not.

And it was then he heard it. He turned slightly, peering back over his shoulder, caught a fleeting glimpse of... something, long and black, moving fast through the air towards him, so fast. Like a bird, but without wings. Closer now, almost upon him... He closed his eyes, braced for the impact.

And he thought of Emily Tuffy, her pretty face, but no longer smiling, instead staring, a spectator, helpless, watching...

Whack!

He heard the dull sound and with it came the searing pain to his face and mouth. He made a short noise in response, a low, anguished *oommpph*. He crumpled to the ground, and there was a loud crack as his old hip broke in two, and with it a shooting pain so intense it momentarily overwhelmed the pain he felt in his face. He lay there, his left leg at a grotesque angle. But he did not make any other sound. He tried to, but nothing came from his shattered mouth.

His vision began to dim, the force of the blow to his face rupturing the minute blood vessels behind his eyes. But then he felt he could see it again, that black shape, moving towards him. Fast. So fast…

And once again he saw Emily Tuffy, her arms reaching for him.

Whack.

And again…

Whack.

And again…

Whack.

CHAPTER ONE

Detective Finnegan Beck was running. Literally. He had already partially completed one loop of the course he had set himself, which was from his house into Cross Beg, along by the river to where the street lighting ran out, then back again. One loop. Less than three miles. That was all. But already he was near to collapse. He stopped, doubling over, hands on knees, drawing air into his burning lungs with short, hollow gasps. This was too much to expect. To open an engine to full throttle when it had been cruising for so long. It was enough to blow a gasket, or at the least a heart valve.

He stayed bent over for a while, waiting for his pulse to settle, then straightened and moved his hands to his hips, closing his eyes, concentrating on each intake and exhale of breath. Trying to think of nothing. But the thoughts were forcing their way back in, along with them the mocking voices that had woken him at 3 a.m.

Finally, his breathing returned to a gentle rhythm, and he opened his eyes. His legs felt strangely hollow, and he was glad for the diversion this sensation gave him. He looked about. Of course, it would be too much to expect that a taxi might be passing at this early hour of the morning. It was. Beck started to walk back along Bridge Street, towards home. He had tried, and tomorrow he would try again. Who knows, he might manage to complete the entire loop.

A trickle of weak light was seeping from the thick grey sky. But was this enough, his early morning jogging, or was he fooling himself? He turned onto Main Street, the buildings ahead like cardboard cut-outs against the hazy light of the new day. A sudden sense of panic began to take hold, and he pushed back against it, telling himself to relax. He made his way along the deserted street, the sole actor on an empty stage. On either side, the trees along the pavements were draped in dresses of twinkling Christmas lights. By now his body should be cooling, but still he sweated.

Beck stopped. The world was silent and completely still, like a painting, and a feeling came to him that he was trapped, here, inside this scene, inside this painting. There was no escape.

Stop it, what's wrong with you?

But he knew the answer to that.

Are you trying to fool yourself?

Again.

Possibly.

Beck knew he was close to the edge.

Just then, the intermittent flashing of a blue light attracted his attention, shimmering across the facades of the buildings, reflecting on the damp street. He heard the snarl of an engine in high gear and looked back along Main Street, saw a patrol car approaching at speed the wrong way along the one-way thoroughfare. As it continued he stepped into the road, stood there, motionless. The car was mere feet from him when it screeched to a halt. The driver's window wound down. A head emerged, that of Garda Fergal Dempsey.

'Boss. Jesus. I could have hit you. What're you standing there in the middle of the road like that for? Seriously, I could have run you over.'

Beck's adrenaline rush began to subside, and he walked to the rear door and yanked it open, got into the car, leant forward.

'Get on with it, Dempsey… I presume this is a real emergency, at this hour?'

'Of course, boss,' Dempsey said, stabbing the accelerator. 'At this hour, ya.'

Beck gripped the front seats tight to stop himself from falling back as the car took off.

There was that particular patrol-car smell, of leather and sweat, mixed in now with the faint aroma of stale sick. Beck didn't recognise the other officer in the passenger seat – which was not a surprise. Cross Beg was a staging post, a short-term stop on the transfer totem pole. No one came here unless they had to. Like him.

'Just got the call,' Dempsey said. 'Postman, name of Jamie McLoughlin, says he found a body. Blood everywhere, is the way he described it.'

Beck shivered, the sweat finally beginning to dry into an icy balm on his flesh. Why was it that patrol cars were incapable of warmth? Either metaphysical or actual? Did they purposely interfere with the heaters at the central depot when the cars were delivered from the manufacturer? Which, Beck had to admit, might not be such a bad idea, when you thought about it.

'Address?'

'Corish. It's a townland. Left turn just before the pub, Mullaney's. The property is at the end of the track from the main road, about three quarters of a mile in. The postman says he'll be waiting for us in his van at the side of the road.'

They went through a red light at the end of Main Street and swung onto the roundabout. Dempsey took the second exit and floored it, catching Beck unawares, flinging him back into his seat. Where he was content to stay. He didn't speak. If there was anything else he should know, they would have told him. He was just glad to have something else to think about, even if that something was a murder.

CHAPTER TWO

The postman was parked, as he'd said, at the side of the road near the pub. They picked him up and took him in the patrol car back to the scene. He was sitting now beside Beck in the rear of the car. Jamie McLoughlin was in his late twenties, a little on the chubby side. Beck tapped a finger on the back of the driver's seat, staring through the windscreen into the funnel of light from the headlamps, two red dots reflecting back at him.

'That's the dog,' the postman said, his voice an almost inaudible whisper. 'Eddie's sheepdog. Max.'

Beck was silent, his eyes raking over the illuminated shapes – the corner of a stone shed, the rusty bucket of a tractor, the edge of a patch of high grass along the side of the gravelled yard – finally settling on the dark shape on the ground containing the two red reflectors, next to which was another dark shape, this one more substantial: the body of Edward Kavanagh.

'He was howling. The dog that is,' the postman said, like he was in a trance. 'That's what got my attention. So I walked over. *Jesus.*'

Beck opened the door. 'Stay here,' he said, getting out. The cold air stung his skin. The squad car was parked before the metal grating between two gate posts that marked the entry to the farmyard.

He crossed the cattle grating, stepping from one rung to the next along the edge, began walking towards the reflected dots of the dog's eyes, making them his reference points, the gravel crunching beneath his trainers. As he drew closer he could distinguish the shape of the animal, noted its head rested on its crossed front paws, that its eyes were turned upward, peering at him. Beck stopped. He turned his gaze to the mound lying next to it, clearly definable now as an elderly man's body, covered in a layer of glistening frost, his arms flat by his sides. He noted immediately the positioning of one leg, as if the hip bone had been snapped out of its socket and tossed to one side, which in a way, maybe it had.

Dempsey got out of the car and Beck heard the crunching sound as he began walking towards him.

'Don't,' Beck called, his voice as sharp as the cold, still air.

Dempsey stopped abruptly and looked at him.

'I wasn't going to,' he said, crouching down. He made a clicking noise with his tongue. 'Here boy. Here boy. Come on, good dog.'

But the dog wouldn't move. It continued looking at them, its head on its crossed paws, its eyes pitiful.

Beck stepped a little closer, staring at the victim, noting now the halo of blood about his head. In the growing light it had taken on a viscous appearance, like a crimson oil slick. He noted the man's hair too. It hung down over one side of the face, the top half drenched in blood. He found himself thinking elderly males don't usually have hair like this man's. This hair was thick and full. Beck imagined, for some reason, the man probably wore it combed back normally. He concentrated on the front of the face. It was angled upward, as if the victim had been trying to see behind him. There had to be something back there, a piece of wood, a stone, to hold it in that pose. Beck could see the outline of the eye socket, pushing against the old, liver-spotted skin, like it would slice through at any moment. The new day still felt unsure of itself, the light hanging above the ground, as if not confident enough to fully settle. But coupled with the lights of the headlamps there was enough now for Beck to fully distinguish the bushy eyebrows, the almost translucent eyelashes. He allowed his gaze to wander, across the flash of frigid, grey dead skin – the dried blood smeared about it like the shadow of receding water at the edge of a tiny lake – to the eye socket, minus its eye, instead filled with a substance that had the appearance and consistency of watery porridge. Across the forehead was a long, deep laceration, but the slight upward angle of the head had ensured that the blood had flowed backward. The pool of it behind the head, he surmised, the result of an impression in the ground acting like a reservoir while the body bled out.

Beck stiffened. He stood there, rigid, bent slightly as if against the wind. He could see what he had not seen in all these years, what his mind had chosen to block, or at least, to obscure – what, no matter how hard he tried, had eluded him. But now, as he stared at the victim lying before him, the way the head was turned, looking back, as if searching for meaning, he saw it again: the face of his dead father.

He turned slowly, took an unsteady step forward and exhaled with a long, loud *whoosh*. He shook his head, as if trying to shake the image free, turned on his heel, his gaze taking a full sweep of the yard, focusing with such effort that it created a sensation like a thumb being pressed in on either side of his head, right next to his eyes. He told himself this was his only opportunity to see the scene as it was. At this moment. As the killer might have seen it too. While the body was where it had fallen, and everything was as it had been. His eyes scanned the farmyard, and he noticed a mismatch of fresh tyre prints across the frozen muddy surface, as well as two sets of footprints, one an animal's – the victim and his dog, most certainly. The victim, walking to his death. He glanced behind the body, across the grass, to a low hedge. Beck wondered at what lay beyond that. Had the killer come from that direction?

He looked at Dempsey. 'Back to the patrol car. This farmyard – all of it – is now a crime scene.'

CHAPTER THREE

Beck wanted to roar, something, anything to clear the image from his mind, to send it back to the frozen wastelands where it belonged. But it would not budge, and he watched as the image altered, like a camera zooming out, revealing the remainder of Edward's body, lying on the hard ground, in that same pose, the human equivalent of a swastika. With a subtle change here and there, that could be his father lying back there. And the image swept him along, taking him back to that time…

Beck's mother had played the piano. Played it so well, in fact, she had been invited to join the Connaught Regional Orchestra – long since disbanded – for their concert in the National Concert Hall in Dublin on one occasion. A review the following day, in no less than The Irish Times, *had called her performance a virtuoso. Afterwards, returning to her humdrum life in a small Irish town must have been difficult. His father didn't care much for music – he was strictly a football and horse racing man. Chalk and cheese really, the two of them. In fact, they had nothing in common; certainly, they should never have married.*

Beck remembered his father, always dressed either in his garda uniform, or his off-duty 'uniform', wool trousers and a plaid shirt.

His mother, on the other hand, always took great care in her dress. She had worn slim-fitting pants before any woman in the town had, and her clothes were always colourful, her lips and nails always painted, and, no matter what the occasion, high heels were always worn, even if merely going to the shops.

It was as if she were making a statement: I'm better than this.

She was attracted to his father, he guessed, because here was a man with a steady disposition and, more importantly, a steady wage. Such things mattered back then. While the attraction for him, his father... well, that was obvious, she was beautiful and everything he was not.

His mother gave piano lessons most evenings in what she called the music room at the back of the house, the sound of tinkling piano keys played out of scale wafting from behind the closed door. All her students went on to become excellent players.

Beck remembered his parents never talked much, and when he was perhaps just five or six, they stopped talking to each other altogether. Instead, they communicated by passing notes to one another through either himself or his sister, Helen. It all seemed perfectly normal, even if it wasn't, of course.

One day Beck came home from school to find his mother sitting at the kitchen table in her dressing gown with the fake fur collar and cuffs. Footsteps sounded on the stairs, heavy steps, heavier than his father's, and Mr Donegan appeared in the kitchen doorway, dressed in a garish purple three-piece suit with a watch chain across the front. He owned a factory for the manufacture of plastic buckets and dustpans. Being a factory owner made Mr Donegan a high-flyer in the bird cage that was Newglass, the town where Beck came from. But Mr Donegan also had a great interest in music, and he sang in the town choir. They said his voice had the most beautiful tones. If he'd wanted, he could have been a professional tenor, that's what they said.

'Talk to you soon, Ann,' he said, smiling. A small man, a little on the heavy side, with a smiling face, a round head and closely cropped grey hair.

His mother smiled too, before looking to her son. Beck remembered her eyes lingered on him, as if trying to tell him something. He knew what that was, now. When his father came home from duty that evening, however, Beck just knew not to breathe a word about it.

CHAPTER FOUR

Superintendent Wilde emerged from his car and strode towards the gateway.

'Everything is as we found it,' Beck said.

'You were running?' Wilde asked, looking Beck over, taking in the tracksuit and trainers.

'Yes. Came straight here.'

'At this hour? One extreme to the next with you, isn't it?'

'I couldn't sleep. Woke up at 3 a.m., tossed and turned until half six, finally got up and went for a run. The postman starts his shift about then. The victim's house is among the first on his route.'

They were standing by one of the pillars. In the cold light of the new day the track from the main road was clearly visible. Also visible through the hedgerow and trees and across a field on his right, maybe a hundred yards distant, was the roofline of a house, a chimney at one end, smoke rising into the air.

Wilde followed his gaze. 'A neighbour?' the superintendent said.

Beck checked his watch. The assumption seemed obvious enough that it didn't require stating. It could hardly be anything else.

'I've only been here twenty minutes and it's just starting to get light,' Beck said. 'I don't know what's what, not as yet.'

Wilde was silent. He looked through the gateway, beyond the blue-and-white crime scene tape loosely tied across it.

'There's two other houses on this actual road,' Beck said. 'We took a witness statement from the postman who found the body. According to him, the victim is Edward Kavanagh, an elderly farmer, lives alone.'

Wilde nodded. 'Where's the postman now?'

'He's gone home. I spoke with his boss. We'll talk to him later, but not now, he's pretty shaken up.'

Wilde nodded again.

'Ballinasloe SOC will be here imminently,' Beck added. 'The Technical Bureau as soon as they can too. And a request has been made to district for more personnel.'

'So, how many we getting?'

'Four.'

Superintendent Wilde placed his hands in his pockets, began rocking back and forth on the balls of his feet.

'Motive: possibly robbery,' Beck said, 'but the scene appears relatively undisturbed, apart from the obvious that is.'

'You didn't check the house?' Wilde nodded in its direction.

'I think it's best we leave things exactly as they are. The less we interfere, the louder the scene might speak to forensics.'

'Jesus, you just think of that line, Beck? Are we sure there's no one in there?'

'I'm satisfied there isn't. We shone torches in from the field at the back. The house is empty.'

'A briefing,' Wilde said, 'will need to be organized ASAP.'

'Um…'

'Um… aren't you coming?'

'Why? That'll tie both of us up, won't it? I don't see the point, is what I'm saying. You choreograph and I dance, as it were.'

Wilde pursed his lips. 'You don't say,' Wilde said. 'Choreograph, eh? Quite the man for turns of phrases today too, aren't you?'

'Pulse will keep me informed.'

'I still want you there.'

Beck nodded, was about to speak, but Wilde pointed ahead.

'For Christ's sake,' he said. 'Someone get that bloody dog out of here.'

CHAPTER FIVE

A few moments later he saw Garda Claire Somers walking up the track from the main road with long sturdy strides, gait erect and confident, a condition Beck knew did not always apply. He thought to himself that Claire had a new vitality about her lately. She looked fresh too, like she'd shed an old skin and a new one had come glowing through. They hadn't worked together in a while. There was nothing to work on. No one was complaining about that. And never would. An Garda Síochána did not do performance targets.

'I left the car on the hard shoulder along the main road,' she said, pointing back the way she had come.

'Come on,' Beck said, heading down the track.

'What? I've only just got here.'

'There are two houses on this track,' he said as she caught him up and, pointing to the side, he added, 'while over there, on the next road along, there's another one. We need to go and pay a visit. But while we're waiting for the Technical Bureau, I need to get home and change out of these, have a shower – it won't take long. You can run me back?'

She nodded. 'Okay. No problem.'

He saw it when getting into the unmarked Focus, wedged between the seatbelt anchor and the driver's seat: a sergeant's exam test sample booklet. She pulled it out quickly as she sat in the driver's seat, sliding it underneath, not looking at him. She started the engine. As she did a U-turn, heading back into Cross Beg, Beck spoke.

'That's nothing to be embarrassed about.'

'What?'

He smiled, enjoying the light moment. 'The test booklet. What's the problem? Even I had to do it once, you know.'

She said nothing, continued to stare ahead, but he noticed her grip tighten on the steering wheel. They drove in silence. On the approach to Cross Beg, Beck turned and glanced out the window at the drab buildings, some with flower boxes of the summer past still hanging from their walls, the contents wizened and dead, and some with Christmas lights now behind their windows and doors.

'I've done it before.'

'What?' He turned from the window, looking at Claire.

'The sergeant's exam,' she said. 'I've done it before.'

'Well, no one gets it first time…'

'Except you. Did you think I didn't know? I do.'

'Okay, you know.'

'I've already failed once. Thought I'd breeze through. But I didn't. So let's just pretend you didn't see that book, that you know nothing about it.' She glanced at him, then back to the road. 'I don't want anyone knowing about this. I'll need a recommendation, of course, and an evaluation, one to ten. It's not for months yet, so there's plenty of time.'

They were almost at his house now.

'A mere formality,' Beck said. 'I'll look after it.'

The car slowed as she pulled in to the kerb.

Beck opened the door, was about to get out. Claire spoke. 'Thanks, Beck. Okay?'

He smiled. 'No worries.'

'I'll wait here.' She yanked the exam test booklet free, opened it, glanced to him again. 'Okay?'

'Of course.' He got out and was about to close the door.

'Have you something on your mind?' she asked quietly, before he did.

He paused. 'What do you mean?'

'I don't know. I get the feeling everything's... not right... with you. I could be wrong. Am I?'

He smiled then, closed the door, walked away. He hadn't answered her question.

CHAPTER SIX

Claire parked again on the road close to the crime scene, and they got out and began walking back along the track. They were approaching the other house now, which was on the right, while the victim's house was several hundred metres further on. They stopped by a low rusted gate; on the other side a moss-covered path led to a two-storey house. Beck went to open the gate, but saw that it was padlocked. He returned his gaze to the house, noted the grass sprouting over the tops of the eve runs, the weeds growing between the stone slabs on the pathway by the front door. He noticed the curtains on all the windows had been drawn shut. The house was empty, abandoned.

'Can I help you?'

Beck turned towards the sound. There was a man leaning over a low wall a little further along. They walked towards him. Behind the man was a small house, with glazed windows and a slated roof, but the white paint of its walls was fading. A council house, no doubt built to replace the crumbling wreck that had gone before. The man had white curly hair on either side of a head that was completely bald down its centre. He was dressed in a knitted V-neck jumper with an orange shirt underneath, buttoned to the neck and with wide lapels. A cigarette hung loose from the corner of his mouth.

'Everything alright up there?' he said when they reached him. 'I've never seen so many cops in my life.'

'And you are?' Claire asked.

'I could ask you the same question.'

Claire took out her ID card and offered it for inspection. The man peered at it.

'I'll take your word. I can't see much without my glasses.'

'We're investigating an incident,' Beck said.

A gust of wind blew the wide lapels of the man's shirt up.

'We won't be releasing any details,' Claire added, 'until we officially confirm the identity and the next of kin have been informed.'

'Next of kin,' the man said. 'So he's dead.' He nodded in the direction of the murder scene. 'It's Eddie, isn't it? He's the only one lives up there.'

They said nothing.

The colour drained from the man's face. 'Jesus.'

'A few questions,' Beck said, 'if you don't mind.'

'Your name?' Claire asked, but the man appeared not to have heard. 'Your name?' she repeated.

'What...? Oh, Dermot Healy.'

She flicked her notebook open and wrote it down.

'Did you notice anything odd,' Beck asked, 'in the last twenty-four hours or so?'

'No.'

'Really?' Beck said.

'You don't believe me?' The man held Beck's gaze.

'How well did you know Eddie Kavanagh?' Claire asked.

Dermot Healy looked past her, said nothing for a moment, then: 'I knew Eddie all my life.' And, shaking his head, he added, 'No nicer man on God's green earth. A gentleman. A true gentleman.' He blessed himself. 'Oh, the Lord save us. *Eddie.*'

'You were friends?' Beck asked.

Healy's eyes narrowed. 'Of course. Me and Eddie were the best of friends... Why're you asking me all this?'

'What we want to know,' Claire said, 'is did he have any enemies?'

'Well, I wasn't one,' Healy answered. 'Or anyone else. Eddie was popular, well liked. By everyone. And I mean everyone. You won't hear a bad word said about him. He was the first to your door if ever you needed help and the last to leave again. He spent two days one time cutting crotchety old Ned Tierney's hay when Tierney broke his arm. Tierney's long since dead now, of course. Eddie did the cutting with the scythe, so it was hard work. He had plenty of his own hay to cut, so he had, but that was Eddie. Do you understand? That was the kind of man he was.'

Beck pointed. 'There's another house,' he said, nodding vaguely. 'Over beyond. I saw it earlier. Can't see it now though, it's hidden behind those trees.'

'That's Tommy's. Eddie's brother's place. You'll have to go out onto the main road to get to it. It's the next left. A dead-end road as well, just like this place. He's the only one living on it... You been up to talk to him yet?'

Claire looked at Beck. 'He may not have heard.'

'He won't,' Healy said. 'With the trees and everything, might as well be at the other end of the county.'

Beck glanced behind Healy's house towards the hedgerow. 'Thank you, Mr Healy... for now.'

'Means you'll be back again soon, does it?'

'Probably,' Beck said, turning, looking along the track. 'By the way.' He stretched an arm and pointed. 'Those, I've been noticing them, all along the ditch there, by the edge of the road. Tyre tracks. Something big pass up here recently?'

Healy's eyes shifted to follow Beck's outstretched hand, then back again.

'It wasn't that big,' he said. 'The road is narrow, as you can see. A van from the co-op in Mylestown. Delivery of animal feed. So what?'

'Thank you,' Beck said, not elaborating. But still, he felt sure. Dermot Healy was lying.

CHAPTER SEVEN

It was a pretty stonewashed cottage, neat, with a black slate roof, the track leading to it unlike that leading to the murder scene, freshly gravelled, the edges trimmed back. It ended in a yard of cobblestones, weed free, bordered by neat hedges. On a raised, gravel-filled section to the left of the house was an antique wooden cart wheel, painted orange with a black metal centre.

Secrets...

The door of the house opened and a man emerged, stood on the threshold looking at them. He was tall and gangly, with a mop of white hair, dressed neatly in a navy sports jacket, check shirt and brown corduroy pants.

'Mr Tommy Kavanagh?' Beck said, stopping by the door.

The man observed him silently, his eyes lingering, then turned to Claire. 'That's right,' he said.

'Detective Inspector Beck. Detective Garda Somers.'

'I recognise you,' the man said, smiling at Claire. 'Saw you at Cross Beg Garda Station one time, when I was renewing my gun licence. I've a good memory for faces.'

'Can we come in?' Beck asked.

'Why?' A change to the tone. 'Has something happened?'

'It's your brother, Mr Kavanagh,' Claire said.

'Eddie. What about him?'

'I'm sorry to have to tell you this,' she said. 'He's dead.'

'Dead?' The old man was motionless, staring at them.

'I'm sorry,' Claire said again.

The old man slumped back against the door, and the skin on his face seemed to sag as Beck reached out, holding him by the arm, as he said softly, 'Let's go inside, Tommy, there's a good man.'

'No, I want to see Eddie. Please. I want to see him.'

'Soon, Tommy, soon. Not now.'

The old man looked at Beck, as if seeing him for the first time, but he nodded slowly and turned, began shuffling back into the house. They followed him into a large room. There was no hallway. A door was in the corner, but this one large room seemed to take up the entire single-storey property. Beck noted an old Jubilee range, and a high, narrow cupboard against one wall by the sink. A long wooden table was in the centre of the room and a TV further along, with a couple of stuffed fabric armchairs in front. Next to Beck was a shelf of cowboy paperback books. He glanced at them as he passed, and suddenly remembered. His father had liked cowboy books – *The Virginian, Shane, True Grit.*

He spotted a copy of *The Virginian,* and felt a sudden sadness.

'Beck, are you alright?' It was Claire, her voice a whisper.

He realised he'd stopped, was staring at the books. He turned and looked about.

'Yes, yes,' he mumbled.

The house was very warm. Next to the Jubilee range was a pair of wellington boots on top of the pages of a tabloid newspaper.

A shuffling sound and a flurry of movement snapped Beck from his thoughts. Just in time, he coiled his arm around the old man's waist as he attempted to barge past. Tommy Kavanagh pushed, but his attempts were feeble. 'Please let me see Eddie. Pleeease…' And Beck could smell the aroma of peat and Brylcreem as the old man slumped against him and began to cry. Beck nudged Tommy Kavanagh gently towards the wooden table and sat him down. He took the chair one side of him, Claire the other. The old man leant forward onto his elbows, began rubbing his hands across his face.

'I appreciate this is quite a shock,' Beck began.

The old man took his hands from his face, and looked at each of them in turn, before placing the hands, palms down, onto the table. There was no sound, only that of his breathing. Claire threw a look to Beck, then spoke.

'We need to ask you some questions.'

Tommy Kavanagh said nothing, just stared at his hands. Then he looked up.

'How did he die? Tell me that.'

'It appears...' Claire said. 'He was... beaten to death.'

She shot another look at Beck.

'Oh, dear God,' the old man said, lowering his head again. 'Oh, dear God. My poor brother Eddie. How could that be?' His whole body shook for a time, before he looked up once more, and his eyes were red and every line on his craggy face was chiselled rough and deep. He said nothing, just looked at them.

'Can you tell us about your brother?' Claire said. 'Was there anyone you can think of who may have wished him harm? I have to ask. Anyone at all, Tommy?'

The old man squeezed his eyes shut again as his chest rose and he breathed in deep. He opened them and exhaled.

'No,' he said, his voice low. 'No. No. No.'

Beck placed a hand onto his shoulder, held it there gently.

The old man fell silent again, looking at Beck, staring into his eyes, searching through them, as if desperate to reach somewhere beyond. 'It's quiet around here,' he said, as if to himself. 'So quiet, nothing ever happens, nothing...'

Beck nodded, and knew that grief often came in waves, in the initial stages especially.

'You can talk to me, Tommy,' Beck said gently. 'You can talk to me.'

The silence settled and lingered before the old man began to speak. His expression told Beck he was going back, dismissing death, seeking comfort in memories.

'We've lived here all our lives, you know, myself and Eddie. Here, in this parish. Agnes, our sister, she's a nun, a Sister of Mercy up in Dublin. After she left, there was just the two of us.' He paused, a faraway look in his eyes, but just as quickly it was gone again. 'Eddie did a bit of farming, and he worked for years in the meat factory until it closed down. He was left the farm you see, because he was the eldest, and I did up this house here, nothing but an old ruin back then so it was.' He forced a smile, a tribute to happy memories. But nothing would ever be the same again. 'I even did up an old cart wheel – can't get those any more, it's over a hundred years old. You saw it out front, didn't you?'

The two detectives nodded.

'That's how it was,' Tommy Kavanagh said. 'There was just the two of us. We led simple lives.'

Beck saw the shadow pass across his face, knew that the terrible reality of what had happened was settling on him once more.

'Tell me about Eddie,' Beck said, trying to delay it, with a smile, a signpost to those happy memories again. It appeared to work, because a smile came from Tommy in return. A weak smile, but a smile nonetheless.

'He was one of life's gentlemen, my brother was… You know, when we were children at school, there was always a bully… but Eddie never got bullied. And he stood up for me. That's the thing…' His eyes widened. 'Everybody liked Eddie. No. They loved him.'

'Did either of you ever marry?' Claire asked.

Tommy Kavanagh seemed surprised by the question. He sat motionless, his expression changing to one of confusion, then he gave a hollow, sad laugh.

'No. I never married. Neither did Eddie. Mind you, he came closer to it than I ever did. Though that was years ago. Anyway, most men around here never married back then. There weren't many women to marry for a start. The women had left, most of them that is, and those that remained, those with jobs, the nurses and teachers and the like – well, what did we have to offer them? Nothing, that's what, except a life of drudgery scraping by on a few stony acres to survive. Don't forget, women in those days had to give up their government jobs when they married. It was the law. So nah, we never married. The only other option for a woman was to join the nuns. That's just the way it was. Agnes, our sister, that's what she did too, joined the nuns. There was nothing here for any of them.' A dark, distant look came over his face then. 'Nothing but loneliness and memories of times past. I never left. I should have, looking back, I know that now. But I didn't. I suppose I wasn't brave enough.'

Beck observed this old man, could almost feel the sense of self-loathing and melancholy from him.

'By the way,' Beck said. 'Just wondering. Did you get a delivery of animal feed of any description recently?'

'Animal feed?' came the surprised response. 'I don't have any animals that I'd need feed for.'

Beck nodded.

'Victim Support will be in contact,' Claire said. 'Would you like that?'

'To talk to, is that it?'

'Yes,' Claire said. 'To talk to.'

The old man nodded. 'Yes. I'd like that.' And his voice began to crack as he repeated, 'I'd like that very much.' But then the wave of grief consumed him and he began to cry again. 'Oh God. Eddie. My only brother… Lord save us. Eddie.' And, shaking his head, he muttered. 'Oh God. Oh God. Oh God.'

They made their way back along the track from Tommy Kavanagh's place. Beck and Claire had waited with him until he had told them he was fine, that he wished to be left alone to pray for his brother's soul. It was only then that they left. The cold winter sun pierced through the clouds, unexpectedly bright, intense and frigid. Beck could see his breath puff from his nostrils each time he exhaled.

'Victim Support should be with him soon,' Claire said, and added, 'Tell me. What's all this about animal feed?'

'What, haven't you noticed?'

'Noticed?'

'You know,' he said. 'Your exam booklet says that you will be asked to provide at least one example of a unique insight you brought to a case. This is your chance.'

Claire lapsed into silence.

'Unique?' she repeated.

'Yes. Can you think of anything?'

The silence lingered. Finally, Beck stopped, and pointed. 'These. Didn't you notice? I didn't either, not at first.'

'What?'

'Tyre marks. Double. From a twin-wheeled vehicle. Wide enough to take up almost the entire track. It's at every place we've visited. I don't believe in coincidences.'

'You heard him. Animal feed.'

'Animal feed indeed,' Beck said. 'I haven't seen any animals, have you? My advice, unless proven otherwise, is to assume that everyone is telling us lies, even Tommy there. But the manual won't tell you that. We need to get to Mylestown. I'll consult the oracle on the way.'

'The oracle?'

When they got back to the car, Beck took the State phone from its cradle in the central console and pressed the yellow button to connect him to the Pulse Operations Centre in Castlebar. His call was answered on the second ring.

'Background checks, please,' he told the operator. 'Stand by for details…'

'Full house,' he said to Claire when he'd finished and was putting the phone away. 'They're all known to the police: Eddie Kavanagh, Tommy Kavanagh, Dermot Healy.'

'Gun licences?' Claire said.

'Yes.'

'Don't get too excited, Beck. You're in the sticks now. Gun licence holders are automatically logged. No surprises there.'

'But I haven't finished.'

'Sorry.'

'Eddie Kavanagh, our victim, handed in his Penno shotgun for destruction two years ago, said he was too old to look after it. But Tommy Kavanagh still has a current licence, for a double-barrel. And…'

'And?'

'Dermot Healy, he had a licence for a Soltz .22 calibre rifle…'

'Had? So? A firearm isn't involved in this.'

'His licence was revoked. Way back in 2004. And the weapon was seized, has never been returned. The reason, I'm getting to my point now, Claire, is – listen up – because sometimes you have to poke about in the leaves with a stick to find an answer. He'd threatened to shoot somebody with it. Dead. You'll never guess who?'

'Um… Eddie Kavanagh?'

'Duly noted. You're correct, of course.'

They passed a roadside sign, one leg buckled like something had crashed into it: Mylestown.

But Beck was thinking of Dermot Healy. Why hadn't he mentioned that?

Animal feed indeed.

CHAPTER EIGHT

Secrets: something kept unknown or unseen by others.

They say Beck's father did not know. After all, who was going to tell him? It was possible – indeed it was likely – Beck also recognised, that even in a small town, a secret might remain hidden from the one who was gossiped about. His father had been a policeman too, so would have known everything – supposedly – but he did not know that. Surely, however, someone had thrown it in his face? Beck considered it more likely that he just did not want to know.

Robert Beck's wife was having an affair with a man of the dulcet tones. An affair that lasted for years. The whole of the rest of the town knew, and it feasted on the gossip.

CHAPTER NINE

The village of Mylestown was really one very long and very wide street, with nothing behind the buildings on either side of it but fields and bog land. It seemed to strive to project an image of grandeur that it didn't possess. In the centre of the village was a small green area with a wooden bench seat. There was a sign there, detailing the village's history, and that it had been built by Viscount Daniel Aldair in the mid eighteenth century from a blueprint. The ambition of the viscount was to recreate a miniature version of the Ringstrasse in Vienna, a suitable place upon which for him to gaze as he passed through from his estate in his gilded carriage. The buildings were indeed impressive, constructed of limestone and granite, some with bevels and gargoyles, others with turrets and red-brick surrounds on their windows and doors. The illusion of European grandeur reminded Beck of a movie set, built in the bogs of southeast Galway. Mylestown stood now looking for the most part faded, its buildings cold and decrepit and practically empty. The place was grey and dismal, as if the surrounding harsh landscape had sucked the life and colour out of it, leaving nothing but its husk behind.

At the end of the street was the Mylestown District Farmers' Cooperative. It occupied one of those old drab buildings, in this case a box-like three-storey structure. The cooperative had occupied the ground floor since 1952, and from then, time had stood still. The two floors above it may as well not have existed; the rows of windows had turned opaque from a decades-old culmination of grime, dust and dead flies.

They parked the car against the kerb outside. Beck could see two huge bay windows on either side of a narrow door at the end of a recess. The windows were crammed with everything from boxes of cutlery to electric heaters and an upright wheelbarrow. They crossed the pavement and went into the building. The floor was bare concrete and just inside the door was a long, dark wooden counter running the length of one wall. Small knots of men, customers he presumed, stood by that counter, dressed in anoraks and dark overcoats, dirty boots and wellingtons. All seemed to be wearing woolly hats. From the high ceiling hung a series of fluorescent lights, but not enough to fill the vast space, the edges lost to gloomy shadow. Two men, middle-aged, in drab blue overalls, moved about behind the counter. They moved slowly, like nothing was ever going to force them to hurry up. One – he was very skinny and tall – stretched to a box high on a shelf like a sloth reaching for the branch of a tree.

Once Beck and Claire had passed through the doorway, several pairs of eyes were upon them. They went to the counter and stood there, blissfully ignored. After a long moment, Beck knocked on the counter with two sharp raps of his knuckles. Business knocks. The very tall one, the sloth, was filling in a receipt. He glanced up, then down again, using his pen to slowly push items one at a time towards the customer standing before him, ticking the items off the receipt. Then he also pushed the receipt towards the man and straightened up, turning towards Beck, raising both eyebrows.

'Guards,' Beck said. 'I need to talk to somebody.'

The man walked over to them. 'Guards,' he said, in a smirking tone.

'Just a quick question about your animal feed,' Beck said. 'Perhaps you could enlighten me about your delivery schedule over the past few days?'

The sloth stared at Beck for a moment, and Beck held his gaze.

'Delivery schedule,' he said then, looking around. 'A *delivery* schedule, is it? Well, excuse me.' He stretched himself to full height, added, 'We don't have delivery schedules around here, *guard*, or any other schedule.' He craned his head to the side. 'We have feck all around here, isn't that right boys?'

'Aye,' an old man said, placing three rat traps onto the counter. 'And rats. Plenty of rats.'

A chorus of laughter rose, sharp and pointed.

'Now that you have that off your chest,' Beck said, fumbling for his wallet, finding it and opening it at the ID pocket, holding it out. 'The purpose of our visit. We're investigating a murder. The victim was found early this morning, not far from here actually, just outside Cross Beg.'

That got everybody's attention. Beck could see the room collectively stiffen. And it fell silent, faces blank. He wondered at the odds of the killer being one of those present, looking at him right now.

'Who?' someone asked.

'Eddie – Edward – Kavanagh. Of Corish. It's unofficial, but we're certain that's who it is.'

The room broke out into loud muttering.

Beck held up a hand, and turned to the sloth. 'Now, I wouldn't ask if it wasn't important. So I will repeat: delivery of animal feed. Tell me.'

The man shook his head a number of times in quick succession, as if trying to shake something out of it.

'Animal feed,' he said, levelling his gaze onto Beck. Beck could tell the fight had gone out of him. 'Animal feed. No. We don't deliver animal feed. Well, we do – we could – but who's going to bother? Not with the ten euro delivery fee, and the two days' notice we require. No, people throw their nuts or pellets or whatever it is into the buckets of their tractors or the backs of their pickups or the boots of their cars. No one pays to have animal feed delivered.

Fertiliser maybe, that's ordered by the tonne, but it's wintertime now, no need for it. Now, how did poor Eddie die?'

Beck ignored him.

'I'd like to ask you all,' he said, turning his attention to the room. 'Anyone here know who might want to harm Eddie Kavanagh? Anyone you can think of at all? Anyone? If you don't feel comfortable talking to us here, you can contact Cross Beg Garda Station confidentially, speak to any officer, or myself. My name is Detective Inspector Finnegan Beck. And this is my colleague, Detective Garda Claire Somers.'

'Are you sure it's Eddie Kavanagh we're talking about?' A man in a long oilskin coat asked. He was standing a few feet away from Beck. 'The gentlest soul you could ever meet. I mean, who would want to do any harm to Eddie? Are you sure that it's him? I was only talking to Eddie the other day.'

'I wouldn't say it otherwise,' Beck said.

'But still,' the man pressed. 'Jeez, he was telling me how much he was looking forward to the midnight mass at Christmas. That he'd say a prayer for me, because I just had a bypass, you see. Always thinking of others was Eddie.' The man shook his head. 'Ah, that's just not fair, so it's not. Not fair.'

No one spoke.

Beck glanced at the sloth. 'You asked me how he died. The answer is, he was beaten, bludgeoned to death, that's how.' He looked back to the room, just as hands rose to cover open mouths. 'Again, if anyone has information – any information at all – contact us, please. Look on it as your civic duty.' He paused, allowing his words to percolate through the room. 'That's all for now. Thank you for your attention.'

He lit a cigarette when they were outside and took a long draw. He was trying to cut down – again. He tried to remember if this was his first or second of the day, then realising it was his fourth, thought: *Damn.*

'Right,' he said, tetchy. 'Mr Dermot Healy. He has a bit of explaining to do.'

Healy was chewing on something when he came to the door.

'A word?' Beck said, dispensing with formalities.

Healy stared at them, caught off guard. Beck could almost hear the cogs turning. His eyes narrowed like those of a suspicious fox.

'Yes? And what's it this time?'

'Like I say. We need a word, need to ask you a few questions, Mr Healy.'

'Mr Healy, eh?' He nodded slowly once, before turning. 'Better come in then.'

They followed him along a short hall into a kitchen. There was nothing here but the bare essentials: a three-ring electric cooker, fridge, a glass-fronted cupboard with a couple of cups and plates inside, and an electric kettle beside the sink. It was icy cold. A used teabag rested in a saucer on the draining board, like it was ready to be used again. Healy crossed the linoleum-covered floor and sat on a rickety chair at a large, white plastic table, the type used in gardens on a summer's day. He looked up at them. There was one other rickety chair on the other side of the table. Beck knew of interrogation rooms with more comfort than this place. He went to the sink and leant over it, placing both hands on the windowsill and peering out through the smeared glass; condensation clung to the edges. He could see a stack of used tyres rising from the wild grass in the back garden, and the base of an old settee with the springs poking out of it, other debris scattered about.

'Make yourself at home, why don't you?' Healy muttered, but loud enough for him to hear.

Beck turned. Claire was sitting at the table in the other chair now. Beck looked slowly about the room again, but everything that there was to see he'd already observed at first glance.

'Secrets…' he said. Beck turned and leant back against the sink, looking at Healy. He noticed he had a very high forehead, and the angle where it folded onto the scalp was sharp, like a precipice above his eyebrows.

Healy's eyes narrowed again. 'Sure, who doesn't have those?'

Beck said nothing.

'You mean secrets in Cross Beg, like?' Healy added. 'Sure that town is full of those.'

'No,' Beck said. 'I mean your secrets.'

Stupid but not stupid, Beck considered. Healy, he observed, seemed like the kind of man who could survive lost in the wilds of Connemara, would know what to do, what to trap and how to skin and eat it, how to light a fire from the sparks of two stones. Beck, on the other hand, would be dead within the week.

'My secrets?' His face folded into false surprise.

'Come on there now, Dermot.' It was Claire. 'Did you think we wouldn't find out? Jesus, give us a break, will ya? Good man.'

'We went to Mylestown,' Beck said. 'The co-op. They don't deliver animal feed, as you well know. You must take us for right eejits.'

Maybe not so clever after all.

Healy held the false look of surprise for a moment longer. Then his hands fell by his sides and his head dropped onto his chest.

'Aw, alright…' he said.

'And the rifle,' Claire said. 'You know? The one seized from you.'

'Aw, alright…' he said again.

'That you threatened Eddie Kavanagh with,' Beck added. 'Where would you like to begin, Mr Healy?'

'I didn't really threaten him. It was all a… a misunderstanding. Yes, a misunderstanding. But the guards didn't see it like that at the time. No, because a firearm was involved. Some firearm, it was an auld yoke I'd had for years, an auld rifle. And Eddie didn't press charges. The two of us would have forgotten all about it. But the guards didn't see it like that. So yes, my rifle was taken off of me, and the place has been plagued with magpies and mink ever since, not to mention the feckin' foxes, and the rats, and the travellers…'

'You would say that, wouldn't you?' Beck said. 'Fact is, you did threaten him. And he was concerned enough to report it at the time, was he not?'

A long, low, croaking noise came from Healy's throat. Then he looked up at Beck. 'You smoke? I could do with a smoke.'

Beck took out his pack and flipped the top, fished out two cigarettes and offered one to Healy. He took it and placed it in his mouth. Beck lit them both up from his lighter. They smoked silently before Healy spoke.

'Look, I was an evil bastard back then. That's twenty years ago now, give or take. The drink, you know, it doesn't suit me. So I don't do it any more… You know what I mean…'

Beck's gaze shifted. He was unsure if this was a question or a statement, so he ignored it.

'The queer stuff,' Healy added. 'Poitín. It was all I could afford. Stuff drove me half crazy, so it did. That's how I pulled the gun on Eddie. I don't even know what it was about. I got it into my head he'd pulled some stroke on me, a fast one, but I didn't know what. So I went round there one night and I told him I'd blow his head off if he didn't…'

Healy held the cigarette between two stubby fingers by his mouth. The smoke curled up into his face. It didn't seem to bother him. Then he lowered the cigarette and looked at Beck.

'If he didn't… if he didn't… I couldn't even remember what the hell I was so worked up about. I didn't know why I was even there. I was standing with me gob open, pointing the rifle at his head. I was a nutcase, that's what I was, and right then, I knew it.'

'Tell me,' Beck said. 'Was the weapon – the rifle – loaded?'

Healy exhaled a long stream of smoke, looked up at Beck, his eyes widening.

'Well ya, of course it was loaded.'

'Interesting,' Beck said. 'That you remember that much. And had the presence of mind to put the rounds in.'

'Presence of mind,' Healy said with a start. 'I wouldn't call it that. It's not that I had the presence of mind for anything. Back in those days, before I knew better, the rifle was always loaded, so it was. What's the point in having it if it's not? I had to be ready, so I had. You never know who's going to call to your door out here in the country. You need some protection… Well, don't you?'

'Whatever,' Beck said. 'But you can't be surprised to know this has placed you on our radar. The fact you threatened to blow his head off. I don't care how long ago it was. Because now that person is dead.'

'I never really threatened him,' Healy said, the fox's gleam back again. 'Didn't you hear what I just said? I wasn't thinking straight, I didn't know what I was doing there.'

'Spare me,' Beck said with a sigh. 'Don't *you* get it? Pointing a gun at a man's head is threatening, for Christ's sake.'

'And now,' Claire said, her voice in the lower register, calming matters, 'why did you lie about having animal feed delivered? Can you explain that?'

Healy fell silent again. He took another draw on the cigarette. It was down to the filter now. Then he flicked it and it tumbled through the air and landed in the sink.

'Well, you're going to find out either way, aren't you, I suppose?'

'We're going to find out what?' Beck asked, putting his voice in the lower register too.

Healy rubbed two stubby hands across his face a couple of times.

Both detectives stared, waiting.

'How can I explain this?' Healy began. As he spoke, he gestured with his hands, underlining certain words with a pointed finger sliced through the air. He had his legs loosely crossed. His eyes had lost their caginess; instead they sought understanding. 'It came one day and parked out on the road there.' Healy nodded towards the kitchen door. 'There was a man behind the wheel. He wasn't local, let me put it like that…'

'You mean he was from another town?' Beck said.

'No, I mean another country. He was a foreigner. That's what I mean.'

'Go on,' Beck said.

'Anyway… he parked out there on the roadway, in a van. I went out and down to the gate, stood there looking at him. "Good day," he says. I didn't know what to make of him. He was a shifty-looking character. I thought he was selling something. And he was. He was selling something. But something I didn't expect. Never would expect.

'Anyway, I didn't say anything. I was just standing there like, waiting, curious, for whatever spiel he was going to give me. Sure, what else had I for doing? Nothing. Just biding me time, that's all. Y'know, sometimes I don't see a living soul out here from one day to the next… now, where was I? Oh yes, I'm standing there watching him. And he gets out of the van. I'm wary of him, watching him the whole time, saying nothing. He spots it too, so he does. He says, "It's okay, brother. I come in peace. I have something special for you, very special."'

He paused, a flush of colour coming to his cheeks. When he spoke again, Beck could hear a slight timbre of excitement in his voice.

'He tells me it's eighty euro. I say, "What's eighty euro?" and he says, "The girl is eighty euro," and I say "What girl?" and he says, "Come, look, brother," and he waves his arm at me to come out beyond the gate. So I come out beyond the gate, and I follow him down the side of the van – by the way, it wasn't like a normal van, it was what you call a camper van – and he pulled the door back and he says, "Have a look, brother," and I was really curious now so I leant in for a gander – careful now, keeping one eye on him too because I didn't know what he was up to, and holy God…'

Dermot Healy looked at them each in turn. 'You'll never guess…?'

They waited.

'No,' Beck said. 'You're right. We'll never guess.'

'It was a woman! A beautiful young woman.'

'And what? What was she doing?' It was Claire.

'Nothing. Just lying there. In the bed. In the camper van. Eighty euro.'

CHAPTER TEN

'Where the hell have you been? I've been ringing.'

Superintendent Wilde was leaning against the gatepost, the crime scene tape that had been tied across it cut at one end and hanging limply to the ground. Beck patted his jacket pockets, remembering his phone was still in the car.

He said nothing for a moment, then: 'The Technical Bureau still not arrived?'

'Just the local boys,' Wilde answered, nodding towards the small van parked by the victim's house.

It was to do with economies of scale, Beck knew. Because Ireland was a small, sparsely populated country, all specialist services were based at Garda HQ in Dublin. It meant now that they had to wait.

'Your pal won't be coming, apparently,' Wilde added. 'Dr Gumbell. He's abroad. Budapest I hear. A conference, on new autopsy techniques or something. Can't say I'll miss the gruff bastard.'

'Ever hear of a travelling brothel?'

'Have I heard you correctly?'

'Yes,' Beck said. 'Dermot Healy, the neighbour just down the road there, says it does the rounds, like an ice cream van, but without the tinkling music... I noticed tyre marks, double-wheeled, at the scene here, and at other locations we visited.'

'Did you now? Good work, Beck.'

'What's more, he'd threatened our victim in the past, with a rifle.'

Wilde gave him a sideways glance. 'Who? This Healy character?'

'Yes.'

Beck watched as a forensic officer emerged from the doorway of the house.

'Did he now?' Wilde said again, his voice softening. 'By the way. How do you like your new office?'

'My new office?' Beck took a moment to consider what he was being asked. In the little over a year he'd been in Cross Beg, he'd been desk surfing. 'It's not new. It's over one hundred and fifty years old.'

'Ah, Christ. You know what I mean.'

'It's an improvement, that's what I'll say. But it doesn't matter, because…'

'Yes yes, I know, you're only passing through.' Wilde finished the sentence for him. 'You're like a broken record, you know that? Anyway, you need to get that out of your head. Once and for all. I was going to tell you about it later, but no time like the present, I suppose.'

'What do you mean?'

'Your transfer back to Dublin, Beck. It's been denied. There. Okay? You're going nowhere. You're stuck here. Sorry.'

Beck stood motionless, impassive. 'In this shitehole? You can't be serious?'

'Unfortunately, I am. Anyway, it's not so bad. Not really. If you could change your damn attitude a little it might help. You'd see there's many benefits to living in a small town like this. You're from a small town yourself, aren't you? I'm getting to know you now, Beck. You may not think it, but you're too set in your ways. It's Dublin or nothing with you, isn't it? The big city.'

'Why?' Beck said.

'I don't know,' Wilde replied. 'Why does anyone become set in their ways?'

'No. I mean why has my transfer been denied?'

'Oh,' Wilde said. He observed Beck for a long time. Then: 'Now you're treating *me* like a fool. You know what the answer to that is yourself.'

'Chief Superintendent Gallagher...' Beck said, but more to himself.

'Yes. Chief Superintendent Gallagher,' Wilde replied. 'No secret, you know. Can't keep a secret in an organisation like this. You can't have an affair with the chief super's wife, Beck, and not expect to be found out. Natalia. That's her name, isn't it?'

Beck was stony-faced.

'Yes,' Wilde said. 'That is her name. What's the man supposed to do? Say, "I think it's a good idea if you come on back and spend some more time with my wife, yes, that sounds like a great idea to me"? I don't think so.' Wilde took a deep breath and rubbed his chin. 'Look. Why don't you find yourself a nice unattached woman? They're out there. Before you get too old. Settle down. Buy yourself a house here in Cross Beg. Property prices are great. Messing with another man's wife is never a good idea, now is it, Beck?'

'Of course, of course,' Beck said. 'I mean, you're right. It's not.'

'Then why do you do it, for God's sake? Tell me that.'

'That's a really good question, but right now I can't think about it. You are right though. Really. I know it. And that's all I can say for now.'

'Hmm. Anyway, I need to organise a briefing. And before you say anything, Beck, yes, I do want you there. You consider them a waste of time, don't you, briefings?'

'An unnecessary duplication is what I said, at times that is, and other times quite vital.'

'I want you there. You know, underneath everything, you think you're better at this than me, don't you?'

Beck looked to his commanding officer, said nothing, his answer in his silence. He scrambled to think of something to say, because he wanted to speak, because, if nothing else, he wanted to maintain a good relationship with his skipper. He liked the man. But he didn't need to speak, because one of the local SOCOs standing by the door of the house waved over to them.

'Come here,' he shouted. 'You can walk across, just make sure you keep to the edge.'

They went through the gateway and walked along the edge of the yard. In the daylight now, the same pattern of double tyre marks was clearly visible, running from the gateway and turning in a wide arch next to a group of outhouses.

The SOCO wasn't wearing a face mask.

'Come in,' he said when they reached him. 'Walk on the floor markers.'

They stepped in. The floor was of bare pine, the boards old and brittle, with gaps between them, square orange markers strategically placed for stepping on. Beck could hear the floorboards creak beneath. The SOCO brought them through the house, showed them the different rooms.

'I wanted you to see there's no sign of any struggle in the property,' he said. 'There's nothing out of the ordinary.'

They were standing in the hallway.

'This is the last room,' he said, and stepped into a bedroom.

The room was small, a dark wood wardrobe and a narrow bed taking up most of it, along with a locker next to the bed with a clock on top. A window looked out onto the front yard.

Beck looked about the room. Yes, all very ordinary.

'Did you look under the mattress by any chance?' he asked, glancing at the bed.

The SOCO's eyes widened and he shook his head.

'In my experience,' Beck said, 'the underside of a mattress often holds things, from old socks to life savings... even if it's old socks, it's worth a look.'

The SOCO grabbed the edge of the mattress and raised it, the duvet sliding down. He held it with both hands, balancing it on its side.

In the centre of the iron mesh bed base was a large red envelope. 'Well, I...' the SOCO began, surprised, as his voice trailed off. Beck took gloves from his pocket and quickly pulled them on. 'Told you,' he said. 'Always something.'

He leant in and picked up the envelope, lifted up the unsealed flap. Inside it was a card. He took it out and placed it on the bed base, opened it. On one side were two crisp one hundred euro notes. On the other, lines of scraggy block handwriting. Beck peered at the words:

My dearest. I want you to know with all my heart that I love you, but that, more than anything, I want to help you. Please take this small token. Perhaps you could buy new shoes, or warm clothes for the cold winter? I want you to think of what I said to you today. I know it will have come as a shock. But think of what I said. Please. You can have a new life. A safe life. A good life. A life of love and happiness. With me. You deserve to be happy, my love. At the very least you deserve that. And so too you deserve all the good that this world has to offer. Yes, I may be old, but I can give you that. And I can protect you. I can save you. Think, my love, of what this old man has to offer. Won't you, please?

'Motive not robbery then,' Wilde said, peering over Beck's shoulder. 'I wonder who this was for.' Then, looking across to the window, he added, 'About bloody time.'

*

The Technical Bureau van loomed like a colossus on the narrow roadway, its diesel engine making a low clonking noise as it idled. The driver's window wound down.

'Will I fit through?'

Claire Somers was standing by the gate pillar. She beckoned with both hands and the big Iveco crawled forward, passing through with inches to spare. Beck's eyes met those of a young man staring out from the rear passenger compartment, with black wiry hair and wearing a tweed jacket. Crime scene investigators didn't normally wear tweed jackets, Beck knew. Only doctors and pathologists did.

The van pulled in along the side of the yard. Inspector Mahony was already at the rear doors when Beck got to it, tugging on the handle and pulling them open.

'This is a crime scene,' Mahony grumbled. 'Not Grand Central Station. You just can't go traipsing around anywhere you want.'

'The local SOCOs said it was okay.'

'Did they now?'

'They looked after the preliminaries... We can't wait for you to get here forever, you know. Impressions were taken of tyre marks, by the way, some of which you've just driven over.'

'I already knew about those, smart arse. What, you think we don't talk?' Mahony took out a forensic suit pack, slid his finger under the flap, opened it up. 'We only stopped once,' he added, his voice bordering on a whine. 'In Mullingar. We got here as quick as we could. Here, excuse me!'

The man Beck had noticed looking out from the rear passenger compartment was striding across the yard towards the body, brown leather medical bag grasped in his right hand. He stopped, turned and looked back at them. 'I beg your pardon?'

'You need the proper attire, Dr Keane,' Mahony said. 'Especially when with the... body.'

Dr Keane looked down; it seemed he was inspecting his brown flannel trousers. The weak December sun reflected off his polished leather shoes. He straightened again. Beck could see the starched collar of his fawn shirt, a perfect Windsor knot at its centre. Beck guessed he couldn't be more than twenty-eight years old.

'Oh. I didn't think. Sorry.'

'What about that dog?' Claire said, pointing.

Mahony looked over. 'Can it talk?' He smiled at his rare attempt at a joke. No one laughed. 'In that case… no use to me. Not now.' He looked towards the house. 'I shall be back. I need to liaise with my colleagues.'

'Keep to the edges,' Beck called after him.

Mahony looked over his shoulder, about to say something, but didn't. He walked away, moving towards the edge of the yard.

Claire took her phone from her pocket, began scrolling through her contacts list. 'I have a number for a dog charity here somewhere…'

The pathologist yanked up the hood of his suit, pulled on the face mask but allowed it to hang beneath his chin.

'How long have you been doing this?' asked Beck.

'I'm actually on secondment to the Office of the State Pathologist,' he said to Beck, 'from Dublin University. I'm just about to complete my residency in forensic pathology. I was meant to accompany the deputy state pathologist, Dr Price, here. But she was called away to another scene. So they sent me… on my own.' He fell silent.

Beck picked up on the emphasis.

'So,' Beck said. 'This is your first murder scene? Solo, I mean.'

'Yes.' His tone was clipped. 'I know what to do though.'

'Yes, I've no doubt.'

They began walking to the body. Dr Keane glanced at the dog when they reached it. This wasn't part of any medical training he'd ever received.

'Once we're finished,' Beck said, 'there should be someone here to take the animal away.'

The dog turned its head slowly and looked at the body, then back to them, and finally lay down, resting its head on its paws, its sad eyes on them. Momentarily, Beck found himself in the past.

Her name was Tizzie. A little Pomeranian with an irritating bark. Irritating to his father that is, who would often shout at the animal to be quiet. His mother would scowl and snap, at either him or Helen, 'Tell your father to be quiet.' The dog's favourite spot was on his mother's lap, but failing this, the back of the settee, which rested against the window, where it could watch the world go by. Beck liked Tizzie, but he wasn't sure if Tizzie liked him. She was indifferent to everybody, with the exception of his mother that is. Right up to the very end…

Dr Keane lay his bag down. Beck snapped back into the present. He looked at the body.

The similarity to his father was uncanny. Beck didn't want to think about it, because if he did, if he focused on it, he knew it would bring it back, all of it. He didn't want that. He couldn't afford that.

'I'll be honest with you,' Beck said. 'Dr Gumbell doesn't usually allow me to tag along for this part.'

'Doesn't he?' Dr Keane was staring at the body, pulling his face mask into place. 'Give me a hand, will you?' his voice muffled from behind it.

The young pathologist reached down and nudged the body backward by the shoulder, turning it onto its side. Edward Kavanagh stared past them, his frozen eyes wide and almost surprised in that dark grey flesh of death. Beck noted the corner of the mouth, the dried blood and the lips that resembled squashed tomatoes, splinters of teeth like the remains of a cheap necklace, and considered that he had been struck from the side. One of many blows. Beck had spotted something. He waited for Dr Keane to comment that he had too. But he didn't.

'Maybe not as I thought,' Beck suggested.

The pathologist was staring at the body.

'What do you think?' Beck asked.

'What...' He turned to look at Beck. Despite his head being covered by the hood and face mask, Beck could see he was irritated. 'Do you mind, Inspector? I'm busy. I'm trying to concentrate here. Maybe Dr Gumbell had the right idea.'

Beck was well aware that those who were unsure sometimes concealed their uncertainty within arrogance.

'Listen,' Beck said. 'All I was asking is: Did you spot it?'

The change in intonation in Beck's voice alone was enough for Dr Keane to take note.

'What do you mean?' His own voice was that of a student being asked to answer a question for which he had no answer.

Beck pointed at the flattened section of grass where the body had been lying.

'That,' he said.

The pathologist looked. He said nothing.

'Do you see now?' Beck asked.

'See what, for Christ's sake? The grass? So?'

'It's not frozen. That's the thing. It's not even stiff. Look around. The grass is still frozen everywhere else. The victim didn't die immediately. That's what it means, doesn't it? He was lying here for a time, unconscious, but alive. Worth noting, don't you think?'

A nerve, very faint, began to pulse next to the pathologist's eye. He spoke softly, his nascent arrogance having disappeared. 'I didn't think of that.'

Beck smiled. Dr Keane hadn't tried to throw it back. He knew plenty would. Dr Keane knelt down, adjusting his face mask. He opened his bag, extracted a vial and held it up to Beck.

'Would you mind, please?'

Beck took it.

'Do you see that?' Dr Keane pointed to the victim's face. 'Beyond the gory abstract, I mean.'

Beck looked. 'No, I don't see what you mean.'

He looked up. 'Ha, ha, my reputation is restored... How do you find Dr Gumbell, by the way?'

'We get on.'

'Friends?'

'You could say that.'

'Didn't think he had many of those. You're not to tell him I said that, please.'

'I won't.'

The pathologist leant over the body, extending the index and middle fingers of his right hand. He rested them on the victim's chin, and Beck watched as he slid the fingers through the gap between the smashed lips into the mouth. He manoeuvred them about for a moment, and when he took them out again, they were gripped on something viscous, short and fat. *A piece of tongue?* Beck wondered. But it was green, and speckled yellow. Was it possible that a tongue could look like that? But then the object began to move. Began to crawl about on Dr Keane's open palm. It was a slug.

He popped it into the vial and screwed on the lid.

The dog began to whine, low and constant.

The pathologist took another vial from his bag and started collecting pieces of teeth.

'If I may,' Beck said, pointing. 'What's that?'

'What's what?' The pathologist looked along Beck's outstretched arm to something small and red poking out of the victim's pocket. Dr Keane placed the vial carefully on the ground and reached for the item, took it out and held it up before him. It was a small, red velvet jewellery box.

'Well, well,' Beck said. 'Can you open it?'

Dr Keane nudged the box open with a finger. Inside it was a gold ring, a cluster of small diamonds at its centre. Beck leant close. The ring appeared to be old, the lining of the box mottled yellow, the name of the jeweller and address printed across the inside of the lid indecipherable, frayed as it was with many letters missing.

'I better pop this in an evidence bag,' Dr Keane said.

The dog was no longer whining now. Instead, a long, low, slow rumble came from between its bared teeth. The pathologist hadn't noticed. But Beck had. He also noticed the fur on the back of the animal's neck rising as it got to its feet, adopting a crouched position. The sheepdog was a deceptive animal, like all dogs a descendent of the wolf, but more wolf than might first appear. Max would fight to the death to protect his charge, or his pack. And right now, he was protecting his pack leader, even if he was dead.

Beck said nothing, but readied himself. When the dog sprang, propelled by its two powerful hind legs, he was waiting. He wrapped his left arm instantly around the neck of the animal and squeezed. The canines gnashed as the dog tried to break free. Beck squeezed harder, but only as hard as he needed to. It took mere seconds for the dog's aggression to evaporate as it began to gasp for breath. Beck turned away, speaking softly into its ear, easing his grip: 'It's okay, boy. There, there. Good boy.' The dog turned its eyes towards Beck, his expression almost human. It was of somebody scared, lost... and broken-hearted.

Beck gently carried the dog towards his car. Until the animal charity arrived, Max would stay with him.

CHAPTER ELEVEN

It was early afternoon, and the whiteboard at the front of the Ops Room had been pulled some distance from the wall so that it stood isolated, as if full of its own self-importance. Superintendent Wilde held a marker in his right hand. He wrote across the top in thick, block letters 'EDDIE KAVANAGH'.

'Our victim,' he announced, and continued by outlining the details of the case, most of which were already available on Pulse. As usual, it was an unnecessary duplication, because, well, that was just the way things were done in Cross Beg.

Beck's mind wandered as Wilde droned on, his sense of unease flittering about, and again realised he was trying to fool himself. *It's there, it's always there, especially now, and you know it, and you're close to losing control. Do something! Before it's too late.*

'Inspector Beck… Beck!'

Beck turned. Wilde was staring at him. So too, he realised, was the entire Ops Room.

The room was silent, like a hungry animal waiting to be fed.

'Does anyone know if prostitutes operate in Cross Beg?' Beck announced.

His question was met with silence, and then… laughter.

'Here, Dempsey,' said a voice. 'You'd know all about that, wouldn't you?'

'Ya,' Dempsey replied. 'Only because you told me, pal.'

'Settle down,' Beck said, gesturing with his hands. 'Anyone?' He looked at Superintendent Wilde. 'Did you tell them about the van? I can't remember.'

Wilde shook his head. 'Can't remember, eh? I was leaving that part to you.'

Beck told the room what Dermot Healy had told him.

An arm rose.

'Yes?'

It was Sergeant Connor. 'There's a couple of auld birds in The Noose they say are up for it. I hear when they run out of money, they'll, y'know...'

'No, I don't know,' Beck said.

'Leave that to your imagination, boss,' Connor said.

'Jesus.' It was Claire Somers, seated midway down the room. 'Say it straight for God's sake, can't you? There's no Mary Poppins in here. Or bishops either. Or whatever else. We're all mules, come on.'

'Quick handjob up the lane,' Connor added.

'How many?' Beck asked.

Connor gave him an odd look. 'What do you mean, how many? How many what?'

'How many women are on the game?' Beck said. 'I presume you do mean women?'

'Yes. Women. A variant of the species, in any case. I wouldn't call it "on the game" as such. There are those two I know of, anyway: Maisy Roche and Dolly Lyons.'

'Those two?' Claire spoke again. 'And who're the men who would go with those fine specimens? And pay them as well? Maisy Roche is a great-grandmother for God's sake, and she hasn't a tooth in her head to call her own...' Claire fell silent, added, 'Oh, Christ,' like she'd just thought of something.

'Enough already,' Beck said. 'Sergeant Connor. Go and talk to these good ladies, please. I'm thinking if there's a travelling pleasure dome about the place, maybe they'll know about it? Pays to be aware of the competition... Yes, you.' Beck pointed to an officer who was waving a pen in the air.

'Mick O'Driscoll, boss, Mill Street Traffic Corp. A character known to us as Sean "Squeaky" Ward was stopped twice last night. It's on the system, but as intelligence only. The second stop was a mandatory alcohol testing checkpoint less than two miles from the murder scene. I tested him myself. The time was twenty-two hundred hours. He blew clean. So we allowed him on his way. He couldn't give us a valid reason for being in the area, got lippy too, said he didn't need one. He's on parole, by the way.'

'What's his catalogue like?'

'He's well known to us.' It was Superintendent Wilde. 'MO for distraction burglaries, mainly elderly people living alone, in isolated locations. Nasty piece of work. Tendency for violence, section threes, usually with an implement found on the property. As far as I know, he's out on probation.'

'What was he driving?' Beck asked O'Driscoll.

O'Driscoll seemed to have to think about it. 'A Renault Master van.'

'You sure?'

'Yes, boss, I'm sure. Big yoke.'

'Was it searched?'

'He blew clean,' O'Driscoll said, looking at the floor.

'So, not searched,' Beck said, his tone a verbal bite. 'The reg?'

O'Driscoll didn't pull out his notebook so Beck knew it was because he hadn't taken it.

'On his catalogue,' O'Driscoll said, 'there's only one Renault Master van. Same colour. White.'

'Okay, ANPR and Pulse alerts on that vehicle, as soon as.'

Beck was thinking. There were now two vans to consider. Bit of a coincidence. And Beck didn't believe in coincidences, not in cases like this.

*

Later, they sat in Beck's office, eating chicken sandwiches ordered in from a local deli that had just started a free delivery service in an effort to drum up business.

Claire was sitting in Beck's chair in front of his computer, Beck himself in another chair, feet up on the end of the desk.

'So you think there's a link?' he asked, taking a bite from his sandwich and washing it down with swigs from a full-sugar can of Coke. 'Between the victim and this travelling brothel?'

Claire peered at the screen. 'I think it's quite probable. If what Healy says is true... Listen to this, from Google: "Married hooker beds thirty men a day in her motorhome". And here's another: "Punters pay one hundred and twenty euros an hour to test the suspension of brothel on wheels". They're out there...'

It was just gone four thirty, and it was already dark outside, the street lighting suspended in the side window of the office like a ghostly apparition. Beck flicked his desk lamp on and the apparition disappeared.

'What?' Beck said, catching Claire's look.

'Eddie Kavanagh. He was a simple man. To all intent and purposes...'

'And?'

'... well liked and regarded. Inoffensive. A lovely man, as my mother would say.'

Beck raised an eyebrow. 'And?'

'According to Investigative Best Practices... you've heard of it?

'Yes, Professor what's-his-name...?'

'Kirk Wzytal – I may not have pronounced that correctly, by the way – criminal anthropologist at Notre Dame University...'

'Yes, yes, that's him,' Beck said.

'... who states there are six prime motivators in the act of murder. One: revenge. Two: robbery. Three: lust. Four: love. Five: deviance, serial killers, etcetera. Six: ill-defined deep-seated resentment, which covers a lot of areas, granted.'

'Can't there be a combination?'

'Not usually.'

They fell silent.

'Don't stop,' Beck said. 'It's interesting.'

'Well, there are a lot of variations within each heading. If I say to you "fish", you think *fish*, but there are thousands and thousands of different fish.'

Beck rubbed his eyes.

'Well, it makes sense to me,' Claire said.

'I didn't say it wasn't making sense.'

'And is it?'

Beck shrugged. 'Kind of.'

'And based on that analysis,' Claire added, 'I would suggest revenge as the prime motivator.'

'That was easy,' Beck said. 'Of course, revenge can be very similar to resentment.'

'Well, it's not,' Claire shot back. 'It's clearly defined... in the book.'

'Ah, the book,' Beck said. 'Yes, yes. I know. The book. Have you anybody in mind?'

'Dermot Healy. Of course. He fits the profile.'

'The profile,' Beck said. 'Of course. But how convenient.'

'Most perpetrators fit one of the particular profiles.'

'Perpetrators,' Beck repeated. 'Is that term in the book too? Anyway, what about Squeaky Ward?'

'By virtue of circumstance he is also a possibility. He was in the right place.'

Beck nodded. 'And at the right time, give or take. And has a history of breaking and entering old people's homes to rob them.'

They lapsed into silence again. Beck checked his watch.

'CCTV. I want you to get what you can, profiles besides, of course.'

'Of course. That's good practice.'

'Good practice.' Beck threw his eyes heavenward. 'Jeez…'

The Christmas lights were glowing in the shop windows as they drove along Main Street. The effect, along with the twinkling lights of the trees, stirred something deeper in Beck than ever before. Christmas really was the most depressing time of year. His legs ached already from his run that morning, and he concentrated on that, feeling the dull pain, lowering his head, trying with all his might to push the images of the twinkling colours from his mind, but they still refused to budge. He shifted in his seat.

'Turn around,' he said to Claire. 'I just thought of something.'

CHAPTER TWELVE

He leant against the gate pillar, lit a cigarette and drew in deeply, watching the tip glow like an afterburner. Beck had asked Claire to drop him here for – well what, exactly? He didn't know, not fully. Beck had never taken the time to analyse this – and maybe he should – but when it came to his job he knew he was driven by both instinct and intuition in equal measure. Neither of which could be learned, or acquired. They just were. So, if there was any reason he had returned here, it was because it *felt* right.

He felt the cold, heavy air on his skin, and watched a star appear in the black sky as the clouds momentarily parted. The atmosphere seemed disturbed, agitated even. He took a last pull on his cigarette and threw it onto the track over his shoulder, stepped through the gateway, and began crossing the yard towards the house. He was halfway when he heard it.

'Don't move, boy, or I'll blow your friggin' head off.'

He recognised the voice immediately. Beck stopped, looking towards the source of the sound, saw the shape step from the darkness and stop. In its hands it held something pointed at him.

'Put the gun down, Tommy, okay? It's me. Put the gun down, there's a good man.'

Tommy Kavanagh hesitated, the shotgun still levelled at Beck.

'What you doing mooching about this place? You put the fear of God into me.'

'I'm sorry,' Beck said. 'I didn't think anyone would be here at this time. Can you put that down now? Please.'

Slowly, Tommy Kavanagh lowered the shotgun, and cradled it in his arms.

'I wasn't here,' he said. He pointed. 'My house is just beyond those trees. I was outside getting turf for the fire. I saw the glow of your fag.'

Beck considered that. 'You can get to your house from here?'

'If I need to. It's a rough path. Only use it if I have to.'

Beck waited a moment before he spoke again.

'You have a key?' he said, nodding towards the darkened property. 'I'd like to have a look around.'

'Why? You people have been here all day.'

There was a clicking sound and then a beam of light sliced through the air. Tommy Kavanagh had turned on a torch, and he swung the light either side of Beck.

'It's okay, Tommy. They're finished. I'm on my own. My colleague dropped me off and left. There's no one else here. A key? Do you have one? I just want to… get a feel for the place, that's all.'

'A feel for the place,' Tommy Kavanagh said, shifting the shotgun into the crook of one arm now. He reached into a pocket and took from it a key. He started walking towards the house, Beck right behind. He put the key into the lock and turned it, pushed the door open, stepped into the hall, and turned the light on. He looked at Beck, and Beck could see the fear in the tired old man's bloodshot eyes.

Beck glanced to the shotgun. Maybe he should have a word with the licensing officer in Galway, have the weapon temporarily withdrawn. The old man wouldn't like that, but still…

The house was cold, a deep, clinging cold. They went down the hallway. Beck paused in the open doorway to a small room. Inside he could see an open fireplace with a tile surround, and a couple of old armchairs gathered about it. He turned on the light and stepped in. There was a dusting of ash in the hearth. He looked about slowly and crossed to the fireplace, peering at a row of old framed photographs on top.

Tommy Kavanagh followed and stood beside him.

'The first one is our mammy and daddy,' he said. 'The other is our uncle, John. He lived in Boston. The third is… her.'

Beck noted the change in intonation at the word 'her'.

Tommy Kavanagh sat down heavily into one of the armchairs and sighed. His body seemed to fold into the chair. Beck knew that elderly siblings sometimes tended to follow each other into the grave. Would this be the case here?

'Her name was Emily Tuffy. Mimi, everyone called her,' Tommy said. 'She was the woman he almost married. He lost his heart to her, my brother did. God love him.'

Beck moved to the mantelpiece and picked up the picture.

'I see,' Beck said. 'But he still kept this.'

'Yes, he did.'

Beck studied the picture. It was not in clear focus, in that way of old photographs. But even so, he could tell that Emily Tuffy was no stunner. Yet there was something about her. She was leaning back against the wall of a house, her hands on wide hips, ample breasts pushing against the fabric of a plain house coat. But it was in her face, it was her smile. Even in the old and fuzzy photograph, Beck could see there was an openness there, a gentleness, and so too a sparkle, a mischievousness. All in that smile. This was a girl easy to fall in love with, Beck imagined, for a man who appeared so gentle and shy. Because opposites attracted. Beck could not help but think of Natalia.

'What happened?' Beck said, his voice startled. He regulated it immediately, and added calmly, 'To her, I mean?'

Tommy Kavanagh observed him, then answered.

'She had been waiting for Eddie to propose. Decided she'd had enough of waiting in the end and disappeared off to America – 1966 it was. They all did back then. Last I heard she'd married a man, Davis or something he was called, living in some place…' The old man fell silent. 'Medicine Bow… yes, that's it, Medicine Bow, I remember, in Wyoming. No one heard from her for years… but my brother never forgot her. Talked about going after her, but never did, of course.'

Beck was about to turn, but his attention was drawn to the next photograph. Of three cowboys standing next to a piebald horse, a lasso in the hand of one.

'The Three Amigos,' the old man said. 'Myself, Eddie and Dermot Healy. That was 1961. A circus had come to town. You paid two shillings and you could dress up as a cowboy and get your photo taken with that horse. Eddie liked it. Different times back then. But anyway, enough talk of old photographs. Like I say, different times. Have you made any progress in the investigation? That's what I want to know. Are you any closer to finding who did this to my poor brother?'

'We're processing everything,' Beck replied, focusing on the practical. 'Technical, and forensics, all other avenues too. We'll study the lot in great detail. It's a case of sifting and analysing. We should know more tomorrow. But I'm hopeful we can make progress over the coming days.'

'With the help of God,' the old man replied in a whisper. And, his voice rising, 'Because if this goes on any longer, no one will be able to rest. It's striking the fear of God into people. I can hardly sleep myself.' He stared past Beck's shoulder and his voice dropped again, as if he were talking to himself. 'Agnes is coming early tomorrow. Our sister. We don't have much family left now. Not any more. Some in England and America. But they're even older than we are, and I don't expect them to travel, for the funeral that is.'

Beck nodded.

'Tell me,' he said, 'what was your brother's relationship with Dermot Healy like? He'd threatened him at one stage, isn't that correct?'

The old man was silent for a while before answering.

'Yes,' he said. 'I have to tell you, we were friends back in the day. But Dermot Healy, he's not right in the head. And that's not just me sayin' it. Everyone knows it. He lives down there in that house of his and never goes out, apart from the odd card night down the pub. Some people can live with themselves and some can't. He's one of them that can't. He wanders about the roads and fields – you could meet him at any hour of the day or night... Look, can I be honest with you?'

'Of course.'

'I don't trust him. You understand that, don't you?'

Beck nodded.

'And pulling a rifle on my brother the way he did.' He patted the shotgun he'd rested across his lap. 'All I'll say is, I'm keeping this yoke with me at all times. From now on, that is. Because Healy down there might have flipped it.'

'He told us,' Beck said, watching the old man's face carefully. 'About the van' – Beck purposely used the word 'the', the illusion of fact, rather than 'a', which left it open to question – 'that calls to people's houses. A certain type of van actually. Strange that we, the gardai I mean, never heard about it. No one was gossiping. People kept it in their belly. Would you know anything? Is it true or not? Is there anything to it?'

Beck noted that while the old man's expression didn't change, a shimmer of red appeared at the bottom of his cheeks and began to crawl upwards across his face. Then he shook his head and looked away.

'I never heard of such a thing,' he said. 'No.'

And Beck knew immediately, because to him it was obvious. Tommy Kavanagh was lying.

Beck waited some moments. The question he had asked still hung unresolved between them. He did not speak now because he wanted the silence to reinforce his suspicion to the old man, to make him realise that he knew he was lying. Despite the heavy silence, the colour of Tommy Kavanagh's cheeks returned to normal. Still, he did not answer.

Beck stood.

'The only thing I'm certain of,' Tommy Kavanagh said, looking up at him, 'is that my heart is broken. I'm trying to just keep myself together. Does that make sense?'

Beck nodded. That made sense. That made perfect sense. Because he was trying to do the same. He knew that grief ebbed and flowed, until eventually it thundered ashore, consuming all before it. When that happened, Beck wondered if Tommy Kavanagh might even survive. And Beck knew, as he had always known, that he had not dealt with his own grief. What he had done was ignore it.

'I'll find my own way out,' Beck said. 'By the way, that pub, out on the road there, Mullaney's, does it ever open?'

Tommy Kavanagh smiled. Beck took it as a sign of contrition for not having answered the earlier question.

'Some days Tim Mullaney doesn't bother opening at all,' he said. 'But tonight he'll be open. He'll be open now in fact. It's card night.'

Beck nodded. He needed to enquire about CCTV.

'Are you going down?' Kavanagh asked.

Beck considered. 'Yes,' he said. 'I think I will.'

'I'll go with you, if that's alright. I need to get out of this place.' A look crossed the old man's face. 'That's provided there's no more talk of this van you're on about. Not tonight. Agreed?'

Beck nodded again. 'What about that?' He pointed to the shotgun.

'That comes with me. I'm not going anywhere without it.'

'Even to the pub?'

'Even to the pub.'

'That's against the law, Mr Kavanagh.'

The old man frowned. 'I need to be able to protect myself.'

'You can't take that with you. I can't allow it.'

Kavanagh looked down at the weapon and patted it, slowly got to his feet.

'Okay, okay. I'll lock it away. You any idea how long it'd take a garda car to get here in an emergency? Too long, that's how long. Way too long.'

'If you—' Beck said, fumbling in his pocket, taking out a pen and a crumpled old piece of paper. He smoothed it out and wrote his telephone number on the back of it. 'Take this. If you have any problems, you let me know about it. Will you do that? You can ring me, anytime, day or night.'

The old man took the piece of paper.

'You don't have to do this.'

'Take it,' Beck said.

Beck was thinking that if the old man did ring, the reassurance he could offer would be preferable to having a spooked Tommy Kavanagh shooting someone.

The old man slipped the piece of paper into a pocket.

'I'll do that so,' he said. 'Thank you. You're a good man.'

CHAPTER THIRTEEN

Light glowed from behind the window on either side of the open door. A spotlight, positioned beneath the sign across the facade, highlighted the name 'Mullaney's' in ornate plaster, painted black. The pub was open for business. Like the Farmers' co-op in Mylestown, inside was a time warp, this time to the 1970s. The bench seating along the wall was of gaudy button-back red leather with high stools by the counter of the same fabric. Framed posters hung from the walls for Capstans, Players 10 and Guinness For Strength, with a smiling toucan balancing a pint of stout on its beak.

'Terrible news, Tommy,' the man behind the counter said when they entered. He had a barrel belly, a white shirt straining against it like a main sail before a full wind. He wore plastic-framed glasses, and his complexion was ruddy. A pack of cigars rose from the breast pocket of his shirt. He extended his hand across the counter. 'If there's anything you need, Tommy, don't hesitate.'

Both men shook.

'I wasn't going to open,' Tim Mullaney said, 'to tell the truth...'

'It's good you have,' Tommy said. 'It's what Eddie would have wanted. And I'm grateful to have someplace to come now.'

'That's what I thought. It'll be good for the boys to have company tonight too. This has put the fear of God into everybody.'

Beck felt certain that if he was to look behind the counter he would find a weapon, a shotgun or rifle, something.

'Aye,' Tommy said, 'it will.' He looked around. 'There's no one here yet?'

'No,' Mullaney said, glancing towards Beck for the first time.

'This is one of the police officers looking to find who did this,' Tommy Kavanagh said. 'Detective Inspector Beck.'

'Beck, is it?' Mullaney said, folding his thick arms. 'That's an unusual name now. Where you from?'

'I don't want to keep you,' Beck said, sidestepping the question. 'I'm enquiring about CCTV. I see you have a couple of cameras outside, on your gable walls.'

The bar owner nodded. 'I do. Had barrels taken. Not the full ones. Have them locked away. The empty ones. Leave them out for collection on a Tuesday night. They're worth seventy euro a piece, they are. The bastards have taken nearly a hundred in the past eighteen months. No one is doing anything about it that I can see…' He fell silent. 'Of course, in the light of what's happened, it pales into insignificance, I grant you.'

'I'd like to look at that CCTV,' Beck said.

'Of course you would,' Mullaney answered. 'But someone's already been. A fella named Dempsey. Came to my house earlier. I don't live here, you see. I live ten miles on the Loughrea side of Cross Beg. I gave it to him, this Dempsey chap. Nice lad he was.'

Good work, Dempsey, Beck thought, *but why the hell didn't you put it under the case number on Pulse like I told you to?*

The pub door opened and a figure in a long dark raincoat entered. His hands were in his pockets and a woolly hat was pulled down halfway over his face. Beck could see Tommy Kavanagh stiffen. Tim Mullaney crossed his arms again and took a step back, leaning against the cash register.

'Hello, Dermot,' Tim Mullaney said.

Dermot Healy pulled the woolly hat from his head.

'Hello there, Tim.' He glanced towards Tommy Kavanagh and nodded. 'Sorry for your loss, Tommy.'

Tommy turned away from Healy as he passed. He leant on the counter with both elbows. 'They say it's usually someone who's known to the victim,' he said, staring at the counter. 'Isn't that what they say?'

Healy pulled a stool out from the other end of the counter, was about to sit down. He paused, turned towards Tommy Kavanagh, opened his mouth as if to say something, but closed it again. Silently he walked back the way he had come, opened the door and stepped out into the night.

Beck made a mental note to have a word with the firearms licensing officer in Galway. Yes. Definitely. That would be a good move to make.

'I'll be on my way so,' Beck said.

'Won't you stay a while?' Kavanagh said. 'Have a quick one? You can't still be on duty, can you?'

A quick one. Beck thought about that. Yes, he would like a quick one. But there would be nothing quick about it. He hesitated, not certain what he would say until he'd said it.

'I need to go. Thank you, I'll be in touch.'

CHAPTER FOURTEEN

In the back of the taxi home, Beck shook his head to stop himself from falling asleep. His natural default setting was like a hamster on a wheel, and he had not stopped all day. It was not that he wished to be like that, but he knew no other way. Because once he stopped, crevices appeared in his consciousness, sucking him in, into his old thoughts, into his old ways. Because they never went away. Always, always, always they were there, crowding about, shuffling their feet, waiting for him to open the door and allow them in. Especially now, at this time of year. So he had to keep running on the climbing wheel, never stopping, not once, never allowing himself any time to think. But he was tired now, and for a brief moment, he thought of nothing.

He saw the small, red car parked near his house through the windscreen as the cab approached it. He felt a sensation like the air being sucked from his lungs before he realised he was actually holding his breath. He exhaled and felt his heart begin to gallop inside his chest, pounding against his rib cage. *Could it be?* he asked himself. His taxi drew up against the kerb by his door and Beck emerged onto the pavement. He paid the driver and looked back along the street. The door of the little red Fiat was opening. A high-heeled pump emerged followed by a long, perfectly shaped leg encased in black tights, the rest of Natalia thereafter. The sight of her was like a sugar rush. He stood for a moment, not quite trusting his eyes, and blinked. Yes, it was true, they were not playing tricks. The sound of her heels on the pavement then, a luscious *click clack click,* getting closer. *Click clack click…*

'You look like you've seen a ghost.' Her tone was contrite yet playful, the dichotomy of this hot and cold woman. Because you never could tell. It was enough to drive a man crazy, him in any case. And he could never understand it. What was it exactly that he found so fascinating about her? He'd tried, but never could work it out. It was everything, both her availability and unavailability. It was the way she walked, a slight pull to one side, her arm swinging across her chest. It was her voice, an audio equivalent of ruched silk. It was her eyes, sometimes so distant she seemed out of reach... It was everything.

A thought suddenly struck him. Strange, he thought, that he had not considered it before, because now it appeared so obvious. He pushed it to the side. He didn't want to go there, not yet...

'Aren't you cold?' What a stupid question. He admonished himself as soon as he'd asked it.

Natalia wore nothing but a very short black dress. Her necklace, a gold pendant in the shape of a heart, twinkled in the street light.

'Of course I'm cold. Invite me in for God's sake, won't you?'

'Yes, yes. Come in. Come in.'

He fumbled in his pocket for his keys. He laughed, walked to the door, turned the key in the lock, glancing over his shoulder, just to make sure. Yes, she really was there.

Natalia smiled. It was a beautiful smile, red luscious lips parting to reveal her perfectly formed white teeth. He looked at her, those small eyes that no amount of clever application of make-up could ever make appear any larger. Those eyes fascinated him.

He held the door open and she passed into the hall, running her hand over the back of his, smelling of hairspray and expensive perfume.

'Beck. My suitcase. In the car.'

'Suitcase?'

'Yes. You don't want me to sleep in the street, do you?'

It was his turn to smile.

'No. Heaven forbid. Let me go and get it.'

She took a step forward, froze.

'What's that?' And then, her voice alarmed, 'Jesus!'

Beck came and stood next to her. He smiled.

'That's a dog. His name's Max. I brought him home earlier.'

Max sat silently, watching them.

'He's very gentle, really,' Beck said, squatting down. He patted the animal's head. 'His owner's been killed, and the dog shelter's full. So... he's here, for now.'

'Really?'

'Yes. Really. Max, say hello to Natalia. Natalia, Max.'

Natalia hesitated, then reached out. As she did so, the dog growled. She withdrew her hand.

'He doesn't like me.'

'It's not that,' Beck said. 'He's traumatised. Just hold out your hand, nice and gentle, let him sniff it. Go on. Try.'

'No. I'll pass.'

'Please. Go on. Do it.'

Tentatively, Natalia stretched out her hand, and held it a short distance from the dog. Max's nose crinkled a couple of times, then he craned forward and sniffed. Finally, his tongue slurped over it a couple of times.

'Now,' Beck said. 'Tickle him behind the ears.'

Again, Natalia hesitated, but she did it, and Max turned his head and pressed into her, closing his eyes.

'He likes you,' Beck said. 'See.'

Natalia smiled.

'Good boy,' she said.

Beck led the way into the living room, and they sat on the settee, side by side. Max followed. He lay on the mat in the centre of the room and closed his eyes, but opened them almost immediately, as if checking that they were still there. Natalia had put her coat on again. It was cold in the room, very cold.

Which made Beck think of the old men living in their stone cottages and council houses up isolated cul-de-sacs, of their cold and miserable lives. Was he getting to be like them, or was he already there?

He wondered why she was here, but he didn't dare ask. The important point was that she was. Natalia began to speak, idle chat, something about the long drive down, and he wasn't really listening. What he was doing was looking into her small pale green eyes, noting the distance, but getting closer all the time. She stopped talking and got to her feet, stretched down a perfectly manicured hand and took hold of his.

'We have plenty of time for talking afterwards,' she said. 'Now, where's the bedroom?'

Beck stood, as Max quickly clambered to his feet, watching them.

Natalia looked down. 'Where does he sleep?'

'We have no formal arrangements. It's actually his first night.' He patted the dog. 'You get the couch, Max. Okay, fella?'

He turned to Natalia, held her waist, pulled her towards him and gently kissed her. 'I've missed you.'

A thought crossed his mind: *Did Mr Donegan once say the same thing to his mother?*

They shared a cigarette afterwards, Beck holding it to her lips as she took short, unpractised puffs. The street light outside through the curtains cast shadows onto the wall behind the bed, the smoke a moving upward spiral. She asked him to open the window when he stubbed it out in the ashtray on the bedside locker. The breeze filtered across the room, carrying more cold air into an already cold room. He got back into bed, and she gave a sharp intake of breath as his flesh touched hers. He could feel the heat of her body warming him, and as they lay there, she told him.

'I've left Jim.' Her voice was a flat monotone and, in case he did not understand, raising her voice, 'I've left him.'

Beck considered what she had said, words he'd thought he would want to hear, but now realised he did not. Because he definitely did not want this.

Yes, she knew him too well.

'Don't worry, Beck, it won't be forever. I know you crave the prize until you actually get it. Then you don't want it any more... No, don't say anything. I understand it, I really do. It's part of the attraction, actually, for me too...'

She lay back now, and the sheet fell away, exposing one perfectly formed breast. People paid a great deal of money to have breasts like those.

She intertwined her fingers with his, placing his hand onto one breast. He could feel the heat of it beneath his hand, the faint beating of her heart.

'Yes. I've left him. I can't stand the sight of him any more, to be honest. And yet, and yet... I don't want to lose him either. That can't make sense.'

'You're right,' Beck said. 'It doesn't. I'm confused.'

'And me. I still want to make it work, is what I'm saying. I still love him.'

'Did something happen?' Beck said. But what he really wanted to say was, *If you don't want to lose him, aren't you going the wrong way about it?*

'No. Nothing. That's exactly it. Nothing happened. Or has happened, for a long, long time. Our relationship is just that, it's nothing. There's a silence to nothingness, you know. A heavy, grinding silence that never goes away. All day long. Day in. Day out. Except for the clock. Tick tock. The bloody antique thing he has on the wall. That silence drives me crazy. I've been thinking about you, Beck. Thinking about you a great deal. So I packed my bags, and here I am.'

She began to cry, very softly.

'Did you tell him?'

Natalia was silent.

'Jesus, you didn't, did you?'

'No,' she said. 'I didn't. Because he wasn't there to tell. He was out with his rugby chums. Again. Spends more time with them than he does with me...'

'But you don't want him to spend more time with you anyway, that's what you used to say. Which is it? You want to be with him or you don't?'

'Are you stupid? Of course I want him to spend more time with me. I want... Do I have to spell it out, for God's sake?'

Beck was silent.

'I want to be loved. Is that too much to ask? I'm pathetic... coming all the way down here to you. I should have known better. Because I know what you want. The unattainable, that's what. And yet you want to be loved too, but you're too damned scared to admit it. So you chose me. Because I'm safe. You're fooling yourself, Beck, but you don't fool me.'

Beck sighed, and felt like crap. Had his mother's lover ever felt like crap too?

'Sorry...'

She squeezed his hand. 'Oh, it's okay. You're not so much a rock in a storm as a buoy, bobbing about, making me hang on tight, like now... He'll wake tomorrow and find me gone. That'll give him a country song to sing, another one to take from his Hank Williams repertoire.'

'He likes Hank Williams?'

'He even visited his grave last year, in Montgomery, Alabama.'

'You go with him?'

'Yes. We had a nice time, actually.'

Beck shook his head. He didn't know that. No one had ever mentioned that the Big Man, Chief Superintendent Jim Gallagher, liked country music. So he would wake tomorrow, the Big Man, to find his wife gone. And it would take him, the commanding officer of the Garda National Bureau of Criminal Investigation in Dublin, less than ten seconds to work out exactly where she was.

Natalia seemed to sense his mood. 'It won't be for long, Beck. I just need to clear my head.'

'Or teach him a lesson.'

'That too… maybe.'

Beck said nothing, thinking.

'No one needs to know I'm here,' she added.

Beck smiled. 'Let's be realistic, shall we?'

'Okay, I'll leave then, book into a bloody hotel, you won't have to worry about it.'

Beck raised himself onto an elbow and peered down at her, gently ran a finger along her cheek.

'You misunderstand me. I don't care about the Big Man. I just never realised that you actually loved him, that's all. Maybe I shouldn't have…'

'What, started all this?'

Beck nodded.

'Don't flatter yourself, Beck. That night…'

Beck thought back – it was almost five years ago now – to the reception at Garda HQ in honour of officers returning from overseas UN duty somewhere or other.

'Who introduced who, exactly?' she said.

Beck remembered she had tugged on his sleeve as he passed, smiling. He'd had no idea who she was. That's how it had started.

'You think I was really interested in that bloody case I con-gratulated you on solving? Get real. Can't even remember what it was now. I was interested in you, Beck, *you*. Because I knew, just knew, that you'd… understand. And you did. And you do. I don't even have to be with you, it's just enough to know that you want me. Sometimes, I even think you need me. That's enough to pull me through, just that, knowing someone wants me. And I know you want me.'

She reached out and rested a hand on his shoulder, pulled him down to her. And for a short while at least, Beck forgot all about Chief Superintendent Jim Gallagher.

CHAPTER FIFTEEN

Beck woke with a start, knew immediately he had been dreaming, as Eddie Kavanagh's mangled and twisted face faded from his mind.

He realised his telephone was ringing on the dresser. He reached for it as Natalia stirred beside him, noted the time in the corner of the screen as he picked it up: 1.45 a.m. It was a number he didn't recognise.

'Yes.' His voice was as thick as wet cement.

'You told me to ring.' The voice on the other end was low, frightened. 'It's Tommy Kavanagh here.'

'What is it?'

'There's someone out there again. In Eddie's yard. It's not you, is it? I can hear them. I'm thinking of going out myself.'

Beck closed his eyes, clearing his mind.

'No,' he said. 'Ring the station. It's not me.'

'I just did. They said it'll take a bit of time, there isn't a car available. What good is that to anyone? You told me to ring.'

Beck took a breath. 'Stay where you are. I'm on my way.'

Silence.

'You got that, Mr Kavanagh? I'm on my way.'

'You better be quick.' And the line went dead.

Natalia was awake now, watching as he got out of bed. He began pulling on his clothes.

'Where're you going?'

'I've got to go out.'

'You can't be serious?'

'It shouldn't take long.' She stared at the ceiling as he extended the palm of his hand. 'Could I have your keys?'

'To the car?'

'No. The Batmobile. Of course, the car…'

'You don't drive.'

'I do. You know I do. I just choose not to, that's all… the keys. I'm in a bit of a hurry.'

'My handbag, somewhere in that fridge you call a living room… Where exactly are you going?'

'Go back to sleep. I'll tell you later.'

'Later,' she muttered. 'It's always later. Bloody policemen, you're all the same.'

He went down the stairs to the living room, found her handbag and took the keys from it, went to the front door and was about to open it when she called, 'Beck.'

'Yes?'

'Take care, darling.'

He smiled. 'Yes,' he called back, and left the house.

Beck didn't like driving, and because of this, he rarely drove. But in Dublin it had never been a problem. Indeed, in the city he considered a car to be a liability. Here it was more of a necessity. He walked along the street to Natalia's small Fiat, unlocked it and got in, fumbled about as he put the key in the ignition and turned it, the engine coming to life. Then he messed about with the controls until he located the headlamp switch. The windscreen had partially frosted over. He fumbled again until he found the wipers. He put the car into gear and moved off. As he drove along Main Street he passed the station. There were no squad cars outside.

The night was clear and sharp. Approaching Mullaney's he could see the pub was in complete darkness. He turned onto the track just before it, pressing down hard on the accelerator for a time, then turned the engine off, allowing the car to coast. Beck squeezed the brake pedal gently as he reached the gateway, pulled the car to the side and stopped. He got out without a sound, walked across the metal grating, taking care to keep to the concrete edge, and moved into the yard. He turned right, along the perimeter of bushes, walking until he reached the gable end of the house. He stopped, listening carefully. But there was nothing, no sound whatsoever. He remained like that, standing still, waiting.

Minutes passed, but he did not move. Because Beck had learnt from his time as a beat cop in Dublin the importance of being patient.

Finally, Beck saw it: a movement, across the yard. There was someone emerging from the side of an outhouse. Beck strained his eyes and watched, discerning the figure at the front of the stone building, an item grasped in each hand. Beck moved back the way he had come, swiftly, on the balls of his feet so as not to make any sound, watching all the time the figure, who was moving slowly towards the gateway. Beck stood concealed in the bushes by the gate until the person was within feet of him, then stepped out, blocking their path.

'Stop. Right there.' Beck was close enough to reach out if they tried to make a run for it.

Instead, Dermot Healy stood motionless, staring at Beck. Beck could see what he was carrying now – the head of a shovel and an electrical extension cord.

'What's the matter?' Healy said, his words slurred.

'I could ask you the same question,' Beck said. 'And I could also arrest you right now.'

'Argh, there's no need for that,' Healy said, wobbling slightly. Beck could smell the alcohol on him.

'You're pissed,' he said. 'What're you doing here?'

'Collecting a few things.'

Beck could see someone else moving towards them behind Healy. It was Tommy Kavanagh. Beck cursed. He had his shotgun, pointing directly at them.

Shit.

'How ya there, Tommy baby?' Healy slurred.

'Shut up, Healy,' Beck snapped. Then, to Tommy: 'Tommy. The shotgun. Please. Put it down.'

Tommy Kavanagh hesitated, but then lowered the weapon, pointing it towards the ground.

'That's better,' Beck said. 'Now. What's this all about? And put those items on the ground.'

'I want him arrested,' Kavanagh said. 'He needs to be locked up. A feckin' murderer walking around like that. No one is safe.'

'I'm no murderer,' Dermot Healy spat. 'Eddie might be dead, but you still need to watch your mouth.'

'See there,' Kavanagh shouted. 'He's threatening me. You heard him.'

'Stop. Both of you.' Beck turned to Tommy Kavanagh. 'Forget about threats, we don't need to inflame the situation any further. He's trespassing, isn't he? You want to press charges?'

Kavanagh nodded. 'Yes, I want to press charges.'

Beck thought about that. Dermot Healy mumbled something to himself.

'That's enough out of you,' Beck said. 'Thing is, Tommy. This isn't your property. So you can't press charges.'

'So he gets away with it, does he? Robbing the place blind.'

'I robbed nothing,' Healy said. 'This stuff is mine. I lent it to Eddie. I'm just getting it back, that's all.'

Beck raised a hand. 'Enough. Dermot Healy, I'm arresting you under the public order act. You're drunk and incapable. You can come to the station with me, sleep it off, and we'll deal with this in the morning. Mr Kavanagh, please go back to your home.

As in, right now. Please.' Beck met the old man's gaze, and held it. 'I mean it. Go back to your house.'

Tommy Kavanagh was motionless for a moment, then turned and slowly began to walk away. Beck needed a squad car. He reached into his pocket for his mobile phone, but thought, *How long's that going to take?* Another thought crossed his mind instead. He put the phone back into his pocket and turned to Healy.

'Put your arms out.'

'What?'

'Just do it.'

Dermot Healy did as he was told and Beck quickly searched him, then grasped a wrist and led him towards the little Fiat.

'If you try anything,' Beck said, 'I have to politely inform you I'll break your two legs. We clear?'

Healy suddenly appeared very sober. He stared at Beck.

'There's no need for any of that,' he said.

They walked to the car. The adrenaline was leaving Beck now, replaced by a deep weariness. They got to the Fiat and he took a deep breath, opened the front passenger door.

'Get in,' Beck said.

Beck handed his prisoner over to the custody sergeant, and once the prisoner log was created, Dermot Healy was placed into a cell, to be held overnight for questioning in the morning. Beck left the station again and drove home.

Max greeted him in the hallway. He patted the dog, and Max wagged his tail. It was the first time Beck had noticed him do that.

Beck climbed the stairs. Max seemed to understand, and went back into the living room.

The house already smelt of her, her perfume, her hairspray, everything. It was as if she had always been there. He went into the bedroom and undressed in the dark, climbed into bed beside

Natalia. She immediately reached for him and he felt her warm hands pressing into his back, pulling him close. They held each other for a long time, silent, neither feeling any urge to speak, instead content to know that at this darkest hour of the night, they each had someone to hold on to. And like this, they fell asleep.

CHAPTER SIXTEEN

The next morning Beck awoke, remarkably fresh, considering he'd had less than three hours sleep. He took a strong mug of coffee in with him to the interview room. It was 7.45 a.m. Claire was already there, sitting opposite a bleary-eyed and subdued Dermot Healy. Beck pulled back a chair but hesitated before sitting down.

'Unofficially, the charge is nonsense,' he said. 'I didn't have to take you into custody, not last night, but I did because your neighbour, who was pointing a shotgun at you, might have blown a hole as wide as the Port Tunnel in your chest if I had not. That's why you're here. Consider you owe me one.'

Beck sat down and took a sip of coffee, placed the mug onto the table, and looked at the time on the interview wall clock. He pressed the voice and video recorder on.

'Interview commencing with Dermot Healy, arrested on suspicion of public order offences on the property of Eddie Kavanagh in the early hours of today, Tuesday 15 December, found in possession of items, namely a shovel head and an electrical extension cord, believed to be the property of the late Mr Kavanagh, but this is to be confirmed... Now, Dermot Healy, what have you to say for yourself about all this?'

Healy stretched his legs out under the table and leant back into his seat, staring at the ceiling. He remained like that for a long time, until Beck was about to repeat the question. Then he spoke.

'You see,' he said, his voice hoarse, 'you can't get beyond the fact that I threatened Eddie. You think because of that...'

'Don't concern yourself with what we're thinking,' Beck said. 'Good man.'

Dermot Healy sat forward. 'You think I was going to harm Tommy Kavanagh?'

'Maybe… but I'm more concerned with Eddie Kavanagh. Did you kill Eddie, Dermot? Did something snap? Did you do it?'

Dermot Healy leant further forward. 'That's way more than public order, that is.'

'So?' Beck said.

'Me and Eddie got on fine. We lived beside each other. We were friends, good friends. Sometimes I helped him. Sometimes he helped me. *Meitheal*, you know what that means, don't you? It's the Irish for community, for neighbours looking out for one another, helping each other out.' He stared at Beck, the whites of his eyes a mosaic of broken red blood capillaries around blue-grey orbs. 'It was a shovel, right? And an extension cord? That's what you said before.'

Beck nodded. Which meant Healy couldn't fully remember what he'd had with him. Made sense. The man had been shitfaced.

'They were mine. I lent them to Eddie… Look, I don't have a clue what possessed me to go round there last night. It wasn't a good idea. Not after what happened. I went round there all the time to get stuff. Eddie came down to me and did the same.' He paused. 'That's why I was there last night.'

Claire cleared her throat. 'You have any proof? That those items are yours? Because right now, it looks like you were in there burgling.'

Which was open to interpretation, Beck knew. Burglary or trespass? A roofed premises with walls – burglary. Or an open yard – trespass. The comment brought a response from Healy, which led Beck to wonder if maybe there had not been sufficient time allocated to allow him to sober up.

'Ya, and I whacked him with a lump of wood. Is that what you want to hear me say?'

Claire glanced at Beck, mouthed 'What?'

'How did you know that?' she asked, looking to Healy. 'That he was killed with a blunt instrument.'

Healy raised his right arm and covered his eyes with a hand, massaging them furiously before taking it away again.

'Well, it was hardly a folded newspaper that did it, was it?'

'The way I see it...' Beck said. 'Think about this, Dermot... Can I call you Dermot?'

Healy said nothing.

Beck took a breath, kneading his words into an affable tone. 'Who do you think killed Eddie Kavanagh, Dermot?' he said. 'Would you have an opinion, because, really, I'm not interested in talking to you about a bloody shovel head and an extension cord?'

'Well, they're mine anyway. Because whenever I buy something, see, I get the manual, and I staple the receipt to it, then I put everything into my manual drawer. And if I don't have a manual I put the receipts in there anyway. So I have everything. Everything. And the reason I have everything is I have feck all, if that makes any sense.'

'Like I said. I don't care about a shovel head and an extension cord. So, tell me. Your opinion, on who killed Eddie Kavanagh.'

'I don't have one.'

'Dermot...' Beck began.

Healy's eyes widened. He stared.

'Stop calling me fucking Dermot. I don't know you from a hole in the wall. You're not my best friend. I don't have a best friend any more. I don't have any friends. And that's the way I like it. I don't need any-bloody-body. Okay?'

The man was rattled.

'Righteo,' Beck said.

Healy coughed. 'You think I'm thick.'

'No, I don't,' Beck said. 'You overlooked some details, but granted, I didn't press you for them, either. Details like... the van.'

'What?'

'I want you to talk to me about the van. Did you avail of its services?'

Healy looked away.

'Avail of its services?' he repeated, facing Beck again. 'All you had to do was ask. I would have told you. Of course I availed of its services.'

'Right,' Beck said. 'And who else did?'

Healy pursed his lips. 'I'm not an informer you know. Don't mind telling you about myself. But I'm not going to report on anyone else. You can forget that. No way.'

'Can you tell us anything else about the van?' Claire asked. 'What make it was? Anything?'

Healy shook his head. 'I don't know what make it was. A Peugeot, maybe. It had a yellow registration number though. I remember that.'

Which meant it was a British-registered vehicle.

'And the girl?' Beck asked. 'Was it always the same girl in it?'

Healy shook his head. 'No, it varied.'

'Can you tell us anything about them?' Claire asked. 'Where they were from?'

'I don't know where they were from,' Healy said. 'Somewhere foreign, they didn't speak much.'

'They didn't speak, or they didn't speak much English? Which is it?' Claire said.

'They didn't speak much.'

'And it was always the same man with them too, was it?' Beck asked.

'No. There was a couple of different ones. Tough-looking dudes, the both of them. Know nothing about either of them, except one had a scar down his cheek – the younger one that is – and the other, the older one, he had a tattoo by his eye, of a teardrop.'

Which held different meanings, Beck knew, the most likely that he had committed murder.

'Younger,' Beck said. 'What age?'

'Mid-twenties maybe.'

'And the older one?' It was Claire.

'I'd say mid-fifties, maybe more.'

'Did the girls seem scared of them?' Beck asked.

Healy turned his head to the side, thinking. 'I wouldn't call it scared. They never seemed... anything. A bit zoned out is the way I'd describe them.'

Zoned out. Beck considered that. Drugged up more like, which made them compliant, but also dependent. It was the way these things often worked.

'Didn't that bother you at all?' Claire snapped. 'I mean, didn't you stop to think about those poor girls, their situation? Well, did you? You ever hear of human trafficking? You think they do it for fun? Do you? They're desperate, for God's sake. Desperate. I've met women in Dublin who, when they're too old to work the brothels any more, end up working the streets along by the Quays, usually to feed a habit. I've seen them after they've been raped, beaten and thrown from moving cars... You look surprised, didn't you think it was possible to rape a prostitute?'

Beck turned to Claire. She glanced at him, looked away, sat back into her chair, folded her arms.

'You don't look so well,' Beck said, assessing Healy.

'I don't feel it.'

'You won't go down to Eddie Kavanagh's place again, will you?'

Healy shook his head. 'No. I won't.'

'We'll wrap this up so.'

'I can go?'

'You can go. Claire, show Mr Healy out. But remember, enquires are ongoing. Make no mistake about that.'

Healy got to his feet. 'Oh, I'll make no mistake about that. Could say the same to you... because you're barking up the wrong tree.'

*

Beck was passing the public office a little later when he heard it. A cough. He stopped in the hallway outside, just past the open door. It wasn't a *cough* cough, more like a someone-is-coming cough. He waited, listening...

'That was close... What was I saying? Look, the car belongs to a chief super's wife. Look, swear to God, the address is the same, she's his wife, there, see...'

Beck stepped back into the doorway. He could see a male and female uniformed officer, both leaning over a computer, peering at the screen. They were oblivious to his presence. He stepped in and walked quietly up behind them, could see that they were looking at the Pulse vehicle screen, the different fields populated by the ownership details of a car, specifically a small Fiat owned by one Natalia Gallagher.

It was his turn to cough now, and two faces turned to him, becoming instantly pale, eyes widening, mouths opening. They reminded Beck of the fish on display in Crabby's supermarket.

'Why so curious?' Beck asked.

Neither answered.

'Well?' Beck prompted.

'I saw it.' It was the female officer. 'The car, I mean. When we were passing your house, earlier this morning. We were on patrol, so I ran the reg. There are not many cars on your street. I was curious, that's all, because I didn't recognise it, wondering what it was, you know, doing there... Just curious, like I say.'

Beck leant in and placed his face centimetres from hers, his face a scowl. 'Your name?'

She looked away as she answered. 'Garda Yvonne Mangan, sir.'

'Look at me, Garda Mangan.'

Her nervous eyes turned to take in his.

Beck smiled then. 'Good work, Garda Mangan. Keep it up. Curiosity is good, it gets answers. Carry on, you two.'

He turned and left the room, feeling their eyes burning into his back.

He had put on his jacket and was about to leave for the mortuary when Claire appeared in the doorway of his office, her sergeant's exam test booklet pressed into her side under her arm.

'Just a few questions. I need to fill these in while they're fresh in both our minds. Won't take a sec.'

Beck looked at his watch. 'I'm already running late,' he said, but went back to his desk anyway and sat down.

Claire sat opposite, placed the booklet on top, opened it, and selected a page.

'One,' she said, pencil at the ready. 'Are you happy with the manner in which the interview with Dermot Healy was conducted earlier?'

Beck scratched his chin, took a deep breath and swallowed down his irritability. Claire was ambitious. Good for her. He reminded himself that so too was he, once upon a time.

'Not particularly.'

Claire held a pencil over the page. 'From one to five, can you rate it?'

'Two.'

'Really? I thought it went better than that.'

'It achieved little,' Beck said.

'I beg to differ. I think he's a strong contender for this.'

Beck closed his eyes. 'Strong contender.' He opened them again. 'It's not a boxing match. I still give it two.'

There was a scratching sound as she wrote on the paper with the pencil.

'Would you say all proper procedures have been adhered to during this investigation thus far?'

Beck paused. 'Really?' he said. 'That's a question?'

'Of course. Don't you think it's valid?'

Beck looked up to the ceiling, as if searching for words, then back down again.

'Hmm,' he said. 'Procedure is nothing other than an established pattern. Doesn't mean you have to stick to it. On the contrary.'

Claire bit the end of her pencil. 'You know, I like that.' She carried on scribbling.

Beck stood. 'Now, I really must go. Keep working at that CCTV. I'll be asking you about it when I get back.'

CHAPTER SEVENTEEN

Beck smoked as he made his way along Main Street to the hospital. In the daylight the Christmas lights draped on the trees had lost much of their vibrancy, appearing now as nothing more than weak smudges of colour. The shop windows groaned with merchandise. Beck could almost feel the desperation in them. Christmas, he knew, might determine whether some would still be in business the following year. He turned off Main Street; the sign on the wall said 'Francis Lane'. At the bottom there was a footbridge that crossed the main Galway Road leading to the hospital. As he walked he paused by a closed-down shop. It was wooden-fronted, with green peeling paint. There was a faded sign across the front that said 'Brady's'. In the empty shop window were a couple of discarded mannequins, one lying on the floor, the other standing, its arms set in a wide, expansive gesture.

Beck couldn't remember the medical term for a repressed traumatic event – usually suffered in childhood – that erupted into consciousness when triggered by an outwardly benign sensory stimulus. In this case, a couple of mannequins.

He stopped, unable to take his eyes off them, with a sensation at the back of his throat, filling up his airway, thick and heavy, like sludge. He coughed twice, but each time he was unable to follow up with an intake of breath, so that he began to choke. A sound came from the back of his mouth, like the cawing of a crow, as his hands grasped at his throat, the fingers pushing in against the flesh from either side. But it was no use, because there was nothing there, no obstruction in the first place, and the sound grew louder as images flashed across his mind, images from his childhood resurrected, carrying him back to that moment…

That moment.

One of many, locked within a vault deep down in the permafrost of his consciousness, leeching out…

Had his mother killed his father? Had she?

Beck collapsed onto his knees, fighting for breath, clawing at his throat as it finally came, and he sucked air into his scorched lungs, making a long *wooossh* sound. He leant back against the wall of the shop as a car passed by, a very fat man behind the wheel, who looked out at him, curious, but not curious enough to stop.

The body of his father smelt of cigarettes and aftershave, although he had never smoked in his life. His father, a cauldron of conflicting emotions, cold and stand-offish, whose only interaction with his children was through his strict authority. His mother pulled Beck away, covering his eyes with her hands. He could smell cigarettes from her too, and that same aftershave.

He kept thinking of the narrow double windows above the back door. These had always been kept locked. But now they were open. And he saw it glint in her hand, the key. And he wondered: Why? And he saw the face of his father. And he thought again: Why? Beck's mother's hands pressed tighter over her son's eyes, shutting out all imagery, but Beck could see the glow of the Christmas lights seeping through, orange and red and green…

Slowly, after some moments, Beck got to his feet, fighting to control his panic. The image of his father's dead body was alongside another. It was the same pose, the same splayed limbs, as those of Eddie Kavanagh. He had an absurd thought: they both had good hair.

He walked on.

Near the footbridge was a Mace supermarket, a sign outside reading 'coffee and croissant €4'. He strode in, two people coming from the other direction stepping out of his way. He walked down the centre aisle. At the end he stopped, his heart racing, his breathing coming in short and shallow spurts.

Where the hell was it?

Facing him were shelves of wine... bloody wine. He didn't want wine.

He walked back down the aisle the way he had come. Just inside the door was the counter, on it a display of lottery tickets, and behind it, a cabinet...

Beck pointed, said to the assistant. 'A naggin.'

She was a young girl. She glanced behind her at the spirits cabinet. 'It's not half ten yet. I can't.'

Beck glanced at his watch. 'It's as good as. By the time you take it out and give it to me it will be...'

She observed him, and in her gaze was a maturity far beyond her years.

She shrugged. 'A naggin?' she said. 'Of what?'

'Of anything... whiskey. And a packet of lozenges. Strong.'

She opened the cabinet and selected a naggin of Jameson whiskey, handed it to Beck. He placed a crumpled twenty euro note on the counter and took the bottle, turned to leave.

'Your change,' she called after him.

'Keep it,' he said.

He paused inside the shop door, twisted the cap, heard the reassuring click as the seal was broken. He turned towards a row of glossy magazines – 'How to change your life in ten easy steps', the headline across one screamed. If only. But still, he paused, staring at the bottle, and heard it, a screaming in his head. He didn't want to do this. Because he knew what ultimately awaited, what always awaited. After the magic carpet ride came the long climb up the sheer rock face of detox to reach normalcy again. But it didn't stop him. He raised the bottle to his lips and the whiskey flowed into him like monsoon rain on parched earth.

CHAPTER EIGHTEEN

The door to the mortuary was closed. Beck stood, hesitating before ringing the bell. He took a lozenge from his pocket, peeled off the wrapping and popped it into his mouth. He sucked on it, ran a hand over his neck, then along his hair. All was good. His senses were just enough out of focus to take away the edges. Which was what he wanted. Because he had rammed the lid back down, and was standing on it now, with all his might trying to keep it from coming off again. He had done what he had to do, the only thing he knew how to do.

He knew he was a cliché, but he could see everything crystal clear at the same time. Alcohol could be his best friend and worst enemy, and right now, his pal had an arm draped around his shoulder: *Don't worry buddy, we got this.* But he knew that if Wilde got one whiff, he'd be suspended quicker than a greyhound out of the traps. No questions asked.

He pressed the doorbell for the mortuary, heard the echo of its chime on the other side. He waited. When no one came he was about to ring a second time when he thought to try the door instead. He pushed. It wasn't locked, and it opened.

He stepped into the foyer. It wasn't an unpleasant smell, but an acquired one, sickly sweet, layer upon layer of odours – chemicals, dead flesh – all coalescing into one distinct aroma that now seemed like it must be part of the building's DNA itself. The building was all grey walls and dark wood panelling. The orderly's booth was empty. The lights were off. Beck heard a sharp metallic sound, and imagined something being dropped into a metal receiver. One half of the swing door ahead was open, held in place by a wooden wedge. He walked through and along a corridor to the door at the end. He could see lights on the inside through the glass panel. He didn't knock. He pushed the door open and entered the mortuary room.

The body of Eddie Kavanagh lay on the autopsy table directly in front of him, a line of crude black stitching meandering up the centre of his torso. Dr Keane was standing at the top of the table, by the head. He looked up at Beck.

'It was an accident,' Beck's mother had told him afterwards – his father had fallen from the window onto the concrete slabs below. She had been very calm about it. Too calm. But Beck was too young to comprehend it, not fully. It was the images that were the most powerful. Her bright red dress, as bright as the blood from his father's head. And that smell, of cigarettes and aftershave.

'But you had the key,' he had said to her. They had been the only ones in the room, so she had to have heard. But she looked away, and never answered.

'Don't you know you can't just barge in here like this?' Dr Keane said.

Beck realised he was staring at the wall. He turned, looked at the young pathologist. 'I've been ringing you.'

'So? It's early. I haven't had time to answer any calls yet. I'm busy. You have to wait until my office contacts you. That's the way it works.' His doctor's eyes lingered on Beck, taking everything in, an appraisal. 'Is everything alright with you, by the way?'

Beck walked to the end of the table, by the feet, turned and faced him. 'That's the way it works, eh, is what you say?' Beck said. 'If I may politely ask, how would you know?'

Dr Keane looked down at his hands, and Beck realised what he was doing. There was that clunking sound again. Dr Keane was stapling a section of scalp back into place, rearranging the grey-white hair like a piece of carpet matting before pressing the stapler down hard again. The doctor placed the index finger of his left hand under his scrub cap and ran it along his forehead. The sweat on the pathologist's skin glistened in the strong, harsh light.

'I had the photographer take close-ups of the ring found in the victim's pocket.' He pressed the stapler down with the palm of his right hand again. *Clunk.* 'They're up on Pulse. The victim's prints are on it, no others. It's an antique, clearly.' He pressed the stapler twice more in quick succession. *Clunk. Clunk.* Then he placed it on the mortuary table by Eddie Kavanagh's head. It was smeared with dark blood and particles of flesh, like gristle, trapped in the crevices of the stapler head. Dr Keane pulled his gloves off and dropped them into the yellow container next to him. 'Hazardous Surgical Waste', it said across the front. He turned and went to the sink, began washing his hands. He pulled some paper towels from the dispenser on the wall and turned back towards Beck as he dried them. He dropped the towels into the regular waste bin and crossed the room again, this time to a steel desk. He sat down, peering at a sheet of handwritten notes. Beck had never seen Gumbell sitting at this desk. He preferred to stand.

'At this point,' Beck said, 'Dr Gumbell would tell me how the victim died, which I would usually have a fair idea of by now anyway, and he would then present me with everything he had, and tell me to not expect any more... but he always did have more.'

'I can tell you something more,' Dr Keane said, and for the first time he gave a weak smile. Beck was surprised to note boyish features breaking through as his expression softened. He peered down at his notes. 'Cerebral vasculitis,' he said. 'Do you know what that is?'

Beck wondered why he didn't just tell him. Maybe he wasn't so dissimilar to Gumbell after all.

'No,' Beck said. 'I don't.'

'It means he had particularly weak, thin blood vessels in the brain. I looked through his medical records. I'm amazed he'd never had a subarachnoid haemorrhage before. Amazed. I would have expected that he would. But he didn't.'

'Before?'

'Yes. In this case, multiple ruptures of blood vessels within the brain, before death occurred, that is, caused, I would suggest, by the first blows. The victim was rendered immediately unconscious, which may explain why it took so long for him to die. And he had suffered at least one stroke. The nerve endings in the brain are torn, and the jaw is broken.'

'Quite considerable force then,' Beck said.

The doctor paused, peering at his notes. 'Yes and no. This is an old body, remember, and like anything that's old... In any case, the brain had effectively shut down. He would have been brain damaged as a result. If he had been discovered earlier he might well have survived, but he would have been a vegetable. I think, considering those circumstances, it's better that he has passed.'

Beck thought *passed* an odd term for a pathologist to use. In his experience, they were coldly blunt. Certainly, they lent the act of dying no mysticism.

'Considering his age, though,' Dr Keane continued, 'he was otherwise relatively fit. And that helped prolong his life, of course, but ultimately it didn't do him any favours here. As I said, it was better that he—'

Beck's father had died immediately. Beck knew that, because moments before he had heard his car pull into the driveway. When he looked, the sight of the Ford Cortina made him want to wet himself. He routinely wet himself, but only at night, in bed, when he was asleep. His mother would shout and scold him the next morning, which did nothing to ease his anxiety around the issue. He felt like wetting himself then because Mr Donegan's car was in the driveway too. And very soon, he knew now, his father would be dead.

Beck pulled up a chair and sat down. 'Time of death?'

Dr Keane looked at his notes again. 'Between 3.00 and 5.00 a.m. is my best guess. But I can—'

'And if I were to press you?'

'If you were to press me, well, maybe knock a half hour off either end, make it between 3.30 and 4.30 a.m. But I consider he was attacked earlier, *much* earlier, I mean, maybe twelve hours earlier.'

'I know,' Beck said. 'Specifically what time have you in mind?'

Dr Keane stood and walked to the autopsy table. Beck followed. Dr Keane indicated to the face. It was a mess. Beck thought of a rubberised zombie mask. Closed coffin for sure. Dr Keane pointed to the long laceration across the top of the forehead, the edges jagged and stiff with old blood.

'Blunt force trauma. The first blow was struck while the victim was standing. It probably did no more than daze him. Then he fell. Repeated blows followed, delivered while he lay on the ground, and are remarkably consistent in accuracy.' He pointed. 'See there, they all are concentrated in the same area with little deviation. Quite accurate. From a distance, it appears to be one massive blow that did the damage. But in fact it was many multiples of.'

'The attacker was strong,' Beck said.

'Well,' Dr Keane replied. 'This is an old body, like I say. Old bones. It wouldn't take much to break them, but still I would hazard at the same time the attacker is perhaps someone young, athletic maybe. I mean, have you ever beaten a rug, thrown it over a clothes line and went at it with a broom handle? It's quite tiring. And to do this amount of damage…'

Beck wondered at the analogy. 'No,' he said, 'I haven't done that.'

'Well,' Dr Keane said, 'it's a possibility worth bearing in mind, I would think.'

He walked over to a locker and opened it, took out another large clear plastic evidence bag. Inside it was a long piece of wood, a fencing stake, cut down the middle.

'The murder weapon,' he said. 'The victim's own, no less. There were a number just like it in an outhouse.'

Beck immediately thought of Sean 'Squeaky' Ward, a litany of section three assaults in his catalogue, usually with implements found on the property and belonging to the person he'd attacked.

'I picked a couple of teeth splinters from this,' Dr Keane said, holding up the evidence bag.

'Wait,' Beck said. 'You said the blows inflicted were remarkably consistent and accurate. But how does that explain the mouth? Did the weapon slip?'

'Maybe,' the doctor said. 'But then he repeated the process. Multiple blows to the jaw too. I mean, look at it. Completely shattered. He really should have died outright. Amazing that he didn't. Amazing.'

'An excess of violence,' Beck said. 'You agree?'

The young doctor nodded. 'Oh, I agree. No doubt. A psycho. Or someone who hated this man so very much to do what he did here.'

'A psycho then,' Beck said. 'Doesn't narrow it down much for me.'

'But it about sums it up,' the doctor said. 'I'm waiting on other results too, of course. Blood splatter analysis, hair fibres. SOC lifted prints from the murder weapon and they're currently running those.'

'And those were the only prints found,' Beck said. 'Correct?'

'Correct.'

Beck considered that. 'Are these the victim's prints?'

He could tell by the doctor's expression that he hadn't thought of that.

'Possibly.'

'In any case,' Beck said. 'If the killer took care to avoid leaving his prints, then that would denote a level of calculation, would it not? Your typical run-of-the-mill psycho is calculating, yes, but also impulsive. This doesn't strike me as being completely either.'

Dr Keane gave Beck a blank look.

Beck glanced at the body on the autopsy table.

But it might be something Sean 'Squeaky' Ward would do.

CHAPTER NINETEEN

The day that had begun under a clear, cold, blue sky had now suddenly darkened, the heavy clouds gathering, shutting out the light. And then it came, cascading from the sky. Snow. Beck stopped for breakfast – he was suddenly ravenous, sitting by the window in Frazzali's. The alcohol had dampened one fire, which was the raw images of the past, but fanned the embers of another, and this was the self-loathing he felt. Beck was neither drunk nor sober, but he knew he was no longer in charge. Now, he was merely along for the ride.

He concentrated on a question. It was this: why had Eddie Kavanagh had an engagement ring in his pocket? He couldn't find an answer to that, so looked out of the window instead, at the line of traffic trailing back from roadworks in the centre of town.

He glanced away from the window. A blonde-haired woman, fresh-faced with striking blue eyes, tight jeans and a sweater, was standing beside him and smiling at him.

'Hello, Vicky.'

In Beck's last big case he had, in all probability, saved her life. They had met at an AA meeting, and for a brief moment had been lovers.

'You're missed at the meetings,' she said.

'I've taken up running instead.'

She smiled. 'Wow. Never considered it could be that easy. AA has got it all wrong. It should be a running club, eh?'

'You could print that as a slogan,' Beck said. *'Keep running back.'*

Vicky didn't smile. 'Don't knock it, Finnegan, okay? That man who was killed, Eddie Kavanagh, he was in the rooms for a while. Everybody comes to the rooms at least once, if you ask me.'

'Really?' Beck said. 'How long ago was that?'

'A few years ago. Though I don't think he had a real drink problem. I think he was just lonely. Not everyone who comes to AA has a drink problem.'

'Really?' Beck said again, and gave an awkward smile.

'Thanks, Beck – you know for what. I just want you to know, my life is a lot calmer now.'

Beck nodded.

'And you?' she asked.

'And me?'

She held his gaze until Beck looked away.

'You have my number, if ever you need to talk.'

A blast of icy wind came through the doorway as she opened it. He watched her walk by the window, could see the drivers in their stationary vehicles turning their heads to look. Vicky might be leading a calmer life, but she still loved an audience.

He paid his bill and left the restaurant. The snow was not sticking, instead turning to slush. Beck pulled up the collar of his coat and made his way along Bridge Street. He lit a cigarette and smoked it in short, distracted puffs. He heard his phone ringing from somewhere deep in a pocket. He reached in and fished about, stopping in front of a property auctioneer's window, took it out, Natalia's name flashing across the screen. He thought of the telephone calls from before, when he would answer and she would not speak, the only sound that of faint breathing on the line. Now she was here. In Cross Beg. Waiting for him.

He answered.

'I didn't get out of bed yet.' Her voice was teasing. He could hear the rustle of bedclothes. 'When're you coming back?'

The hollow sound of a dog's bark in the background.

'Did you feed Max?'

'What?' she replied, as if stepping on a nail. 'Did I feed Max, you say?'

He paused. 'Yes. Could you? There's a shop right on the corner.'

'Feed the dog…' she repeated.

'Afraid so.'

'How romantic is that? I'll feed the dog, but also, you get here, before I change my mind.'

He peered at the display of houses and apartments up for sale and to rent, heard the click on the line that told him Natalia had hung up. He looked up above the door, at the garish sign: 'Charles Bastic, Residential and Commercial Property Specialists'.

Beck flicked the stub of his cigarette into the gutter next to the wheel of a brand new, gleaming red Mercedes Coupé, opened the door and stepped inside. The office was surprisingly dim and gaudy, the carpet a mixture of purple and black swirls, a high wooden counter in one corner, behind which sat a man who Beck immediately considered looked like he didn't belong there. The type Beck imagined would be more at home in a swanky Southside Dublin hotel or on the waterfront in Marbella. He was in his late thirties, Beck guessed, fair hair parted down the centre, tanned complexion – the result of a recent holiday? – and was dressed in a grey suit with a pale blue shirt, yellow tie with a gold pin across it, and a yellow pocket square. He observed Beck's approach but didn't smile.

'I know you,' he said then, placing his hands onto the counter, his jacket sleeve riding up to reveal a Rolex. 'I do, don't I? Know you?'

'Have you ever been arrested?' Beck asked.

For a fleeting moment something crossed the man's eyes, but then it was gone just as quickly and he gave a half smile.

'You're the cop, the guard – what's your name, Peck, Leck…? No, I have it, Beck. Right?'

Beck nodded.

'Charles Bastic, at your service,' he said, standing, extending his hand. 'My receptionist has just stepped out. How can I help you?'

'Just looking in your window,' Beck replied, taking Bastic's hand and shaking it. The grip was overfamiliar, firm. 'At your houses for sale, that's all.'

'How much you want to spend? Take a seat.'

Beck smiled. 'Straight to the point, aren't you? I won't stay, just an enquiry.'

'You want some brochures?'

'Maybe.'

Charles Bastic nodded. 'Have a look around. Then we can have a word.'

Beck's phone rang. He took it from his pocket and answered without checking the screen, expecting Natalia's sultry tones to waft into his ear. But they didn't.

'Where the hell are you?'

It was unlike Superintendent Wilde to get agitated. And there was something about the tone that didn't sound right, like it was forced. Did he have someone with him?

'Where am I? I've just come from the hospital. Preliminary autopsy results…'

'I want you here. Ten minutes. In my office.'

The line went dead.

'You're a busy man,' Bastic said.

'Another time, perhaps.'

'Of course.'

Beck went outside, but turned right, away from the station.

Natalia awaited. Wilde could wait.

CHAPTER TWENTY

Natalia's eyes were half shut, her skin glistening, the edges of her lips raised in a slight smile.

'God, I've missed you,' she purred, her arm draped across his chest.

She lay back and stretched her arms up above her head in what was beginning to be a habit, resting them against the wall. Her left leg rose and came to rest on top of his. She closed her eyes, seemingly in a state of bliss.

Beck knew there was much more to this than met the eye, he just didn't want to admit it. Not now. Because for now, in this moment, everything was just, well, fine.

Beck dreamt, but there was no imagery, merely a voice, *that* voice, that rasping, mocking, familiar voice, from way in the past, booming across the void of his slumbering consciousness. *No it's not fine, you gobshite. Look at you – in bed with another man's wife. Remember Mammy? In that cute red dress, so tight she could hardly walk. And she only seemed to wear it when he wasn't around, Daddy that is. And when she wore it she always stank of cigarettes and aftershave. Who was in that room when Daddy went sailing through the window? Guess we'll never know the truth, not now... Here, Beck, you sick hoor, you stink of cigarettes too, don't you? And that smell, sweet like aftershave, except it's alcohol. Work it out for yourself, you imbecile, you cretin, you moron...*

Beck's eyes snapped open.

'Beck, Christ, are you alright?'

'What...? Oh, I must have nodded off.'

He blinked, realised he was sweating, and his jaw hurt – he'd been grinding his teeth. There was the sound of cackling laughter, fading, fading, then gone…

He took a long, deep breath.

'Sorry,' he said. 'Sorry. I was… dreaming.'

He threw back the duvet and got out of bed, her foot sliding from his, and stood on the cold floor. He felt woozy, and like an animal bloodied, he wanted more. He squashed the feeling down… He didn't have to drink, he told himself. It could be different this time.

But that was the problem.

It *was* different this time.

Beck laughed, an involuntary gesture.

'What?' Natalia was staring at him. He was struck by her expression: like someone who'd stepped too close to the edge of a cliff on a windy day.

He cleared his throat. 'I've got to get back to work.'

'Finnegan.'

'Yes?'

She sat up, gathering the sheet about her. 'Won't you tell me? What's going on.'

He considered for a moment. 'Can't you guess?'

'We all struggle, you know…'

'I know,' he said.

'You told me once. That this time of year, Christmas, stirs something in you. I'd like to help. Won't you tell me? What happened?'

Beck shivered, feeling the cold now. Natalia reached out and placed her hand on the back of his, stroking it gently.

'I will. But just not right now. It's too close. I mean, it's too…' His voice trailed off.

Natalia placed a finger to his mouth. 'Shh, it's okay. You don't have to say a word, not until you're ready. I'm going to lie here a little longer. What time will you be home?'

Home. Definition: a place where one lives permanently, especially as a member of a family or household.

'I... don't know,' he said, forcing a smile. 'I don't know.'

'Let's make it six. Okay? That's a good time, isn't it?'

'Yes. Let's make it six.'

He kissed her softly, and left the room. He made his way along the landing to the bathroom. He was about to get into the shower when Max nudged the door open and stood there, watching him with his big, sad eyes, cocking his head to the side, as if studying Beck. Beck stared at the dog, and Max slowly approached, sat in front of him. Beck ran his hand over the animal's head, and Max looked up at him with that same sad expression, definitely studying him.

'You trying to understand me, boy?' Beck said. 'Are you? Even if I don't understand myself.'

He patted the dog once more, then ran the water in the shower.

In the kitchen afterwards, Beck made a mug of instant coffee, and fumbled through the cupboards until he found it. He told himself he wasn't going to start again, that what he wanted – okay, what he needed – all he needed, was enough, just enough. A snifter. A settler. The hair of the dog. As he poured some whiskey into his coffee, the real dog, Max, was sitting there again, in the doorway, his head cocked to the side as before. Beck drank his coffee and reassured himself he had everything under control. He glanced at Max, who was still staring at him. Beck shook his head. *It's only a dog.* He glanced to Max again... Those eyes, almost human. *Jesus.*

As he left the kitchen, he considered that he and Natalia were choosing to ignore the tsunami building up just off shore, a tsunami they knew was bound to be heading their way. Definition of tsunami: a long, high sea wave caused by an earthquake or other disturbance. Yes, Beck considered, that would sum up Chief Superintendent Gallagher just about right at this moment.

CHAPTER TWENTY-ONE

'Wilde has been looking for you,' Claire said when Beck entered the Ops Room. 'He's not happy… You don't look so good, is everything alright?'

'Something came up,' Beck said, managing to stop himself from smiling at his own private joke.

'Where the hell have you been? It's the afternoon now, for Christ's sake.'

'Not now, Claire. Anything I should know?'

She sighed. 'The postman. Jamie McLoughlin. He was in, wondering when we're going to interview him.'

'And…'

'I told him someone would be in touch. In an investigation of this nature a material witness such as he should be given priority, don't you think?'

Beck considered her words, like she was reading from an official bulletin. Had he been like this when he was preparing for his sergeant's exam too?

'Is he on Pulse?'

She shook her head. 'Not so much as a parking fine,' Claire said.

'The boss. In his office I take it?'

'Yes.' Claire pushed the exam booklet to one side. The heading on the page was: *When best practices are not adhered to, or are ignored, choose one of the following…*

Beck could hear footsteps behind him as he walked away, moving quickly. A hand on his shoulder now. He stopped, turned around again. Claire was standing inches from him.

'Jesus, Beck, don't just walk away like that. The CCTV, remember?'

'Oh yes, of course.'

'I got something. A camper van, twin rear wheel axle just like you said.'

Beck nodded. 'Where?'

'In town. Twice. Turning onto Bridge Street from Plunkett Hill. I have the reg number. And, wait for this, also turning up the track by Mullaney's on the CCTV Dempsey collected.'

Beck thought about that. 'Did you run it?'

'It's British.'

'Get in touch with the PSNI liaison officer in Lisburn then. The contact details are on Pulse.'

'Oh…' She looked at him in an odd way, seemed about to say something else. If she was, she had changed her mind, because she said nothing.

'I'll see you in a few minutes, okay?' Beck said.

'What's up?' she asked then. 'Where the hell *have* you been?'

'I'll see you later.' He turned, ignoring the question.

He strode out of the Ops Room, and Claire watched him go. He went along the corridor to the stairs and bounded up them two steps at a time, into the antique section of the station, got off at the nineteenth century. He walked along the creaking floorboards until he reached the door with the brass name plate on it that said: 'Superintendent Wilde'. Just before he went in, he popped another lozenge into his mouth.

He was about to knock when the voice on the other side said, 'In.'

Beck opened the door and was surprised, very surprised, to see that seated behind the desk was not Superintendent Wilde.

Instead it was a man with neatly combed black hair, heavy jowls and big ears on a big head: Chief Superintendent Jim Gallagher. His bushy eyebrows raised themselves in an almost perfect V shape.

'Why do you look so surprised, Inspector Beck?' Gallagher said. 'Did you really think I'd just let this go? That I wouldn't come after her?'

Beck said nothing. When confronted with a bear, the advice was to stand still, not make any sudden movements and avoid all eye contact. Beck ignored the eye contact bit, stood looking at Gallagher.

'Don't just stand there, man. Take a seat, for Christ's sake.'

Beck crossed the room and sat down, wondering how the chief superintendent managed to get his shirt looking so dazzlingly white. The crease lines along the sleeves appeared sharp enough to slice lemons. Beck wondered how a man noted for being such a strong and decisive leader had failed miserably to hold onto his wife.

Beck felt nothing now but a profound sense of shame. His shame was all-consuming and stifling. The chief superintendent didn't have to say a word. The silence was enough. It was Beck's torture. Beck wondered if the chief superintendent could sense it.

He seemed not to, for if he had, he surely would have allowed Beck to wallow in it further.

'Can't you get a woman of your own, Beck, is that it?' he said.

Beck thought about what the chief superintendent had said and found himself strangely humoured by it. Didn't the man get it? It was about so much more than that. It wasn't about a woman, any woman, it was about *a* woman. Couldn't Gallagher understand this? If he couldn't, then it was no surprise he could not understand his wife. Beck himself couldn't fully work it out. Not completely. So he tried now, for the first time.

'If I may?' he began. 'Because we have something in common, do we not?'

Chief Superintendent Gallagher's expression was one of agitated surprise.

'I'm not going to lie,' Beck added.

'Well, that's a start.' The chief superintendent's tone sounded like a schoolyard retort to hurt pride.

'I did not contact...' Beck was about to call her by her first name, but thought a little more of an impersonal approach was best '... your wife. She contacted me. In fact, she has been contacting me for quite a while. Silent phone calls. Which I didn't answer – well, mostly I didn't answer – or she hung up before I could. Granted, it takes two to tango, but I...'

'Shut up.' Gallagher's cheeks glowed. 'This is my wife you're talking about. *My* wife. You're blaming her now, is that it?'

'I was about to say,' Beck said, 'that I did not resist. Your wife has a certain allure, a very powerful allure. I find it irresistible, to be honest. There, I said it. I find your wife irresistible. But that has a lot to do with my dysfunction in seeking the unobtainable, and there is nothing more unobtainable than another man's wife. Is it wrong? Yes. And do I feel guilty? Yes. As to whether I wish it had never happened? No, I don't, to be honest. Natalia is a wonderful woman, much too good for me.'

'You've got that right,' Gallagher said.

'But...' Beck said.

Chief Superintendent Gallagher's face was inscrutable, and Beck hesitated before continuing.

'Where is your place in all this, may I ask? If you want her back, why don't you go and get her yourself?'

Chief Superintendent Gallagher clenched his fists. They were big fists, fists that Gallagher had never been slow to use.

'Don't fuck with me.' His voice was like a rumble of thunder. 'She's mine, and I want what's mine. Until she asks for a divorce, that's the way it stays.' His expression softened, as did his tone. 'Because I love her.' His voice softened further still, becoming tender and brittle enough to break. 'I want her back, Beck, won't you help me? I'm asking you. I'm laying my soul bare here. *Please.* I don't care how you do it.'

Beck took a deep breath. 'Why can't you do it yourself?'

Chief Superintendent Gallagher sighed. 'Because if I do, I might push her even further away. She's heard it all before. But this time I mean it. Because this time I know she means it too. She will leave me.'

'Like I say,' Beck said, 'you should go around yourself and talk to her.'

But his words lacked conviction.

The chief superintendent shook his head. 'I don't want her to even know I'm here. I'm going straight back to Dublin after I finish with you. I came here to ask you that one question. Help me to get her back. I won't be talking to you again about this. You either will or you won't. My coming down here was not planned. I'm acting on emotion, and I don't like that. To me, that's dangerous. Tell her whatever you want, but just make it happen, okay? And don't make it obvious.'

Beck pursed his lips. 'For a matter so, as you say, emotional,' he said, 'isn't this all a little devious? Wouldn't some straightforward honesty be the best approach? Like I say, simply go and talk to her. I think that's what's needed, what Natalia needs.'

Beck saw it immediately. As countless gougers had seen it in countless interview rooms through the years. Gallagher's expression was changing, the features compacting as he tightened his facial muscles, the mouth becoming a thin, pinched line. He spoke, a rumble through those lips that hardly seemed to move.

'I give and you take, Beck. I say and you do. It's simple. Got it? So if you want to keep the one thing keeping you from begging on the streets, your job, you'll make sure Natalia comes back to me. She's not interested in you. You're a distraction, that's all, and I always thought she could have done better myself.'

Beck didn't answer.

'Have you fucking got it?' Gallagher suddenly shouted. He gave a twisted smile.

Beck nodded. He got it alright.

CHAPTER TWENTY-TWO

'Sergeant Robinson,' Claire said, appearing in the open door of Beck's office. 'PSNI Lisburn just returned my call. The camper van is registered to a Mr Jeffrey Agnew of Bangor, Co. Down. They contacted Mr Agnew on my behalf, who says he sold it about three months ago. To a "foreign gentleman", that's how Sergeant Robinson says Mr Agnew put it. The buyer paid cash. Mr Agnew said there was some confusion over paperwork. His belief was that he deliberately had been confused by the buyer. In any case, the van is still registered to Mr Agnew, and he has no details of the person who purchased it.'

'I see,' Beck said. 'So, it's driving around illegally, because a foreign vehicle must be registered in this jurisdiction within thirty days.'

He went to the window and looked out. The snow was falling again, the sky heavy and dark.

'Beck...'

He turned. 'Yes?'

He began massaging his temples. 'Yes?' he said again, tetchy.

'What's up?' She crossed the room and stood by his desk.

He looked at her. A number of seconds passed between them in silence. But just then, his desk phone rang. The shrill sound echoed through the high-ceilinged old room. He went and picked it up. He covered the mouthpiece with his hand.

'Not now,' he said to her, and, into the telephone: 'Hello.' He listened, then: 'Okay. I'll be right down.' As he hung up he spoke.

'Two ladies have presented themselves at the public office counter, as mentioned by Officer Fergal Dempsey at the briefing yesterday. Remember, from The Noose?'

'I remember.'

'Yes.' Beck, moving towards the door, was glad for the change of subject. 'Come on, let's see what they have to say for themselves. I think they should be able to shed some light on this travelling brothel. Maybe give us something we need.'

CHAPTER TWENTY-THREE

They were sitting on the hard wooden bench seat against the wall just inside the station door. They both had their arms folded, mouths tightly clamped shut. They were Maisy Roche and Dolly Lyons.

'Ladies,' Beck said, going and standing before them. 'I'm Detective Inspector Beck.' He gestured towards Claire. 'And this is Detective Garda Somers. Let's go and talk somewhere a little more private, shall we? Follow me, please.'

They stood, arms remaining tightly folded and lips pressed together. Beck led the way down to the basement and into Interview Room Two. It was larger than number one and airier. He indicated two chairs before the interview table and they sat down. Then he closed the door and he and Claire sat on the opposite side, facing them.

'If I may ask?' Beck said. 'Your names please, ladies?'

'Maisy Roche.' Her voice was raspy, like a moped engine climbing a hill. She had greasy, badly dyed blonde hair, the grey roots visible down the centre of her head and stretching a quarter of the way down the strands. She had on a frayed coat with wide lapels and buttons of different-coloured thread. She wore no make-up at all, and her complexion was ruddy, the skin cracked like a dry riverbed. Beck had no trouble imagining her propping up the counter in The Noose.

'Dolly Lyons,' the other woman said, softer spoken and smarter in appearance, her raven-coloured hair held off her forehead by a diamante band. She was heavily made up and wore a leopard-skin brown raincoat with a pink silk scarf. She was classier in a down-at-heel sort of way, though the bar wasn't very high in this case.

They were similarly aged, though, Beck considered, early to mid-sixties he guessed.

'How did you hear that we wanted to speak with you?' Beck asked.

Maisy unfolded her arms again and placed her hands on the table, staring off behind Beck with her bloodshot eyes. Beck could detect it now, the faint aroma of alcohol.

'I heard. Youse hear about things in a town like this. It's not hard.' She had a thick Dublin accent.

'You're from Dublin?' Beck said.

'Where the girls are so pretty, love, ya.' She made a gurgling sound. Beck realised she was laughing.

'It was Maisy here who told me,' Dolly added. She fixed her gaze on Beck now. Her eyes were clear and bright, and her accent West-of-Ireland lyrical.

'I see,' Beck said, turning back to Maisy. 'And what exactly did you hear we were interested in, Maisy?'

Maisy shrugged. 'Something about a bleedin' camper van. Going about with a bird in the back. Doing the rounds like, ya. Youse want to know 'bout it, ya. That's why we're here, ya?'

'But why would you want to speak to us?' Dolly said, the emphasis on the *us*.

Beck blew air into his cheeks. 'OK ladies, I won't lie,' he said. 'Your names were mentioned...'

'By who?' Dolly interrupted, placing a perfectly painted long fingernail against the corner of her red lips and raising two eyebrows, plucked to within an inch of their lives.

'You know I can't say,' Beck said, 'but...'

'Then it mightn't be true,' Dolly added. 'Passing comments about us like that. The cheek of them. Going off with men...'

'Is that what you were doing?' It was Beck's turn to interrupt. 'Going off, as you put it, with men?'

Dolly folded her arms tightly across her chest again. 'Yes. It's been said about me for years.' She turned to look at Maisy. 'Hasn't it, Maisy?'

But Maisy didn't respond. She was completely still, staring at the wall.

'I mean,' Dolly went on. 'I mean, it's not enough that I'm a happily married woman. With grown children, I'll have you know. But I'm supposed to be regularly pimped out by my husband of all people, by Alfie Lyons… Did you never hear of such a thing?'

'I'm not long in Cross Beg,' Beck said, and regretted his words immediately. Because he considered his inference to mean that if he had been here for a time then he would have heard. He pressed two fingers against his temple, trying to hold in the pain.

But Claire said, 'I never heard that, Dolly. And I've been here a while.'

'Well that's reassuring at least, I suppose,' Dolly said, 'because I don't need my husband or any other man to pimp me out. I can look after myself. And if a man wants to be friendly with me and give me a little something in return, a gift like, well then, that's his and my business only, isn't it?'

'Um,' Beck said. 'I suppose it is.' He glanced at Claire and found she was already looking at him.

'But not that I would, you understand,' Dolly added quickly.

'Of course,' Beck said. 'Not that you would.'

'What about you, Maisy?' Claire asked gently.

'What about me?' Her tone changed, becoming a defensive shield.

'Why would your name be mentioned to us?'

Maisy shrugged and held the collar of her old coat tightly about her neck with one hand.

Silence.

'I don't care,' Beck said. 'I just want you to know that. What both of you may or may not get up to. My only interest is in a brothel camper van, if I can call it that. That's my sole interest, okay?'

'Then why do youse want to talk to us?' It was Maisy.

'Because you might know something,' Beck said, his words sharper than he'd intended.

'And why would we know?'

Beck leant forward now, placed his elbows onto the table and tented his hands beneath his chin. 'Maisy, I'm being polite here, aren't I?' he said.

Maisy said nothing, staring straight ahead again, at the wall.

Dolly spoke up. 'Yes, you are being polite. But we should expect nothing less.'

'Yes,' Beck said. 'That is correct. You should expect nothing less. Will you answer my question or will I have to tell you?'

'Tell us,' Maisy said, her eyes wide.

'The way I heard it,' Beck said, 'both of you work in that business too. There, I said it. That's what I heard.'

Dolly made a strange whistling sound through her nose and suddenly got to her feet.

'How dare you,' she said. 'I have a good mind to sue the gardai for what you just said… and I very well might. I mean, how dare you. I would never, *ever* stoop to such a thing…' She looked at Maisy.

Maisy caught it. 'What? And I would, is that it?'

Dolly's mouth opened, about to say something, her face stretched so tight the plucked eyebrows were becoming almost vertical.

'For God's sake, Maisy,' she said. 'Everyone knows it, don't they?'

Maisy got to her feet now too, and stabbed a finger through the air at Dolly.

'Missus high-an-fooking-mighty herself, is it? They call youse The Recliner 'cause there's no car you can't get into without the bleedin' seat goin' back, ain't that right missus? You think you're above the rest of us.'

It happened so quickly that Claire didn't notice until it was almost too late. As Dolly swung an arm through the air, the long, painted nails at the end of it as lethal as a cat's claws, heading for Maisy's face, Claire dived across the table and pushed her back just in time. Dolly stumbled against her chair and both she and it toppled against the wall. Dolly began sliding to the floor, and as she did one knee struck the back of the chair and she cursed aloud, her coat and dress riding up to reveal black stockings and a pair of garters.

Beck was already moving around the table. As Maisy stepped forward, raising a hand and about to bend down, about to slap Dolly across the face, Beck wrapped his arm around her waist and yanked her back. She smelt like an old ashtray.

'Steady on,' he said. 'Steady on. One move from either of you and you'll be in the cells, understand?'

Maisy pointed a finger and gave a hoarse laugh.

'There,' she said. 'Did youse see the get-up? Wrapped up and ready to go she is… the floozy!'

'Shut up!' Claire said. 'The both of you!'

A voice came through the intercom in a corner of the ceiling by the door. 'Everything alright in there? You need a hand, boss?'

Beck waved towards the camera: all under control.

'Sit, ladies,' he said.

He released Maisy, hooking his foot around the leg of the fallen chair and pulling it towards him. He set it upright again and offered his hand to Dolly, helped her to her feet. She stood motionless, staring at Maisy, her nostrils flaring.

'Now,' he said. 'Sit down. Both of you.'

'Read my lips,' Beck said when they were all seated again. 'And let it sink in. I don't care what either of you are getting up to. I. Don't. Care. What I care about is that bloody camper van. Do either or you know anything about it? Yes or no? Tell me.'

Dolly shook her head, but Maisy sat motionless.

'Right,' Beck said. 'That's what I call a conundrum. Which is it, ladies? You know or you don't?'

Maisy and Dolly looked at one another.

'What the hell?' Maisy began. 'Makes no difference now, does it?'

Dolly said nothing.

'What is it, ladies?'

Dolly looked away, towards the door, then back to Beck. Then she turned her head towards Maisy. 'Enough, Maisy, yes?'

Maisy did not reply.

'Don't know why I give a damn,' Dolly began. 'But I do. This is strictly between these four walls?'

'Yes,' Beck said. 'Between these walls.'

Dolly said, her tone businesslike, matter-of-fact, 'I'll tell you so.'

Maisy shifted in her chair, looked towards the door.

'I heard about it couple of months ago,' Dolly said. 'I mean, when you think of it...I wish I'd thought of it.' Dolly fell silent, stretched her hands out before her, looking at her nails. 'If you have a service, why not go direct?' She paused. 'They're foreigners,' she continued. 'I mean, they'd have to be. Who's going to do that? Only them. Albanians, I heard, or maybe Bulgarians. Something 'arians anyway. They're flat-out busy too, from what I hear, calling to all the lonely old boys. Wish I'd thought of it... bloody foreigners. I mean, I wish I'd thought of it.'

'Do you know the girls?' Claire asked.

Dolly shook her head. 'I told you, they're foreigners.'

'Bulgarian?' Beck asked.

'I don't bleedin' know,' Maisy said. 'Does it matter?'

'It might,' Beck said.

'They're young wans,' Maisy said. 'I mean the girls. No ones bothering with us now since they've showed up.'

'Speak for yourself,' Dolly said, sounding put out.

'Ladies, please,' Claire said. 'Not again. Have either of you seen this van?'

'Naw,' Maisy said. 'A fella told me.'

'And you?' Beck asked Dolly.

Dolly shook her head. 'No, but the quicker you put an end to all this the better for us.'

'Why didn't you come forward with this before?' Beck asked.

'I'm no snitch,' Maisy said.

'Listen to her.' Dolly laughed. 'The only reason you didn't say anything is the same reason I didn't.'

Beck rubbed the back of his neck. 'What are you getting at?' he asked.

'Nothing,' Dolly said. 'Said far too much already.'

'That won't do,' Claire said.

'No,' Beck said. His mouth was dry. He tried to swallow, but coughed instead. 'It won't.'

Dolly pursed her lips.

'Withholding information,' Beck said. 'You'll be here a while so, while we get this sorted out. Both of you.'

'I'm not bleedin' staying here,' Maisy said. 'I've things to do.'

'It's up to you, ladies. But you don't leave here until you tell me.'

'Is that bleedin' so?' Maisy replied.

'Yes,' Beck said. 'That is so.' He knew, however, in reality, it wasn't.

'There's nothing much to tell,' Dolly said.

'Jesus.' Beck found himself getting angry now. 'Stop the games. The both of you. Tell me what you know. Speak.'

'Hmm, forceful, aren't you?' Dolly gave him a wink.

'Fook sake,' Maisy snapped. 'Charlie Bastic. There. I said it.'

'Well, I didn't.' Dolly said.

'Fook you,' Maisy said.

'Charles Bastic?' Beck repeated. The flashy estate agent.

'You're getting no more outta me,' Maisy said.

'Or me.' It was Dolly.

'So why'd you mention his name?' Beck asked.

'I heard it, okay? Don't ask me from who. If you want to talk to me any longer,' Dolly said, 'then arrest me, but I want a solicitor. Clear?'

'And the same goes for me,' Maisy added.

Beck smiled. 'There's no need to be like that, ladies.'

'Bit late for the charm now,' Dolly said, getting to her feet. 'We've been more than helpful to you. Do you want us to do your job for you completely, is that it? Come on now, surely you can work it out for yourself?'

Beck knew it was no use.

'Okay,' he said, getting to his feet too.

Some moments later he was standing outside the station door, watching as they walked away along the street, normal relations restored by the way they were leaning into one another, animated in their discussion. *If only I could hear what that particular conversation is about*, Beck thought. He turned. Claire was standing behind him. He hadn't noticed her follow him out.

'Charles Bastic,' he said, taking a pack of cigarettes from his pocket. He took one out and lit it, took a long draw. 'Well, well. Tell me what you know about him.'

'No smoke without fire,' Claire said. 'That's what I'd say about him.'

He angled his head as he looked at her. 'And what does that mean?'

'It's cold,' she said, and gave a shiver.

Beck liked the cold. And it seemed to ease the pain in his head. He took a couple of long draws on the cigarette and tossed it half smoked into the gutter.

'He's supposed to have lost it all,' she said as they walked slowly back into the station. 'During the economic crash, I mean. Ended up penniless. But he made it all back again. Quickly. Like, really quickly. No one quite knows how he did it... but there were rumours.'

'Rumours?'

'Actually it was more than rumours,' she said as they crossed the foyer. 'We received information, and took it seriously enough to obtain search warrants for his office, home and various properties he owns. But we never found anything…'

'And what were you looking for?'

She shrugged, folded her arms tightly across her chest. 'Not quite sure… drugs possibly. That's what we thought, at the time, but we weren't certain. He never could explain how he made the big time again. Like I say, no smoke without fire. But we couldn't find it, the fire I mean.'

They stopped at the security door. Claire punched in the code and they went through. As they walked along the corridor a uniformed officer appeared in the doorway of the Comms Room.

'Squeaky Ward, boss,' he said, 'they're chasing him.'

They walked quickly in. An officer was standing by the window holding a handset. Beck and Claire stood listening to the voices from the patrol cars:

'Zulu Yankee Five One, I can see him, he's moving fast…".… Where are you, Zulu Yankee Five One? Still on the Ballinasloe Road…?' '… Shit no, he's turned off onto the L353, where's that go to?' 'Tango Seven Seven One. He's heading to Larkhill, I can catch him at the other end…' 'Zulu Yankee Five One pulling back. It's too risky. He's driving like a lunatic.' 'Tango Seven Seven One. I have him in visual. I'm on the L353. I've come out directly behind him.'

The sound of static, followed by silence, then: 'Crash, crash, crash. He's in the ditch. Standby…' They waited. 'Have the bastard. No apparent injuries. Prisoner in custody.'

CHAPTER TWENTY-FOUR

Beck and Claire were waiting in the custody area when Sean Ward, aka 'Squeaky', was brought in, handcuffed between two uniforms, missing one sneaker and hobbling. The custody sergeant looked him over, then glanced to the uniforms.

'Which one of you is the arresting officer?'

The officer gave his name and details of the arrest, added, 'The suspect's on probation, Skipper, I believe.'

'I see that,' the custody sergeant said. 'Yes, I see that here on Pulse.' He peered over his glasses at Ward. 'Anything important we should know about you? Any aliments? On any medication? Anything?'

'Aye, I got ailments,' Ward said, the reason for his nickname becoming clear, as his voice sounded like he had just taken a mouthful of helium. 'Me foot's busted.'

'Cell two,' the arresting officer said. 'Mr Ward. You're required to change into a paper suit the officer here will provide you with…'

'A paper suit,' Ward said. 'What for?'

'Your clothes are being taken for analysis, Mr Ward,' the custody sergeant said.

'No way. I want me solicitor.'

'You can have your solicitor,' the sergeant said. 'But first… look, are you going to make this difficult now or what?'

Ward was a small block of a man. He wore a sweatshirt and jeans, and that one sneaker. His head was shaved. Beck could see his body stiffen. Yes, he was about to make this difficult.

'Can I speak to you on your own?' Ward suddenly said to the custody sergeant.

'You can speak here. That's the best I can offer you.'

Ward leant in, and as he whispered, Beck could swear he saw a trace of a smile cross the sergeant's lips. The custody sergeant said something in reply and Ward nodded his head in turn. Then the uniform took him away.

And finally the custody sergeant nodded towards Beck and Claire. 'You want to interview him first?'

They stepped up to the desk. 'Yes...' Beck said.

'Interview Room One. Table's bolted to the floor in there, just in case...' He leant towards them now, waited for them to lean in to him. 'He told me something. Get this...'

They waited. 'Get what?' Beck added when the sentence remained unfinished.

'He's wearing women's knickers. I told him the matter would be treated with sensitivity. Gas, or what?'

Beck was impressed. The custody sergeant had managed to keep a straight face the whole time he spoke.

They made their way slowly to Interview Room One, giving Ward enough time to change into the paper suit.

Ward was leaning back in his chair when he went in. The paper suit made a rustling noise as he folded his arms.

'I want me solicitor,' he said.

'We'll get you one,' Beck said. 'You are sure? You do want one?'

'I'm sure. I want one.'

'Not going to make any difference. You're heading straight back to prison, you know that? Bolt cutters, gloves and a balaclava were found in the back of your van... Don't give me that look, like it's a big surprise. That's why you took off. Broke the conditions of your parole.'

Ward turned his head. 'I know that,' he said. 'Still. I want one.' And, turning back again: 'Otherwise you're going to lob a heap of new charges on me, get me a couple of years added to the end of me sentence. I know how you lot work. Think I came down in the last shower. No way.'

'It wasn't me who arrested you,' Beck said. 'That's a separate matter. I only want answers to a few questions, that's all.'

'I don't give a damn,' Ward said. 'I'm not answering anyone's questions. Get me me solicitor.'

Ward folded his arms and pursed his lips, set his jaw at an angle and dropped his head.

'Right,' Beck said. 'You leave me no choice. Comfortable, are they…? Women's knickers. I was told.'

Ward's head shot up. He looked at Beck. He didn't look such a hard man any more. But Beck didn't have time for or any interest in sympathy for Ward, or in working out what deviant, socio-economic or whatever other reasons or circumstances caused him to do what he did and to wear women's knickers. Maybe he had a skin condition. But in the world that Ward inhabited, wearing a pair of ladies' underpants was enough to mark him out, make him a source of merciless, endless ridicule. His life wouldn't be worth living.

Ward glanced at Claire.

'Don't worry,' Beck said. 'No one knows. At this time, that is. At this time, the matter is being treated with the discretion and sensitivity our operational guidelines demand.' Beck looked at Ward and held his gaze. 'But that may change…'

Squeaky slumped back in his chair, squeaked, 'Bastards.'

Beck nodded to Claire, who turned on the recorder and listed the time and preamble.

'A murder investigation.' Squeaky's voice was a perfect falsetto.

'You were in the vicinity,' Claire said.

'We know that because you were stopped twice at garda checkpoints,' Beck clarified. 'A traffic checkpoint and a mandatory alcohol testing. Explain.'

'It weren't me.'

'How do I know that?' Beck said. 'I'm weighing up odds here and I'm thinking they're stacking up. Against you.'

Ward looked at the floor, and said nothing.

'The man was beaten to death,' Beck said. 'You like to beat people, don't you, Squeaky?'

'Don't call me that.'

'Old people,' Beck said. 'Isn't that right... *Squeaky?*'

Ward looked up. 'I said, don't call me that.'

'Why? What you going to do about it? Beat me up too?'

Claire shifted in her seat, threw a look at Beck.

Ward was silent for a moment. 'I were somewhere else,' he said then. 'When that man were killed.'

'Where?' Claire asked.

'I were in Ballinasloe. I only came over to Cross Beg in the evening. And I didn't stay long. D'ya think I'm stupid or what? Would I have drove the main roads if I were out robbin'? I'll give ya the reg and ya can trace the van from Ballinasloe all the way over to the town, then trace it all the way back again. And I'll make it even easier, I'll give ya the names of all the places where there are CCTV cameras, cause I know where they all are, every one of them.'

'I bet you do,' Beck said.

He stared at Ward. There was an intelligence there, he knew that, an aberrant intelligence, the career criminal's intelligence, a way of thinking that continually posed both a statement and a question: *How am I going to get what you have?*

'Why did you come to Cross Beg that night?' Claire asked. 'And how long did you remain here?'

Ward began stroking his chin.

'Is that on CCTV too?' Beck asked.

Still, Ward stroked his chin, silent.

'I take it it's not then,' Beck said.

'I'm on another kind of camera,' Ward said. 'From the place I went to. They have one on the wall so they do, just inside the door, to see who comes in. Tiny thing, most of the punters don't even see it. But I do, so I do.'

Again, Ward lapsed into silence.

'I was there for about a half hour,' he said, as an afterthought.

'All the way from Ballinasloe,' Beck said. 'For a half hour. Where?'

'A house in Cedar Grove... number six.'

The way he said it, like it was an answer they should both already know. He looked at them, from one to the other.

'You know?' he said.

'No,' Claire said. 'We don't.'

Now Ward grinned, which altered his face, lent him an innocence that didn't belong. Beck could see how this might fool people, charm them just enough to allow him to gain entry to their property, where the smile would disappear and the mask would come off. Because lurking just beneath the surface was the real Sean 'Squeaky' Ward.

'Some of the boys call it the Purple Palace you know, because of the lights.'

Beck took a breath.

'Call what the Purple Palace? Tell us.'

'It's a whorehouse, for God's sake. Some coppers ye are. How do ye not know that?'

Beck was speechless. He had no answer for that.

It was possible, he thought again, in a small town, to keep big secrets.

'A what?' Superintendent Wilde spluttered.

'A brothel, boss,' Beck said. 'Or whorehouse, to use his term.'

They were sitting in Wilde's office. The blinds were drawn and only the desk lights were on. Wilde sat back, half in shadow. His jacket was off and his shirt sleeves rolled up. The radiators made a clicking sound, throwing out more heat into an already stuffy room.

'In Cross Beg?' His tone was like he'd just been told of a two-horned unicorn.

'Yes,' Beck said.

'How... I mean, Jesus... How's that possible?'

'Think about it, sir,' Beck said. 'Who's going to tell us about it? The punters? I don't think so.'

Wilde was silent for a moment. 'You think there's a link?' he said then. 'To Eddie Kavanagh's murder?'

'Well,' Beck said slowly, mentally shuffling through a stack of case files. 'I find a serious crime often has tentacles. Where they reach to we only find out afterwards.'

Wilde gave him a look.

'Yes,' Beck said, 'I think there's a link. Most definitely.'

Wilde shook his head. 'Surely there are neighbours, for God's sake... And a mobile brothel too, makes us look like fools... Where is this place by the way?'

'Cedar Grove.'

Wilde leant forward. 'Cedar Grove, eh? Nice area. Secluded houses. Suppose you don't know who owns the house, do you?'

'I do. I checked.'

'And?'

'Charles Bastic.'

The commanding officer jumped to his feet.

'That bastard! I see what you mean about tentacles. He's a slippery one that fella... Right, get some bodies together. I'll have the warrant ready by the time you leave. I want that house searched top to bottom. Bastic! Maybe now I'll finally get the bastard.'

CHAPTER TWENTY-FIVE

They arrived in three cars and parked along the street just down from number six. Cedar Grove, just a half mile from the station, was a horseshoe-shape small estate of twelve exclusive properties, each on its own half acre or so plot of land, set back from the road, and each hidden from the other by high trees and ivy-covered walls. Number six had a neat lawn running in front to the pavement, while to the side a driveway swept up and ended in a large curved area by the front door. On either side of the driveway was a row of lights set into the neat bushes. The house itself had the appearance of a Swiss mountain chalet, but without the wood. The roof was high, with a sharply angled central section, and another section on either side of it sweeping up and down in a soft curve.

Beck got out of the car and closed the door gently, raised his arm and indicated for the others to follow. It was dark now, and two upstairs lights were on, one downstairs, as well as the porch light. He led the way along the driveway, the lights casting the approaching police officers into an abstract of bobbing shadows. He could see a couple of large cars parked by the door.

Beck motioned for two uniforms to go round the back. He gave it a minute to allow them time to get into position, then fisted his hand and banged on the door, at the same time pressing the bell and keeping his finger there.

'Open up. Open up. Guards.'

He waited. The burly officer with the door ram was getting into position, readying himself to smash the door down. Then there was a voice from the other side. Beck recognised it as Dempsey's. 'Back inside, you two. Move. Go on now. There's no one leaving.' Heavy footsteps sounded, approaching the door. Then he heard the sound of a latch turning, then another, and the door swung open and Dempsey was standing before him.

'The back door opened and two males attempted to leave,' he said. 'Like rabbits out of a burrow, boss.'

Beck stepped into the foyer and moved aside, allowing the four officers behind to come in, one of them Claire. There was a smell in the air, like bleach and perfume. Fixed to the ceiling, just as Squeaky Ward had said, was a discreet CCTV camera trained on the door.

'What have we got?' he asked Dempsey, looking at a long wooden table towards the rear of the foyer with a sculpture of a mermaid at its centre. He looked around. The floor was deep pile carpet, a wooden staircase in the centre, LED lighting set into the steps like something from the Starship *Enterprise*. By the staircase was a leather couch and hanging from the wall were framed paintings illuminated by soft under-lighting. Dempsey led the way along a corridor and they passed a series of doors.

'They're locked, boss,' Dempsey said. 'I checked.'

He led them into a kitchen, an expanse of tiled flooring and walnut wood fitted cabinets, a long breakfast counter in the centre ringed by a gleaming handrail and wooden high stools, two of which were occupied.

Sergeant Connor was standing by the back door, watching over the two men. They both covered their faces with their hands, peering out from between the fingers.

'Who have we got here?' Beck asked.

They dropped their heads, staring at the floor. Beck noted the similarities: mid to late thirties, well-cut suits. Not the types you'd expect to have to pay for it. Unless… They both slid from their stools and stood, shoulders slumped.

'Let me guess,' Beck said. He detected a subtle change, a stiffening of postures. 'Both married, yes? Come on gentlemen, talk to me. Either of you realise how silly you look right now?'

The one nearest to Beck dropped his hand. He had scared blue eyes and red hair, a gold wedding band on the second-to-last finger of his left hand. The other man – his hand remained over his face – was bald and a little overweight, perspiring, the forehead between his fingers bathed in sweat.

'Christ,' the man with the frightened blue eyes said, sounding like he was about to burst into tears. 'I did nothing wrong. Honest to God. Look, can't I – we – just go home?'

'Name?' Beck said.

'Ah, come on.'

'Name?'

'Paul… McCartney.'

'Spare me,' Beck said. 'If that's not your real name, sunshine, you'll be going straight to the station.'

'OK. OK.'

'So, what is it?'

'James… James O'Malley. Honest.'

'Where you from, James?'

'Sligo.'

'What brings you here?'

James shuffled his feet, said nothing.

'Yes,' Beck said. 'I know it's kind of a stupid question. All that way, eh?' He turned to the other man. 'And you?'

Finally, this man dropped his hand from his face too.

'John Rogers,' he said. 'We came down together.'

'I see,' Beck said. 'We'll be checking your identities, by the way. Anyway, how did you hear about this place?'

'Hear about this place?' O'Malley said. 'What do you mean? We're just visiting.' O'Malley's eyes all of a sudden didn't look so frightened any longer; there was a hardening of his voice too.

'Yes,' Beck said. 'But visiting for what reason?'

'There's no law against people visiting wherever they choose,' O'Malley said, standing tall now, meeting Beck's gaze without flinching.

'That's true,' Beck said.

'And indeed, whenever they choose,' O'Malley added.

'Well now,' Beck said, 'that depends.'

'Certain circumstances, maybe…' O'Malley's voice trailed off.

'You sound like a solicitor,' Beck said.

'That's because I am. We both are. And now, if you don't mind, we're going to leave, and there's nothing you can do about it.'

'One moment,' Beck said. 'I'm afraid you're not. If you really are both solicitors you should know you are required to remain here until I ascertain if this property is being used for the purposes of prostitution, the procurement of which is illegal, by the way, as you no doubt well know. I have a search warrant and all persons on said property are required to remain until otherwise directed to leave by a member of An Garda Síochána.'

'Brothel,' O'Malley said. 'I don't know what you're talking about. Are you inferring…? Listen, I'll have you know we are on this property for legitimate, private business reasons, details of which I don't wish to divulge to you.'

O'Malley looked to his friend, but Rogers only patted his brow with a damp tissue.

'I bet you are.' It was Claire. 'Here on business, that is. Yes, I have no doubt you're here on business.'

Rogers looked away, but O'Malley spoke.

'I hope you're not…'

'Inspector.'

Beck turned. A uniform was standing at the door. He added nothing more, just looked at Beck.

'You will wait here,' Beck said. 'The both of you. Sergeant Connor, Dempsey, make sure they don't go anywhere. Claire, you come with me.'

O'Malley was about to speak, but closed his mouth again. Sergeant Connor nodded.

They followed the uniformed officer out into the foyer and he led them up the winding staircase. In a recess on a wall of the landing was a sculpture, a classical reproduction of some kind or other. The officer headed down a corridor to the left. Midway along he stopped at an open door. Beck could see the wash of purple light spilling out like a sensory fog. When he looked in, the imagery brought to mind *Apocalypse Now*, the Vietnam war movie. It had contained scenes of whorehouses in Saigon, scenes just like this: a room of shifting shadows, the neon circle of ceiling light creating a sense of otherworldly malevolent mysticism. There was music in the background, a rock tune, Led Zeppelin maybe, the drums distinctive, a slow percussive powerhouse. The bed was massive, but the girl was so small, lying directly in the centre, her arms spread out on the pillows either side. Beck noted her hair, long curling blonde locks, and determined it was a wig. He stepped into the room. He could see the windows were draped in heavy curtains. There was a smell, a cocktail of rubber, oil and perfume. On a dresser was a bowl filled with condoms and leaning against it was what looked like a horse whip. Claire was behind him, and they walked over to the bed and looked down at the girl. He was struck by her eyes; the pupils were perhaps the largest he had ever seen, floating about, back and forth, up and down, without any anchor, looking at him but seemingly seeing nothing.

'I've been waiting for you, baby,' she said in heavily accented English. 'You going to love me good, baby? Come on, baby.' Then, to Claire: 'You too, honey.'

What was she, nineteen, twenty years old maybe, tops?

He turned, feeling a rage building up inside him.

'Stay with her,' he said to Claire. She nodded, and he walked out of the room into the corridor.

The uniform was standing there.

Beck took a deep breath, held it, then exhaled slowly.

'There's a couple of girls in another room,' the uniform said. 'Two young fellas too. Nothing but their boxers on.' He pointed. 'And further down, at the end of this corridor, there's a kind of office. We found a man in it, a foreign national.'

Beck nodded. 'Show me. The girls first.'

Beck followed the uniform. The room was similar to the one he had just left. Standing directly inside the door were two young men, early twenties at most, shirts now haphazardly tucked inside the waistbands of their trousers, shoelaces undone. They stared at the floor sheepishly.

'Downstairs,' Beck said, jabbing a finger at each of them. 'Now. Go on. Get out.'

The girls looked to be in their late teens, slim, delicate features, both very pretty, and black-haired – one shoulder length, the other in a bob cut. The long-haired girl was lying on top of the bed, leaning against the wall, smoking a cigarette, wearing a red baby-doll nightgown. Her eyes were distant and vague. She didn't speak, merely smiled at Beck, pulling on her cigarette. The other girl sat on a chair, her arms hanging by her sides, her head slightly drooped. She was dressed in a sheer negligee. She didn't seem to notice them.

'Come,' Beck said softly to both, beckoning with his hand.

The long-haired girl was about to pull on her cigarette but froze. The other girl raised her head slightly.

'Come,' he said again.

But neither moved.

'It's okay. Come. Follow me.'

Slowly, they both got to their feet and stood, silently staring at him.

Beck walked to the door and stepped out into the corridor. The girl with the bob cut followed. He noted her gait was slightly unsteady. He looked into her eyes. They were lost to the stratosphere. But the other girl froze on the threshold of the door, staring out at him.

'You've never left this room, have you?' he said, wondering if the girl understood what he was saying.

But she nodded, and said softly, her voice slurred, 'No.'

'Come,' he said, beckoning. 'It's okay.'

She craned her neck out and looked up and down, as if seeing a whole new world. But she didn't cross the threshold.

'Come. It's okay,' Beck said, smiling.

Slowly, she stepped out into the corridor, and Beck led them down to the room where Claire and the other girl were, the uniform following. When they entered, the other girl said something to them, in a language Beck did not recognise, but her tone was sharp. Which surprised him. The other girls both replied in the same language, but their tones were meek, subservient. Both of them crossed the room and sat on the bed. The girl with the blonde locks began speaking rapidly, glancing at Beck.

'Stop,' Beck said.

She smiled, and ran a tongue across her lips.

'Honey…' she said.

'Split them up,' Beck said to Claire. 'This wasn't a good idea. Find out where they're from. Don't let them talk to one another. I'll be back.' He looked at the uniform. 'This office. Show it to me.'

It was a small room, nothing in it but a table and some chairs, and a microwave on a large upright cardboard box with the words 'This Side Up' printed along the side. A medium-sized man, tanned, was sitting in a chair with a hard expression, smoking a cigarette, his legs stretched out before him, his head resting back against the wall. Beck's gaze was drawn to his right eye, a tattoo next to it. Of a teardrop. Beck remembered what Dermot Healy had said, about the men in the camper van – one had had a teardrop tattoo, the other a long scar on his cheek. No, he didn't believe in coincidences.

The air was thick with cigarette smoke, but despite this, Beck fumbled in his pocket for his pack, before realising it was in his jacket, which was in the car. A pack of Marlboros was on the armrest of the chair the man was sitting in. Beck picked it up, opened the pack and tapped one out. The man smiled, held out his lighter, flicked it to life.

Beck leant forward, but instead of lighting his cigarette, he wrapped his hand around the man's wrist, and squeezed. The man's expression altered, the smile disappearing. Beck squeezed tighter and tighter. A few feet away, the uniformed officer leant against the wall inside the door, watching, two hands behind his back. Beck pulled the man to his feet, realising that his instinct had been correct, that this was the way the man expected police would behave, this was what he was used to, but more than anything else, this was what he understood.

Beck placed his face centimetres from his. He could smell his breath, like stale puke. He spoke slowly, stretching his vocal chords into a deep, low vibration.

'You will tell me,' he said. 'I know you speak English.' Which was a lie, merely a hope, the best way Beck knew of getting the man to speak if he was planning on playing the idiot.

The man stared, looking confused now. Perhaps he really didn't speak English after all.

'You will tell me,' Beck repeated, and the man slowly nodded. It was Beck's turn to smile.

The uniform spoke, his voice low and calm. 'Steady there, boss.'

Beck released his grip on the man's wrists, pushed him into the chair.

'Now,' he said. 'Who are you? Have you got ID?'

'I have passport, yes.'

'And the girls? Have they got passports?'

The man did not respond.

'That's a yes or a no question,' Beck said.

Still, the man did not speak.

'I have passport,' he said.

'Get your passport.'

The man glanced behind Beck, towards the door. 'I cannot. In safe. Boss Man has code.'

Beck thought about that. 'Boss Man?'

The man opened his arms wide. 'He own all this. This house. Everything.' The man lowered his voice. 'Maybe the Boss Man give you money? How you say, make problem go away.'

'Say that louder,' Beck said. 'So this nice officer can hear.' Beck pointed to his uniformed colleague.

The man said nothing.

'You don't want to?'

The man shook his head.

'What nationality are you?' Beck asked.

'Bulgarian.'

'And what about the other one?' He pointed to his cheek. 'The one with the scar on his face. Where is he?'

Surprise showed on the man's face.

'Yes,' Beck said. 'We know about him.'

He looked away.

'And the van?' Beck said. 'I don't see it outside.'

'Van?' He looked back again.

'Yes, the camper van. We know about that too. Don't play me for a fool now.'

The man folded his arms. 'A van is not illegal. He take it. Antoz. The one you ask about. My nephew. He go. Somewhere. Maybe he find girlfriend, no?'

'Antoz,' Beck said. 'He's the one with the scar?'

'Yes.'

'Okay. And this Boss Man. Why's he got your passport?'

'Because I give him. To look after. That is all.'

'Really?' Beck said. 'Hmm. And who is he? What's his name?'

The man's mouth clamped shut.

'Give me your cuffs,' Beck snapped at the other officer, and, to the man: 'I don't believe you don't know the code. I think you do. Last chance.'

The officer unclipped the cuffs from his belt, handed them to Beck. Beck opened a ring and made to place it on the man's wrist.

'Withholding information, that's the charge… Come on, put out your wrists.'

'Okay. Okay,' the man said before Beck could snap the ring shut, and then smiled, a fawning smile. 'I have code. But I swear, I no know his name. Boss Man. He no say. No tell me.'

'Open the safe.'

It was small, on the shelf next to a CCTV monitor. The man took out the passports. The safe was otherwise empty. Which didn't surprise Beck. He was confident any cash would be secreted somewhere else, probably outside the property, because the first object of interest in a robbery or police raid was always a safe. The man handed the passports to Beck. There were five in total.

'Your name is Sergey Domi,' Beck said, selecting one, studying the photograph. 'Born 1958.' He handed it to the uniform, but kept the others. 'Stay here and run this through Pulse. Don't let him out of your sight.' He looked at Sergey. 'CCTV camera downstairs. I want the footage.'

'Seventy-two hours before cut,' Sergey said. 'Okay?'

'I want it. You'll get it for me?'

He nodded.

'Now.'

He was about to leave the room when Sergey spoke. 'But I see his car,' he said.

'Whose car?'

'The Boss Man's.'

'Really. And…?'

'Mercedes…'

'… Red. Coupé? Brand new.'

Sergey smiled, displaying crooked, blackened teeth. 'Yes. Fast red car, vroom vroom.'

Beck went out onto the corridor and down to the bedroom.

The girl with the golden locks was dressed now, sitting by a dresser next to the window, which was covered in heavy drapes. The other girls sat side by side on the edge of the bed, watching Beck.

'She says her name's Britney,' Claire said, nodding towards the girl.

'Does she now?' he said, handing her the passports. 'See who these belong to.'

Claire took them, opened the first, flicking through it, while Beck moved in front of the girl, hunkered down onto his knees so that he was at her eye level. Her eyes danced over him and beyond, then darted away.

'You want to leave this place? With us?' he said. 'Do you understand? We will take care of you.'

Her mouth opened a little, then closed. She turned her head, a jerky exaggerated movement like a drunken person might do. Then she looked at him again, and he had the sense she was trying to concentrate, trying to understand him.

'Do you understand?' Beck asked. 'Do you?'

Beck stared into her eyes, wondering what secrets they held, what sights they had seen, trying to understand how she had ended up here.

'No,' she said, her voice faint.

'No. You mean you don't understand? Is that it?'

'No,' she repeated. 'I do not want to leave.'

'You don't. Why not?'

She shrugged, turning her head with that exaggerated movement again. 'This my home.'

She looked beyond Beck, and he could see something else in her eyes now: fear.

'You call yourself Britney.'

She smiled. 'Britney... you like...' And her voice fizzled out.

'Britney. You have family, in Bulgaria?'

She laughed and pointed vaguely, her arm quivering. 'Yes, far away, over the rainbow. Yes. Somewhere far, far away.'

'Listen to me carefully,' Beck said. 'Are you being held here, against your will? Forced? Forced to stay here?'

Again, she laughed. 'I came on ship, baby, a cruise ship.'

'This is your chance,' Beck said. 'You can leave with us. All of you. You will be safe. We will look after you. You can return home, to your family. You have a family, don't you? A family who loves you? Who miss you? This is your chance.'

And then she did something Beck had not expected. She covered her ears.

'NO! NO! NO! I stay here. Not go home. Never. Go away. Leave me.' She glared at him as she screamed, 'LEAVE ME!'

He could only stare back, and shake his head.

He looked to the other girls. 'Either of you?'

'My home,' the girl with the long black hair said. 'Here. I stay here too.'

The last girl nodded, but did not speak.

Beck squeezed his eyes shut, trying to make sense of it. None of it made sense. He thought of starlings. He had seen some one time, trapped inside a large shed. They had gone in one by one, and slowly their numbers increased until there were perhaps twenty. But for some reason they could not leave again. Instead they flew madly about, twisting and turning, right up to the threshold of the open door, but never crossing it. And just as they had entered, one by one, they died. These girls reminded him of those starlings.

Beck opened his eyes and shook his head. *Concentrate,* he told himself. *Concentrate.*

Claire finished going through the passports. 'It's them.' She looked down at him. 'And they're all over eighteen.'

So, free to make their own choices.

She handed the documents to Beck.

The blonde girl's real name was Liliya Abadzhiev. He studied her photograph, and was surprised. Because it wasn't a wig – her hair was real, the same as in the passport photo. The other girls were Petri Duboitz – her bob cut was the same – and Ivet Savov – whose hair was shorter in her photo. But there was no doubt, it was the girls.

Beck stood, his knee bones creaking as he straightened, and looked at Claire. He indicated for her to follow as he led the way out into the corridor.

'We'll need transport to take them in,' she said when they were outside.

Beck shook his head. 'We're not taking them in.'

'No?' Her voice rose.

'How's that going to work?' he said. 'They'd be out again within the hour. If you have any other ideas, tell me, really.'

'Well…' She pointed to the room. 'They don't want to be here, surely.'

'They say they do. Are they lying? Prove it.'

'They need protection, you know that.'

'They've got to want it.'

'But how can they decide? They're out of it. Look, if we can take drunks into custody for their own protection, why not these girls?'

'Aw, Christ, Claire, drunks out on the public streets, falling in front of traffic. We don't pull them in from their homes, now, do we? This is different. Otherwise we'd be taking in half the population of the country every Saturday night. You heard them, this is their home, that's what they said.'

Claire clenched her fists.

'Damn it, Beck, there must be something we can do.'

'Maybe, but not now. A sting. Catch it all on camera and audio. But then what? Preliminary charges of…? Prostitution? Remember, it's not a crime now. But running a brothel is. As is paying for sexual services. So, we need the girls to give evidence, at the very minimum. Anyway, let's just say we get all that and we prepare a case for the DPP. We wait. Then…'

'That's enough, Beck. I get it.'

'… by the time the DPP reaches a decision, let's assume it's to proceed, we call round here, and…? They're all just waiting for us? No. I guarantee you this house'll be as empty as a Monday morning church. You think I like it any more than you do? No, I don't, but that's the way it is.'

Claire was silent. He knew how she felt – he felt the same way too.

'Then why the hell are we here?'

'Because of Eddie Kavanagh,' Beck said.

'The mobile brothel?' Claire said.

'Of course. Has to be a link.'

'Then bring everyone in for questioning.'

'We can do that here. But they'll tell us nothing. Why would they? We need something, and we don't have it – not yet.' He scratched his head. 'Take their passport numbers. If they try to leave the country that'll be enough to stop them – if need be. That's the best we can do. For now. Look, Claire, this is a murder investigation. Everything else, *everything*, is on the back-burner.'

She nodded. Beck turned and went back into the room where Sergey was.

'Nothing,' the uniformed officer said. 'Or nothing outstanding, should I say. No European or international arrest warrants, although he may have had minor criminal records in other jurisdictions, but no bench warrants exist in Ireland.'

So, he was free to go.

'Check these,' Beck said, handing the other passports to him. 'If you find anything, let me know.'

He went back downstairs to the kitchen. O'Malley and Rogers were standing there, shuffling their feet, fidgety.

'Names,' Beck snapped to the younger men standing a little down from them.

'Richard Farrell,' said one.

'Paul Tierney,' said the other. They were clean-shaven, well dressed, smelling of quality aftershave.

'I won't lecture you boys,' Beck said. 'You know it. Look at me.'

They glanced at Beck.

'You watch porn?'

Neither spoke, but they flushed red.

'Listen to me,' he said. 'You both listening?'

They nodded.

'It's not like that in real life. What did I just say? Repeat it after me... *It's not like that in real life.* Now, either of you have sisters?'

A slight nod of the head from one.

'Those girls, in those rooms – imagine they're your sisters. They're somebody's sisters, and daughters. You think they like what they're doing? Well?'

'No.' The answer came in unison.

'They do it because they're desperate,' Beck said. 'Repeat it after me... *They do it because they're desperate.*'

He stared at them then, from one to the other, long and hard. Then he turned to the older two, did the same. He shook his head, and walked out of the house.

CHAPTER TWENTY-SIX

In the glow of the floodlights in the car park at the back of the station, the snow drifted to earth, thousands of invading tiny winter paratroopers. Beck felt like the inside of his head was an amalgamation of misaligned wires, all crackling and misfiring, sending his thoughts into a frenzy of images.

'Damn,' he said, looking at the seven missed calls on his phone screen. 'I forgot. I was supposed to be home by six.'

'*Home?*' Claire said. 'I want to say something. But I don't know if I should.'

'Say it.'

'I don't think she's good for you.'

'I know that already.'

Claire opened the door to the station. Her car was parked out front of the building. 'I'm going home,' she said.

'If I may ask, how are things with you and Lucy?'

Lucy was Claire's wife.

Claire smiled, a heartfelt smile that lit up her whole face. 'You know. When it's good, it's really good,' she replied. 'And it's been really good for a while now. I'm going to tell you something. We've been in relationship counselling, because we needed it, and that's tough... Who likes to hear the truth, and have to face up to it? But it brings results, amazing results.'

Beck looked away.

'Jesus,' she said. 'I wish you'd tell me what's going on with you. Sometimes I think you're falling apart, do you know that?'

Beck said nothing. He was about to say that she sounded smug, like someone telling a hospital patient how great it was to have good health. But he didn't. She hadn't meant it like that, he knew. It was the way he had chosen to hear it.

She lingered a moment.

'See you tomorrow, Beck. Get a good night's sleep, for God's sake.'

She went inside and the door banged shut behind her. He watched her walk down the corridor through the glass panel in the top of the door and disappear round the corner. Then he turned, crossed the car park, and walked down the narrow street at the side of the station that would take him onto Main Street.

He needed something. Just enough. No more. Just enough. Two faces stared at him, floating on the air: his father and Eddie Kavanagh. *Christ, I look just like him, my father*, Beck thought.

He walked through the town until he found himself standing in front of a pub, that distinctive stale sweetness on the air. He went inside, felt a dry, fragile heat from a few paltry sods of turf in the hearth. A coat and cap were arranged on a stool by the counter, but then Beck noticed another face, that of the man inside peering out at him. It gave him a start. A white-haired old woman rose from a low stool behind the counter, watching him, two knitting needles on either side of a wool suspension bridge in her hands. He smiled, but her expression did not change.

Just enough. No more. Just enough.

'Good evening,' he said.

She silently stared.

'A brandy,' he said. 'Double.'

She turned, picking up a glass from a stack on the shelf. He watched her reflection in the mirror running along the wall. Her eyes were focused on the glass as she pressed it against the optic, once, twice. She turned, shuffled over and placed it before him.

Beck picked up the drink, sipped it once, for appearances' sake, placing a twenty euro note on the counter. As she rang it up on the till and placed the note inside, he knocked the drink back in one swallow, and pushed the empty glass across the counter so that it was ready when she turned back to him. 'Again, please.'

She showed no reaction, merely lifted the glass, repeated the procedure, and so did Beck. This time, when he replaced the glass onto the counter, he took a deep breath. The gusher had stopped. He turned his head, took in the silent coat and hat next to him, the face lurking within like the face of a hobbit.

He left and began making his way home, between the serried rows of lanky buildings on either side of the street, appearing to huddle against each other for warmth.

For now, he thought of nothing.

The house was in darkness when he entered. What appeared to be a shadow passed from the living room into the hall and came to him. It was Max. Beck switched on the light and stood listening. There was no sound. He had a feeling he was alone now. He patted the dog and walked to the kitchen, Max trailing behind. The musty smells of the house had been replaced by that of perfume, unmistakably Natalia's, and spices. Indian spices. The table in the kitchen was set for two. The plates he recognised as those from a set of six stored in a cupboard that he had never used. The cutlery and two glasses gleamed. The room had been cleaned, and was gleaming too. Not that it had been dirty to begin with – he had not used it sufficiently for that. He walked into the hall again, and down to the stairs. He placed a foot on the first step and paused, listening again. Nothing but complete silence. He tried to remember if Natalia's car had been outside, but couldn't be certain that it was. He turned on the light and climbed the steps and at the top crossed the landing to the bedroom door. It was closed.

He passed by it and went to the bathroom, took off his clothes and left them in a pile on the floor. He stepped into the shower and turned on the water. It was frigid, jolting him, temporarily pushing any thought trails from his mind so that when the warm water began to filter through, his mind was empty, without even an echo, and as the steam rose, he began scrubbing himself clean.

When he finished, he dried, wrapped the towel around his waist and went to the bedroom. In the weak shaft of light from the landing he blinked. She had not left. He could see the smooth contours of her body beneath the duvet, facing the wall.

The silence festered then. After a moment, Natalia spoke.

'Go away,' she said, her voice bruised.

And Beck could feel it, the craziness of this relationship. Now that she had just told him to leave, he didn't want to. He wanted instead to roar with the frustration and confusion of it all. He crossed to the bed and sat next to her. He waited. Would she speak? Or would she ignore him? The thought of her ignoring him made him crave her even more.

'What really got me,' she said then, her voice made up of a thousand parts, all sharp and broken, 'is that you couldn't... you couldn't even be bothered to tell me, to let me know. Was that too much to ask? You couldn't even be bothered to ring. I mean, I thought you... I thought you bloody cared. You told me you did. But you led me up the garden path, isn't that it? Didn't you?'

Beck reached out and held a hand to her shoulder. She shrugged it off.

'And you're drinking. I can smell it. You left an empty bottle in the kitchen. That's really your mistress, isn't it? You're a mess.'

Yet, he thought, *you're still here.*

'There's a murder investigation,' he said. 'It takes over. You know how it is. And I'm too long on my own. I don't think. I didn't think.'

'Bloody right,' she said. 'You didn't think. And you're right, you are too long on your own. Ah, Jesus, what am I doing here? I left my husband for you.'

'Um, on that topic...' Beck said, and suddenly she was sitting bolt upright. Beck noticed the satin nightdress, the prominent nipples pressing through. He fell silent.

'What topic?' she demanded.

But all Beck could say was 'I'm sorry,' faced with the overpowering lust he felt again for this woman. And Natalia, sensing it, slid down beneath the duvet, gathering it about her, tucking it in under her body with extravagant movements and loud pats of her hands, turning her face to the wall again and closing her eyes.

Beck stood, and turned slowly, began walking towards the door. He reached it, was about to step out of the room.

'No,' she said. 'Don't leave me.'

CHAPTER TWENTY-SEVEN

It was 2.30 a.m., and Sergey could not sleep. He paced the floor, the air heavy with cigarette smoke. Outside the snow was falling. It was then he heard it.

Tap, tap, tap.

He looked to the living room window, then to the door.

Tap, tap, tap. Louder now, more insistent.

Sergey cursed under his breath and sighed. He went out into the foyer, walking over the deep pile carpet, as soft as moss, to the front door. He turned on the outside light and it flooded in through the glass, sending shafts of white across the darkened floor in front of him. He looked through the peep-hole and saw a person standing there, his back to the door, shoulders stooped. Sergey began to turn the latches, then slid the bolt back and pulled the door open. It was like opening the door to a freezer, with it a sudden gust of air that sent a flurry of snow inside.

But there was no one there.

He shuddered, dressed as he was in shorts, a T-shirt and slippers, and cursed again.

Another icy blast of wind sent a shiver through him, and instinctively he folded his arms tightly across his chest, and leant forward, peering out into the night. It was then he heard it, a sound like the rustling of leaves. But it was not the rustling of leaves. Because there were no leaves. He listened, and heard it, unmistakable, a voice, whispering, but he couldn't catch what was being said.

He stepped out onto the porch in a slow, tentative movement, and crossed it, feeling the damp through his slippers as his feet cut into the smooth, stiff snow with a soft crunching sound. He took a number of paces forward and stood there, still listening. He caught it then, a fleeting shadow through the air at the very corner of his vision, and as he turned he saw it, emerging from the blackness, illuminated briefly in the light from the porch, long and slender, moving fast...

Whack!

The first blow took the top of his ear clean off, but still, he did not fall. He stood dazed, feeling a warm liquid flowing down his cheeks, wondering why his feet were so cold but yet his face, that liquid, was so warm.

Whack!

He began to tilt slowly to one side, and then to topple, crashing through the snow into the ground face first, striking the asphalt with a dull thud, the white about his face deepening immediately to red.

And as he lay there it came again.

Whack!

Whack!

Whack!

CHAPTER TWENTY-EIGHT

Beck awoke with a start, staring into the darkness, which was diluted by the light of the street lamp from outside the window. His breathing sounded as if someone were frantically pumping air into a bicycle tyre. He took a gulp and held it, grappling with the rising panic, trying to force it down again, but it was too strong, and kept coming, unstoppable, the crackling echo of laughter growing louder and louder. He looked around. There was no one laughing. *Am I going crazy?* He shook his head, realising he was still sleeping, trapped inside a dream.

'No!' he cried, shaking his head. 'No!' And then his eyes snapped open and he was really awake – staring into the eyes of Natalia. 'Jesus.' He made to push her away.

'Stop! You're having a nightmare. A nightmare, Finnegan, a nightmare. Relax, for God's sake.'

He lay there, panting, listening to the hollow sound of his frantic breathing. He turned, pulled back the duvet and got out of bed, stumbled across the room and out onto the landing, closing the door behind him. He went downstairs and into the kitchen, the panic sweeping through him, dropping onto the floor by the cooker, opening the door of the cupboard where the cooking oils were kept.

Somewhere in there…

He rooted around, and way at the back found it. He fumbled with the top and screwed it off, raised the bottle of cooking brandy to his lips, was about to drink, when suddenly he felt it, a sense that he was being watched. He turned. In the doorway, sitting in that still and silent way of his, was Max, head cocked to one side, watching.

'Jesus, Max. You gave me a fright, boy.'

Beck looked to the bottle, then to Max. The dog came and sat next to him.

Beck told himself, *Just enough, no more, just enough.* Still, he hesitated, looking to the dog.

'Just a little,' he said, wondering why he was telling an animal. 'Just a little.'

He could hear it then, a low whine.

Beck raised the bottle to his lips, resisting the urge to gulp it down, took a deep swallow instead, then put the bottle back into the cupboard and stood. He went to the table, sat down and lit a cigarette. It was still dark outside, and for a fleeting moment the moon broke through the clouds and it was framed in the window above the sink like a painting. He knew she was standing there. Standing in the hall just outside the door. He took a long draw on the cigarette, watching as he did so the orange glow reflected in the glass.

'Thought you were trying to give up,' Natalia said, breezing into the room, her voice heavy with false cheeriness.

'What?' he said. 'The cigarettes?'

She pressed the light switch on and the moon disappeared from the window as the florescent bulb came to life with a sound like crinkling paper. She crossed to the sink and reached for the kettle, turned on the tap and pushed the spout into the flow of water. Standing in her satin nightdress in this drab kitchen, filling a kettle of water, she appeared as incongruous as a groomed poodle eating discarded chips on a grubby pavement.

Beck felt better. He had outrun the hurricane for now, but the hurricane was fast, and would come again. If he listened, he could hear its deep rumble from not far off in the distance.

Max had gone beneath the table. He was lying there, the white tip of his tail poking out. As if he belonged there.

Natalia turned from the sink and leant back against it.

'What? You're staring,' she said.

Beck took a last pull on his cigarette, taking it to the edge of its filter, stood, then went and opened the back door, flicked it out into the darkness.

'Could you leave that open?' she said, the cheeriness evaporating. 'Let in some fresh air, for God's sake... Beck.'

He paused by the door, the cold air slapping his senses. 'Aren't you cold?' he asked.

The kettle was boiling now, the steam rising and curling against the ceiling like a miniature fog.

'Finnegan' she said. 'You were like a complete nutcase in there. I've never seen you act like that before.'

He stood, went to her, slowly brought up his hand and gently rested it against her cheek.

'It's always like this,' he said.

She turned her eyes away. Without make-up, they appeared even smaller than usual.

'What do you mean?'

His hand was still resting against her face. She brushed it away now.

'You've got to open up to me,' she said. 'Tell me what's going on.'

She watched him. He took a deep breath, and felt a tightness coil inside him.

Natalia spotted it immediately.

'I'm beginning to question *myself*, now,' she said. 'Have I a fundamental flaw, a blind spot when it comes to men? First Jim, now you, and a couple of others along the way.' She shook her head. 'I don't seem to learn, I keep making the same damn mistakes.'

He was about to speak, but she continued.

'I can't stay here a moment longer,' she said, 'if you don't open up. If you don't tell me. Talk to me. I want to know. I want to help you… Jeez, I want to help myself.'

Beck was silent a moment, then: 'I can't.'

'Okay. Then find yourself somebody else. Because I've had enough. I'm going back to Dublin.'

Beck said nothing. Because he knew there was nothing to say.

CHAPTER TWENTY-NINE

'Good morning, Cross Beg gardai. How can I help?'

The words just spoken were written on a laminated sign displayed on the wall above the phone and, lest anyone still forgot, Superintendent Wilde had underlined each twice, and written next to them in block letters 'NO EXCUSES'. Above the sign was another, the Garda Mission Statement: *Working with Communities to Protect and Serve.*

'Um...' said the voice on the other end of the line.

'Yes. Cross Beg gardai. How ca—'

'I might be wrong...'

'Go on, sir, you might be wrong.'

'But...'

'Yes, but...' Irritation was creeping into the uniformed officer's tone.

'... when I was leaving this morning, a little while ago... Listen, can you just wait a sec? I'll pull onto the hard shoulder...'

'Sir, it's not a good idea to use your mobile phone while driving. It's against the law, actually. If you were...'

There was the sound of static on the line, then: 'Look, I don't have time. I'm going to work, but I think there's someone lying on the ground back there, just outside the front door... It's the house in the middle. It's hard to be certain, I noticed it as I was passing. I just happened to glance in... and while I'm on about it, there's a lot of comings and...'

'Sir, what do you mean, someone's lying on the ground? Outside what door? Of what house? And what's wrong with them?'

'The house in the middle, Cedar Grove. It looks like well, a body, and the porch light is on.'

'Your name please?' the guard said. 'I'll send a car over.'

But the caller had already hung up.

CHAPTER THIRTY

Beck walked along the darkened street. The snow was smooth and unblemished, except for a corkscrew of tiny prints of what he guessed had been a cat disappearing into an alleyway. When he turned onto Main Street the twinkling Christmas lights turned the scene into a living picture postcard.

At the station he could see tyre marks of vehicles that had been parked outside. Something was up, because every car was missing.

Frank Cosgrove, the longest-serving garda in Cross Beg, was behind the public counter. Beck could see the steam rising from a mug next to him as the old guard sat reading a newspaper. He turned his white-haired head to look at Beck.

'Where is everybody?' Beck asked, leaning on the counter, staring down at the newspaper. He was surprised to see that Cosgrove was reading the horoscopes. The old guard's eyes were heavy from recent sleep. He glanced to his newspaper. 'A body. Cedar Grove. Don't know what it is yet. Maybe a drunk thrown out by his wife... or something.'

'The horoscopes tell you that?' Beck said.

Cosgrove glanced at him, gave him an odd look. Beck was sucking on a lozenge.

'If there was anything to this I'd have heard by now,' he said. 'A drunk thrown out by his wife, that's what I'd say... Here, you have a cold there, boss? You're sucking an awful lot of lozenges lately.'

'What number house?'

'I don't know.' He shrugged. 'Not as yet.'

A voice came through the radio as if on cue.

'Frank, we have a male, deceased. Outside number six. You got that, Frank…?'

Cosgrove pushed against the counter and used his feet in a spider-stroke movement to propel himself across the floor in his wheeled office chair.

Beck was going out the door of the station again when Cosgrove called after him.

'The horoscope says the day ahead will be filled with surprises, and not all of them pleasant. Did you hear that now, boss?'

CHAPTER THIRTY-ONE

It took Beck less than five minutes to walk from the station to Cedar Grove. The town did not stir – there was no sound, no movement, just the crunching of his boots in the snow. He thought that for the second time this week the pre-dawn had brought with it a grim surprise.

As he turned into the estate he could see the flashing blue lights of a squad car shimmering across the houses, lighting up driveways and gardens. Beck cursed. He didn't want an audience. The offending squad car was parked against the pavement, two others midway down the driveway of the house they'd searched the night before. Beck stopped and opened the squad car's door, leant in and turned the roof rack off. With the darkness restored, he made his way towards the house, checking the time: 7.45 a.m. Was it going to stay dark as night forever today?

There were six uniformed guards and a sergeant milling about outside. Almost the entire day shift. Two he recognised, Dempsey and Jane Ryan.

'Who checked the house?' Beck asked.

Silence.

The sergeant shifted. Beck didn't know him. He was young, recently promoted, newly arrived in Cross Beg.

'No one checked,' Beck said. 'Is that it?'

The door was wide open; he could see snow had accumulated on the floor just inside.

'We just got here ourselves,' the sergeant said. He nodded towards the body lying some feet to the left of the porch, his voice scrambling for authority. 'We need to get him covered.'

Beck nodded. 'But this house needs to be checked for the living first. There were people here last night. And can someone tape off the bottom of the driveway?'

'Crime scene the body too?' The sergeant posed the statement as a question.

'Yes,' Beck said. He looked at Garda Ryan. 'Put on gloves, and come with me.'

They walked to the front door. By the porch was a stiffened slipper, sole side up, next to it a mush of footprints. Casts had been taken of the prints at the scene of Eddie Kavanagh's murder. But taking casts would likely prove impossible here. Soon, with the coming of the new day, the prints would either melt or be covered in fresh snow.

Beck took out his phone, which was an old model with a cracked screen and useless for taking photographs.

'You have a smartphone?'

Garda Ryan nodded.

He put his phone away and pointed in a circular motion. 'Take some photographs in this vicinity here. Concentrate on the viable prints, okay?'

She said nothing, reaching into her jacket pocket. It made a squelching sound as she fumbled about. Then she took out her phone, which was as large as a small tablet.

Beck peered across to the body of the man he had spoken to just the previous evening, dressed in a T-shirt and shorts and one slipper. He thought of the teardrop tattoo. Things had come full circle for this man, he considered. The stiff body lay in a Hollywood death pose, arms and legs splayed, head on its side. Beck imagined he had tried to crawl away. He stared at the face. He knew the blows had not been as precise as those delivered to Edward Kavanagh. He could tell the nose had been broken, pushed to one side, and there was a deep laceration by one eye, the one without the tattoo, that had taken away half the socket, the eyeball sitting in it like a loose coin. *Who the hell are you, Mr Psycho?* Beck thought. *You come like a ghost, leave no trace behind, except, of course, the results of your rage, a rage that could almost be sensed on the air.* Beck stared at the body, grateful that this time, at least, it did not stir those images of his father. He did not wonder why, he was just grateful.

'Come on,' he said, after Garda Ryan had clicked off a series of shots. He went to the doorway, paused, staring at the CCTV camera. At first glance it appeared to be intact, but he could see the lens was smashed, the glow of the red activation light absent. He went into the house, heading for the staircase. 'We have no choice,' he said, when he saw Garda Ryan pause in the doorway.

He started up the steps, Garda Ryan hurrying to catch up. At the top they paused, then Beck walked to the first door, the one where Britney had been found the night before. He turned the handle. It was not locked. He pushed it open, fumbling for the light switch. The room illuminated with a purple neon glow.

It was empty.

He crossed to the built-in wardrobe running the length of the wall opposite. He slid the door back and peered inside; nothing but a couple of laundry baskets and some blouses hanging from plastic hangers on a rail. Garda Ryan went to the bed, got down onto her knees and looked underneath.

'Clear,' she said, getting slowly back to her feet.

They left the room and went along the corridor to the next door. It was ajar, purple light spilling out. They entered.

The girl with the long black hair, Ivet Savov, was lying on her side on the bed, wearing the same baby-doll nightie as before, naked, her hands clasped between her knees. Beck took two strides and reached her. She appeared to be dead, but remarkably uninjured, pale and stiff looking. He nudged her shoulder and it was pliable as she gently fell onto her back. Beck extended two fingers and placed them onto her wrist. Her lips had turned blue, the edges crusted in a dry yellowy foam. An overdose? He felt it then, a faint but regular beat.

'She's alive,' he shouted. 'Come on. We need to get her to a hospital. Call an ambulance. Now!'

Beck strode towards the door.

'Where're you going?'

'Checking the other rooms. That ambulance. Now!'

He rushed out. The last door along the corridor was open. He went in. Darkness, save for a wedge of light slicing in from outside, enough to drape the body in a half shadow. It brought to mind an exhibit, in a wax museum perhaps. The body was on the floor, slumped back against the side of the bed. There was no doubt, it was very much dead. Beck would have said it was facing him, except the body didn't have a face – what it had was an abstract of red, purple, yellow and white, which was bone and teeth splinters reflecting the light from the corridor, and all framed within a perfect bob cut, remarkably intact and untouched: Petri Duboitz.

This was not a museum exhibit. This was a murder scene.

The sound of footsteps running along the corridor outside, slowing, entering the room, stopping next to him.

'Check every room,' Beck said to the uniform, who was bringing up his hand and covering his mouth. 'Don't touch anything.' He stared at the body, considered: *Psycho. Yes. One very sick psycho indeed.*

Ten minutes later, when he stepped out of what was now a very contaminated crime scene, he saw that a tarpaulin had been strung between a bush and the branch of a tree towards the bottom of the garden, at just the right angle to shield the body near the door from view of the street.

He looked along the driveway. The new day was at last dissolving the dark, bright enough to distinguish the cold heavy clouds lumbering across the sky. The roof of the world was low and ominous and dark. Beck felt as if he could almost reach out and touch it. At the end of the driveway was the vista of the humpback that was the central green area of the estate, pockmarks of green breaking through the snow, and in the foreground streaks of grey and black that were the roadway and pavement.

There were only twelve houses in the estate. At this time of day one thing was certain: everybody would be home. He saw Claire's car pull up on the road outside. She got out and began running, half sliding, down the driveway.

'I heard about it on the way over,' she said when she reached him. 'Jesus.'

'Quickly,' Beck said, pointing. 'House to house. I'll start to the left, you start to the right, we'll work our way out.'

'Let me get my breath first.'

'Everyone is home at this hour,' Beck said, starting to walk away. 'Hurry.'

CHAPTER THIRTY-TWO

'My name is Detective Inspector Beck,' he said when the first door opened, extending his Garda ID card for the woman to see.

She yawned. She wore a short nightdress beneath an open dressing gown. It didn't seem to perturb her in the least that a strange man was standing in front of her. From behind came the sounds of children, the rattle of crockery and a man's voice: 'I told you, that's enough, Rosaline, put it down and eat your breakfast. There's a good girl.'

'Beck?' she repeated, and he nodded.

'Number six…' Beck pointed.

The woman yawned again.

'Of course, it's right there.'

'Yes,' Beck said. 'Next door.'

'But it's not actually next door, *next door*,' the woman added, 'if you see what I mean.' She gave a self-satisfied smile. 'All the houses in the estate are *detached*, next door is just a term. We're in our own little world here. I should think so too. You know how much houses here sell for?'

'I was going to add,' he said, 'because you live next door, that maybe you might have heard something? During the night that is?'

She stepped into the doorway and looked out, left and right, an instinctive reaction, because there was nothing she could see.

'Why? Has something happened? Like I said, it's not next door, *next door…*'

'Didn't you hear the commotion? Earlier on. The flashing blue lights and sirens… everything.'

She shook her head. 'No. We were at the back of the house.' And with a grin, added, 'It's a big house.'

'Someone's been killed,' Beck said, if only to wipe the stupid grin from her face. 'Two people. Murdered.'

That did it. One hand flew to her mouth, the other began gathering the dressing gown about her. 'Oh my God. Are you seeeerious?'

'Yes. Unfortunately. Beaten to death actually, it appears.'

Her eyes widened, both hands covering her open mouth now. She suddenly looked very pale.

'Are we safe?' she said from behind her hand, 'I mean, this is the second one, isn't it?' And, her eyes narrowing, added. 'And why haven't you caught anyone yet? I mean, that old man who was killed round here the other day.'

'Did you see or hear anything?' Beck pressed. 'Last night. Anything unusual at all? If you could just think.'

She took a step back into the hallway, reaching for the door. 'I've thought about it. I heard nothing. But there's a lot of comings and goings in that house… and I don't have anything more to say.'

And with that, the door shut in his face.

Beck had no success with the next three houses either. In each was the usual morning frenzy as agitated families got ready for the day. He knocked on his last door, the furthest from the murder scene, with little hope. He wondered if at least a district SOC unit would be at the scene when he returned.

The man who answered was elderly, balding, but fresh-faced and twinkly eyed, dressed in flannel pants and a cardigan, wearing brown leather shoes, a pair of half glasses hanging around his neck on a gold chain. Beck went through the formalities, introducing himself, offering his ID for inspection, and was about to explain why he was at the man's door at such an ungodly hour when the man spoke.

'Something serious, is it? I saw the cars arriving earlier. Like something out of *Hill Street Blues*. You remember that, do you, from the telly? Few years ago now, of course.'

'An unfortunate incident,' Beck said. 'What looks like a double murder. At number six. I don't expect you hap—'

'A double murder,' the man said, like he was impressed.

'Did you happen to see or hear anything?' Beck continued, mentally preparing to turn and leave.

'The house with the motorhome,' the man said. 'That one?'

'Motorhome.' Beck's voice was louder than he'd intended.

'Yes, pretty big one too. I've always wanted one myself, of course, but they're not practical, not really, are they? They don't park it nearby, they leave it away from the house. Don't know why, there's plenty of space. I usually see it around the corner actually, like they're hiding it or something…' The man scratched a corner of his mouth. 'You asked if I heard anything last night,' he said.

'Yes.' Beck felt a kick in his chest. Was this going somewhere? 'And did you?'

'My dog. Fifi. She's sleeping now, of course, because it tired her out. And myself too. Never stops barking. Getting on a bit now, so doesn't usually bark as much, but she barked last night. Boy, did she bark. And it doesn't take much to wake me, not since my wife passed away… Anyway, what was I saying? Oh yes, the dog woke me. I told her to shut up and go back to sleep, but she didn't. I was a little cross with her, to be honest. So I had to get up. I found her in the kitchen, barking by the door. I opened it and she bolted out into the bushes at the end of the garden. A moment later I heard a shout, then a yelp. Whoever it was must have given her a kick, the bastard. So I put the light on and went out myself and had a look. Then I saw Fifi running towards me, and I could see someone – a man – crossing the field on the other side of the bushes, heading away, more a silhouette really, because the light wasn't great, but I could still make him out…'

The man's voice trailed off. 'Just a fleeting glimpse, mind… Oh, and something else.'

'Yes?'

'There was someone with him. A female. He seemed to be half dragging her along behind him… and…'

'And?'

'Long curly blonde hair, she had.'

'Really?' Beck said. 'You could make all that out?'

'Oh, yes,' the man said. 'I mean, couldn't miss it really, hair like that.'

'No,' Beck said. 'I suppose you couldn't.' He began fishing in a pocket for a pen. 'If I could. Your name and telephone number, please?'

Beck was pleasantly surprised to see the big Technical Bureau van pulled in at the top of the driveway when he got back, Inspector Mahony and the pathologist Dr Keane suited up and standing by the open rear door.

'Impressive,' Beck said. 'That you got here so quick.'

'Well, that's made my day,' Mahony said. 'Impressing you. We got as far as Ballinasloe before we were called back. This strengthens the case for a regional full forensics capability if ever there was one. Is there something in the water in this town? Like a bloody Stephen King novel – bloody, literally.'

Dr Keane shifted his medical case from one hand to the other. 'Two bodies,' he said. 'That correct?'

Beck nodded. 'Afraid so.'

'No entry,' the young pathologist added. 'You understand?'

'Of course he understands,' Mahony said. 'The place looks a mess. No access, Beck, strictly forensics only. We'll see what we can salvage. No exceptions to the rule.'

'Yes, of course,' Beck said, wondering how to begin looking for a missing person who may not be missing at all. But he hoped she was. It was better than her being dead.

Claire was standing to the side, flicking through her notebook. 'I've got nothing from door to door,' she said.

He filled her in on what he had learned. 'The mystery man,' he added then. 'We need to have a word.'

'The mystery man?'

'Bastic,' he said.

CHAPTER THIRTY-THREE

The same gleaming red Mercedes Benz coupé was parked outside the offices of Charles Bastic. When they went inside an intense-looking young woman was sitting behind the counter, typing furiously onto a computer keyboard. She was brightly dressed in a cream-coloured blouse, red neck scarf and cream jacket. There was a gold name tag pinned to her jacket – 'Sue', it said. She used a finger to rub something from the corner of her eye as she looked up at them with a *do-I-really-care?* smile.

'Can I help you?'

'Hopefully you can,' Claire said.

'Is Mr Bastic around?' Beck asked. His voice sounded hoarse, and he coughed. 'We need to speak with him. Urgently.'

'Right here,' a voice said from behind.

They turned. Bastic was standing outside the open door to an inner office. Beck glimpsed a desk and chair behind him. He was dressed in another well-cut suit, this one brown, with a fawn shirt and tie, and thick gold cufflinks.

'Come in, please,' Bastic said, moving inside.

The office was large, and Bastic sat behind a massive wooden desk in a gigantic button-back leather chair with wide armrests.

'Take a seat, please.' He pointed to a couple of small, plain wooden chairs in front of his desk, both of which combined would not make up half of the seat he was in. On the top of the desk was a family photo. Beck noted it was not turned towards Bastic, but turned outward for visitors to see. It was of Bastic and a pretty blonde woman, a chubby little boy in Bastic's arms, and a little girl in the blonde's. Beck noted that no one, not even the children, was smiling. He felt pressure at the back of his head, circling outward, a dull pain beginning to build.

Bastic sat sideways in his seat, leaning an elbow onto the armrest, running his other hand through his fair hair.

'You'd have heard by now,' Beck said.

He could tell by Bastic's expression that he was wondering how to deal with this. It was what people did when they had something to hide. Calculated.

'You mean…'

'Yes,' Beck said. He felt something at the back of his mouth and swallowed. 'At your property, Number Six Cedar Grove. Two people, dead, beaten to death; one person, female, in hospital with a suspected drugs overdose; and one person suspected missing – we're starting to look for her as we speak, but it's difficult. We have no details.'

Bastic held Beck's gaze, not blinking. 'But it isn't my property,' he said. 'It's leased to me.'

'Which begs the question,' Beck said, '*why* is it leased to you? What do you need it for? Come on, Mr Bastic, don't take me for a fool.'

Bastic shook his head. 'I'm not taking you for a fool. It's a terrible business.'

'What is?' Claire asked.

Beck noted Bastic didn't look at her when he answered. Rather, he looked at him. 'Are you alright?' he said to Beck. 'You don't look very well.'

'Don't worry about him,' Claire snapped. 'Just answer the question.'

'What do you think I mean?' There was a note in Bastic's voice as he turned to Claire now – condensation perhaps. 'The deaths of those people. What else?'

Bastic's eyes returned to Beck, and Beck did not speak, but allowed the silence to churn through the room.

'So?' Bastic said.

Still, Beck did not speak.

'Listen.' Bastic's tone became one of exasperation. 'What is this? Are you going to sit there like that and say nothing, just continue to stare at me?' Bastic's eyes widened, like he couldn't swim and had suddenly stepped out of his depth. Finally, he looked away.

Beck took a deep breath. 'I'm wondering,' he said.

'Yes, you're wondering?' said Bastic.

'How you plan on playing this. Because I know you're playing this.'

'I beg your pardon?'

'Your property is a brothel,' Claire said. 'You telling us you didn't know? Come on now, a successful businessman such as yourself?'

Bastic acted like she wasn't in the room.

'Mr Bastic,' she said. 'I'm talking to you.'

Looking straight ahead, without turning to her, he spoke. 'Are you?'

'Yes. I am.'

He sat back in his oversized chair. Beck wondered why Bastic had ever thought that chair was a good idea. He looked like a kid sitting in it. Bastic finally turned to take in Claire and smiled.

'I don't know what you're talking about,' he said.

'I think you do,' Claire replied.

Bastic looked up to the ceiling, then down again, glanced at both detectives, then finally his eyes settled on the door.

'If you're going to say something like that,' he began, 'you'd better be able to prove it.' Then, slowly now: 'Because I take grave exception to my good name being run through the mud.' He looked at Beck. 'Grave exception indeed, if you get my meaning. If you were ever to make such an accusation public, I'd have to defend myself... by all legal means possible. Do I make myself clear?'

Beck laughed, and the effort caused pain to shoot up into the top of his head.

'Something funny?' Bastic asked.

'Listen to you,' Beck said. 'I know you know.'

'What do you mean "I know you know"?' His voice was even more surprised. 'I didn't say anything.'

'Exactly,' Beck said.

Bastic opened his mouth, but closed it again. Before he could recover, Beck spoke.

'It was sub-leased then, the property. Who was renting it from you, Mr Bastic?'

Beck saw the look drifting across Bastic's eyes again, as he thought of the right words to use.

'You shouldn't have to think about it too long.' It was Claire.

'Because you heard what happened,' Beck said. 'We've just been talking about it, so it's in your mind. You've had time to think already, Mr Bastic. So, who was renting your property? It's a straightforward question. Simple, actually.'

'Is that why it was searched last night?' Bastic said.

'Spare me,' Beck replied. 'You're as vague as fog. I have to tell you, Mr Bastic, this is not good. Not at this moment in time. So again: Who was renting your property? Last chance. Otherwise you're off to the station. Withholding information should do it.'

'You can't do that. Threatening me like…'

Beck said nothing.

'Sergey something or other,' Bastic said then, his voice a verbal retreat. 'Look, I'm not quite sure what his last name is… There was no paperwork. Straight cash, okay? They paid their rent on time, I had no complaints. That's all I care about. Model tenants, actually.'

'Domi,' Beck said. 'I hope I'm pronouncing that correctly. Sound familiar?'

Bastic appeared as if he were thinking about it. 'Yes,' he said, voice dripping with feigned surprise, 'you know it does. Yes, I think that's it.'

'Of course,' Claire said, her words coated with sarcasm. 'And who actually owns the property?'

Bastic looked down at his desk, then up to the ceiling, said nothing.

'Who owns the property?' Beck asked. 'This is trying my patience, I have to tell you.'

'Okay,' he said. 'I own it.'

'You made hard work of that,' Claire said. 'Yes, you take us for fools alright. Well, we're not.'

'It's an arrangement my accountant suggested,' Bastic said. 'Okay? Perfectly legitimate. It lowers my tax liability, but, and to me this is just as important, cloaks my property portfolio…'

'It what?' Claire said.

'Makes it difficult for people to know what I own,' Bastic said. 'People in this town, if you have more than they have, you wouldn't believe what they can be like. This way makes my life easier.'

'I bet it does. Now, pay attention, Mr Bastic, because our patience is wearing thin,' Beck said. 'Who else was in that house?'

'I don't know,' Bastic said. 'He had a nephew, I think.'

'Antoz?' Beck said.

'Yes. Yes. That's him. Had a scar on his cheek, but you probably know that already.'

Beck shifted on the hard wooden chair.

'The girls,' Claire said. 'Who are they?'

It was his expression, fleeting, but impossible to miss nonetheless: a tightness of the mouth, a distance in the eyes, an all too familiar expression to Beck.

'What girls?'

'Bastic,' Beck snapped, two cymbals crashing in his head as he raised his voice, 'you're full of shite, do you know that? Yes, of course you do. Don't give me any of your auld guff. The girls. You know the girls I'm referring to. Who are they?'

Bastic jumped to his feet. 'How dare you. Coming in here, accusing me... accusing me of, well, I don't know what exactly. I'm a respectable businessman. In a town like this a reputation is everything. Who do you think you are? I'm going to talk to my solicitor about this, most certainly I am. Now' – he pointed to a pile of paperwork on his desk – 'I have lots of work to catch up on. I want you to leave. Now. And you can expect a letter from my solicitor. Very soon. I guarantee it.'

Beck allowed himself a smile. 'The false indignation. You're so bloody predictable, Bastic, you know that?'

An indignation that wasn't even enough to pump some colour into the man's cheeks.

'Is that your Mercedes outside?' Beck asked.

'What's that got to do with anything?'

'It is. Thought so. What's that cost? We're talking a hundred thousand euro easy. Correct?'

'So? It's none of your bloody business.'

'Do you own it? Or is it leased?'

'I own it. What, you jealous? That's it, isn't it?'

'No, I'm wondering where you get your money, Mr Bastic. A town like this, property prices not being great, the way I see it, you'd have to earn a lot of commissions to cover a hundred thousand euro.'

Beck got to his feet slowly, very slowly, kneading his lower back with his fingers as he did so. 'I mean, these chairs. Christ, what's that about? Meanwhile you're sitting there like a king on his throne.'

'People don't have to sit there for very long,' Bastic said. 'That's the whole idea. They can sign the papers, seal the deal and get the hell out of here.'

'Yes,' Beck said, walking towards the door. Claire got up and followed. Beck turned, his hand on the doorknob. 'Clever. Conniving of course. But clever. And for a man concerned with not appearing to have more than anyone else, well, that car of yours… I don't believe much of what you're telling me, Mr Bastic, is what I'm saying. And spare me the false indignation.' He turned the handle. 'By the way, we spoke to Mr Domi, you know, our murder victim – no, you wouldn't know that because you didn't ask – when we searched your property at Cedar Grove last night. He referred to someone as the Boss Man. You wouldn't know anything about that either, would you?'

Bastic glared and shook his head.

'No, I didn't think so either,' Beck said. 'That would be too easy, wouldn't it?'

'And,' Claire said, 'you can account for your movements last night, can you?'

'My movements. Why? You think I had something to do with this?'

'Well…' Beck said. 'I don't know what to think.'

'Of course I can account for my movements. I was at home. My wife will vouch for it.'

Beck nodded. 'Of course. That too. She will.' He paused. 'You have all the answers, Mr Bastic, don't you? Anyway, we'll be on our way. For now… Oh, just one more thing.'

'What?'

'A witness said they saw a motorhome parked at the house in Cedar Grove. You wouldn't know anything about that, would you?'

'A motorhome? No, I don't know anything about a… What type of motorhome?'

'Oh, a sudden interest there, Mr Bastic?' Beck said.

Bastic said nothing.

'You're curious, aren't you?' Beck added.

Bastic looked away.

'No. You don't know anything about it, do you? You might think you're clever, Bastic, but I can read you like a book.'

'Well, read this. I told you, in a town like this, reputation is everything. You implicate me, I'll sue. I'll take it to the High Court. Believe me.'

'Oh, I believe you alright,' Beck said. 'But you're wrong if you think that would stop me. Or anything else. Nothing would. I'm not bringing you in because it'd be a waste of time – you know your way around an interview room – for now, that is. But I'll be back. Understand, Mr Bastic?'

Bastic said nothing. He understood.

*

CHAPTER THIRTY-FOUR

'Frazzali's,' Beck said as they stepped out onto the street. 'I'll meet you there. Get a window table and watch Bastic's office. Order me some food. I won't be a minute, need a packet of cigarettes.'

'They sell ciga…' Claire began, but Beck was already walking away along the street.

He made his way to Crabby's supermarket quickly. Beck had gotten to know Maurice Crabby over the course of a previous investigation. So when he entered now and told Crabby he wanted a naggin bottle of Paddy whiskey – enough to fit discreetly inside his jacket pocket – Crabby looked at his watch, an unspoken reference to it being before time for the retailing of alcohol.

'You were doing so well,' he told Beck. 'I even saw you out and about jogging a few times. What happened?'

'I'll be jogging again, soon,' Beck said, not answering the question.

'You will?'

'I will.'

Crabby pursed his lips. 'Give me a minute.' He left in the direction of the off-licence section. When he came back he handed the bottle to Beck.

'Take it easy on that,' he said, 'for God's sake.'

Beck took a crumpled note from his back pocket, but Crabby waved it away.

'Call it my good deed for the day, or not so good, whichever way you want to look at it. But get yourself sorted.'

'Thank you,' Beck said, and left the shop.

Outside, he went into an alcove by the door, turned his back and opened the bottle. He saw his face reflected in the window as he drank in short, quick gulps, and felt nothing, neither shame nor regret... nothing at all. He noticed a set of eyes on him from the other side of the glass. It was a child, a little boy, leaning against the leg of a woman who was talking with another. The child had a soother in his mouth, and he took this out, holding it before him, as if offering it to Beck. Beck lowered the bottle and smiled, placed it inside his pocket, turned and walked away.

Claire was sitting at the same window table in Frazzali's that he had occupied the previous day. The restaurant had just opened, and people were filtering in. Beck sat opposite her. She gave him an odd look.

'What?' he said.

Her gaze lingered.

'Nothing,' she replied, but not sounding certain.

'Bastic. Did he come out?'

'No. By the way, I ordered you a sausage sandwich, and an Americano. A mug, correct?'

He smiled. 'Perfect.'

'Your face is flushed.'

'I ran, didn't want to keep you waiting.'

He knew she didn't believe him.

'Don't you think we're wasting time?' she said. 'Sitting here. A murder investigation is acutely time sensitive. Professor Kirk Wzytal calls this the "hot phase". He says—'

'As opposed to the forty-eight hour window.'

'That too.'

'I've just pressed pause,' Beck interrupted. 'To give me time to think. Also, I find if you rattle someone's cage, sometimes they jerk their knee.'

Claire looked at him, was about to say something, but just then the waitress placed their order on the table.

Beck poured some milk into his Americano. He felt suddenly totally aware of everything, an acute sharpness to his senses. The sound of someone taking a spoon of sugar from the bowl at the table behind him was like a shovel into sand.

'Those girls,' Claire said. 'At Cedar Grove. They're forgotten about, aren't they? I mean, Christ – I want to help them, but I can't. It's like they're invisible, to everyone except those making money off them… or taking pleasure. It's pathetic, and I'm angry about it.'

Beck took a sip of coffee. 'And me. The tentacles of crime, like I've said, stretch everywhere, in this case all the way across Europe to some backstreet bar where those girls were first sold.'

'I want to do something.'

'Of course,' Beck said. 'But what?'

She gave him a look.

'Seriously,' he answered, putting his mug back onto the table.

She lifted her milky coffee, blew on the froth, making a hole in it, then took a sip, replaced the cup into its saucer, wiped her mouth with the back of her hand.

'The briefing…' she said, with an air of resignation.

'Bloody briefing. Let's just go through things here first, shall we?'

Beck brought his sausage sandwich to his mouth, and was just about to take a bite.

'Well, well,' he said, peering through the window. 'I think Bastic just jerked his knee.' He stood, wrapping his sandwich in a napkin. 'Come on, he's on the move.'

Their unmarked Focus was parked a little way down Bridge Street. By the time they reached it, the red Mercedes had gone. Claire drove to the end of the street, turned onto River Walk and floored it. The Focus rattled and groaned but still galloped along like an old race horse stretching its legs. At the end of River Walk was a set of traffic lights, on green. Claire hit the brakes, slowing the car right down. And Beck knew why. Because Bastic's Mercedes was approaching the intersection from the other direction. The lights turned red now. Claire coasted to the stop line as Bastic's car passed before them, heading for the bridge. Bastic was staring ahead, his face pinched. He hadn't noticed them. Beck lowered his window and placed his arm out, held up the palm of his hand to other traffic as Claire went through the red light, crossing the junction. He saw a woman in a small blue car staring at him, stopping, holding up the traffic behind, which was what Beck wanted. Claire swung across the junction onto the bridge.

'What's this about anyway?' Claire asked. 'He's not breaking any laws.'

'You heard him. He said he had lots of paperwork to do. Then he takes off right after we leave. I don't believe in coincidences, not at a time like this. I don't think you do either.'

Bastic turned left on the other side of the bridge onto Riverside Drive. Claire kept a distance, allowing a car to pull out, placing it between them and the Mercedes. At the end of Riverside Drive, Bastic turned onto the Coast Road. Claire, however, continued straight on.

'We're losing him,' Beck said.

'Maybe not,' she said. 'I'm taking a chance he's heading to Mulla. That's the Coast Road he's just taken. This is a main road, and it's a straight run. If I put the foot down, we should get there before he does, pick up where we left off.'

Beck nodded.

Claire rattled the car along. So close to the sea, the salt air had turned the snow on the road to slush, and it soon unfurled before them to the seaside village. And soon too, Beck could see in the

distance the dunes and beach draped between the land and the
sea like a scarf underneath the dark sky. Claire pointed a finger.

'See, over there,' she said, 'the Coast Road. See that truck?'

Beck looked, spotted the top of a box truck moving along
above the hedges in the near distance, and behind it, just about
visible, the roof of a red car.

Claire whipped the Focus faster.

They passed the junction with the Coast Road just as the truck
approached it and stopped. Beck watched in the wing mirror as
they drove by, could see the truck move out onto the main road
behind them, and following was Bastic's red Mercedes.

Claire slowed as they entered the village.

Beck was silent.

Boats on stilts sat on either side of the old stone harbour slipway,
taken from the water for the winter months. As they approached Beck
heard the distinctive metallic chomping sound of a helicopter – by
the sound he guessed a large one. He leant forward, peering through
the windscreen. A red and white coastguard chopper rose into the
air from the other side of the harbour wall, a vertical ascent, and as it
gained height, Beck could see an orange buoy hanging from beneath
it. It hovered briefly before descending again, fast and straight. They
rounded a bend and a hill rose in front of them, buildings on either
side, a mixture of private houses, a couple of cafés and pubs and a hotel.
Beck noted the name of the hotel as they passed: The Atlantic Arms.

He glanced in his wing mirror. The red Mercedes was rounding
the bend at the bottom of the hill now. Ahead was a crossroads.
Beck looked in the wing mirror again. The Mercedes was gaining
on them.

'Pull in,' he said.

'Where?'

Beck pointed. 'There. Now.'

Claire turned the wheel sharply, the car lurching through
the open gateway of a private house. She pulled a hard right

and stopped the car behind the garden wall. A woman's face immediately appeared at a window, peering out at them. Claire smiled, gave a slight wave of her hand. The woman pressed her face against the window, turning to some unseen person, talking, animated, pointing.

The red Mercedes passed by. Claire reversed, and moved forward again, out through the gateway. Bastic had turned right, was pulling away fast.

Claire turned at the crossroads after him. 'He's got a clear road, hardly any snow here. We'll never keep up now, he's too fast.'

Beck didn't speak. He was enjoying the adrenalin rush, the surge of endorphins a whetstone sharpening his dulled senses. He reached for his phone, scrolling through his numbers. It was so crazy it might just about be possible... He found the number, pressed call. It was answered on the second ring.

'Pearse Street Comms.' The voice was harried.

'Finnegan Beck.'

There was a brief pause. 'Beck! That you?'

'Listen. Listen. I don't have time. You have cross services access there, don't you?'

'Course.'

'Put me through to Coastguard Command. I need to speak to someone. Now. Please.'

The comms room operator didn't ask questions. The comms room dealt with serious business. He said just two words: 'Stand by.' There was a clicking sound, then that of another telephone ringing, just one ring, and: 'Operations.' The female voice was alert, efficient.

'My name's Detective Inspector Beck, Cross Beg Gardai. You have a chopper in Mulla, Co. Galway? I need to communicate with it.'

'It's on an exercise with the RNLI. I can't just let you—'

'Please. I need to speak with it. Trust me. We can fill in the blanks later.'

Silence. Beck could sense her brain processing the situation. The red Mercedes was getting smaller and smaller in the distance. Still, silence. He was about to speak again when his ear suddenly filled with the roar of engines, with it the rhythmic *clack clack clack* of helicopter rotor blades. A voice came through the noise, distinct and calm.

'Coastguard helicopter. Who's this?'

'Detective Inspector Beck. We're involved in a chase. I need your help.'

Claire turned to him and gestured with her hand: *What the hell?*

'It's a red Mercedes,' Beck said. 'Travelling north out of Mulla. We're behind it, but we're losing visual. I believe it might be connected with three murders in the last forty-eight hours in Cross Beg.'

'This is highly unorthodox.' The calmness was unwavering.

'You're right. But can you help or not?'

The loud drone of the engines and the *clack clack clack* of rotor blades seemed to go on forever.

'Gaining altitude,' the voice said. 'Travelling north you say. How far out?'

'It left Mulla within the last five minutes, thereabouts.'

A change in pitch of the engines, the drone losing its deep bass sound, becoming sharper, like a low scream.

'North. Can you be more specific? Have you GPS?'

'No GPS at this moment, sorry.'

Nothing then but the sound of those engines, accompanied by the *clack clack clack*. Beck waited.

'Three thousand feet.' A different voice this time. 'Roger that. Northbound.'

Again, nothing but the sound of engines.

Then: 'What you driving?'

'A blue Ford Focus,' Beck said.

'Flash your lights.'

'Flash your lights,' he said to Claire.

'We have visual,' the voice said then. 'Hello down there. My name is Captain Eoin Davey, and I'll be your pilot today. Give us a wave.'

The noise in the phone suddenly grew so loud Beck had to remove it momentarily from his ear. It was only then he realised the sound wasn't coming from the phone. It was coming from above, from the helicopter, which rumbled directly overhead, passing them by. The car vibrated in the downdraught. He watched it streak away, bank sharply to starboard, climbing at a steep angle.

'Visual on red Mercedes,' a voice said. Beck didn't know if it was Captain Davey speaking on this occasion. 'One point five kilometres directly ahead. Maintaining position to port of vehicle at six o'clock, three hundred meters... You have a radio designation, caller? I can communicate with your car radio. It'll be easier.'

Beck glanced to Claire. She nodded to the radio handset.

'It's written on it,' she said.

'Yes,' Beck said. 'Stand by.'

'Standing by.'

'Oscar Yankee Zulu One Nine Nine Seven, frequency Zulu Tango.'

'Roger that.'

A moment later the voice came through the car radio receiver.

'Coastguard helicopter. You receiving, Oscar Yankee Zulu?'

Beck snatched the receiver from its hook, pressed the talk switch, brought it to his lips. 'Receiving. Loud and clear.'

'The road you're on leads to the N51. The car has just turned onto it, heading north-west.'

'North-west,' Beck said.

'Roger,' the voice said. 'It's turned right. Heading in direction of Galway.'

Beck glanced out the window. If Bastic was involved in nothing more than a rush to a dental appointment, he'd have some explaining to do.

'Don't ever do that again,' Claire said when the helicopter had relayed the information and headed back to base: the red Mercedes was parked in the Galway Industrial Estate. 'This Jason Bourne stuff. I'm sure you've just broken every rule in the book... only you, Beck, only bloody you.'

He laughed. He didn't want the adrenalin rush to stop. Not now.

He was about to tell her to have some faith, but faith in what or whom he had no idea, so said nothing.

CHAPTER THIRTY-FIVE

'Well, well,' Beck said as they drove in through the gateway. 'What was I saying about coincidences?'

Claire turned and saw what Beck was looking at: a camper van parked against the wall just inside the entrance to the industrial estate. She could see it had twin rear wheels, and a yellow registration plate.

'And there's the car,' Claire said, pointing ahead to the red Mercedes. Beck saw it too. As they drew near, he could see a sign outside the building it was parked in front of: A1 ENGINE REMANUFACTURING. There was another building a little way down from it, with the sign DIGITAL SOLUTIONS over its door. Claire pulled in behind a car by the entrance.

Beck was struck with the dilemma: *what now?*

The expression on Claire's face posed the same question.

'Let's have a look,' Beck said, opening the car door.

He pulled up the collar of his jacket and got out of the car, lowering his head against the light fall of snow. Bastic's car was the only one outside A1 Engine Remanufacturing. When he reached it he saw a road ran down the side of the building, leading to a yard behind it, bordered by a high wire-mesh fence. They started down the roadway. Beck stopped by the corner at the end of the building, peered around it. Side by side in a row at the rear of the yard were a dozen or so cars, their front ends smashed in, write-offs Beck guessed, high-end BMWs, Audis and Mercedes Benz.

Still, there was no law against that. A gust of wind sent a sudden flurry of snow across the yard. It was just after midday, but it was dark as early evening. Beck thought again of coincidences. They were stacking up. But that wasn't enough to secure a search warrant. Or anything else. He had to make a decision. Right now, he really only had one option, which was to sit out front for as long as it took and watch the building. But even that option wasn't available. For one, Superintendent Wilde would be required to sanction it, and the local district commander would have to be informed and agree to it. Beck didn't have time for any of that.

He cocked his head.

'Hear that?' he said.

Claire listened, and shook her head. 'No.'

Beck raised an index finger, still listening. Had he heard something? He couldn't be sure. He thought he had, from somewhere inside the building. He closed his eyes. It had sounded like a…

'Aagggghhh.' It came again. And again: 'Aagggghhh.' Louder this time, much louder, a primordial sound, of male vocal chords reaching registers only ever designed to be achieved when about to be devoured by a Tyrannosaurus Rex. Beck reached for his phone. Because now he could dispense with instinct. This was logic. And logic told him to call for backup. He pressed the number for the divisional Comms Room as he rounded the corner.

When he'd finished the call and was putting the phone away, he noted the roller shutter at the back of the building was not properly closed – it hung open by a couple of inches. He pointed at it.

'Give me a hand pulling this up.'

They approached it, bent down, grasped the edge at either end, and pulled. The door rose smoothly on well-oiled rollers. There followed a moment frozen in time. During which Beck, free of all thoughts except for this moment, saw all, every detail, like he was examining a photograph or a clip from a movie, set on pause. He saw a car – actually, the grey shell of a car – on a raised lift.

He saw what appeared to be spare parts for the vehicle laid out neatly on the floor next to it. He saw at one end of the building two gleaming Mercedes Benz, and at the other a trio of crashed cars similar to those outside, all damaged at the front end. He saw a man tied to a chair too – sallow-skinned, on his cheek a scar in the shape of a half-moon – turning to look at him, his expression a mixture of surprise and terror, but also one of pleading. And he saw Bastic, in his tailored suit, standing to one side of the chair, incongruous within these surroundings, while standing on the other side was a stocky bald man in dirty overalls: a hardman. The hardman was holding a blowtorch, its nozzle angled towards a lighter poised in his other hand. Bastic said nothing, and in that long frozen moment Beck knew what he was doing: calculating, weighing up the odds. And Beck, in his silence, was doing the very same. But then, the frozen moment passed, sounds and movements restored: *action.*

The bald one with the blowtorch, the hardman, stared at Beck and Claire.

'What the…?' he began, but a sound diverted his attention. It was sirens, approaching fast.

'Steady on…' Bastic began, but his voice fell away.

Just then, the bald one dropped the blowtorch, and it clanged onto the floor, followed by the sound of his frantic footsteps, heading for the door. He gave Beck a wide berth, running by Claire instead. If he had considered her the safer option, he was wrong. As he passed, Claire extended a foot and wedged it expertly between his feet, turning it to the side, and his arms flayed as he tumbled to the floor, landing with a loud *plooomp* sound. He moaned, trying to get back to his feet. Claire rammed her shoe into his back, forcing him back down, and kept it there.

'Easy there, big boy,' she said.

The squad car skidded to a halt, its bonnet protruding through the doorway, the sound of its siren a piercing squeal within the enclosed building. Four uniforms got out, two with telescopic batons drawn and extended. They began advancing, unable to decipher who was who or what was what. Beck savoured the moment, because he rarely got to experience the business end of policing from a criminal's perspective. He had to roar to be heard as he presented his ID wallet for inspection.

'Can someone turn that damned siren off?'

CHAPTER THIRTY-SIX

Beck considered the superintendent to be the youngest he had ever seen, mid-thirties at most; he had never come across one below the age of at least fifty before. *Whizz-kid.* He was a little short of six foot, wiry, immaculately groomed. He was standing to the side of the custody area in Galway city's main garda station, Mill Street. There were multiple processing booths in the counter. A busy place. Cross Beg had only one.

'Inspector,' he said, and turned, stepping towards the wall by the double doors he had just come through. The echo of a cell door shutting sounded, along with it a muffled shout. 'A word, please.'

Beck went and stood next to the superintendent, who observed him gravely, plucking at his lower lip with two fingers.

'My name is Superintendent Browne, second in command here at Mill Street. Care to tell me what this is all about?'

'I don't rightly know myself.'

The superintendent raised and lowered his eyebrows in an exaggerated movement: *Oh, really?*

'Let's talk out here,' he said, turning and pushing through the double doors.

Beck followed onto a brightly lit corridor.

'You heard?' Beck said. 'The three murder investigations. In Cross Beg?'

The superintendent continued plucking his lip. 'Of course.' As if saying: *What do you take me for?*

'There's a bit of background to the investigation, which might explain why I'm here.'

'There is?'

'Yes,' Beck said. 'One of those just brought in, Charles Bastic. We followed him here, to Galway, to the industrial estate.'

'All the way from Cross Beg?'

'Yes, sir.'

The superintendent raised his eyebrows.

'The house in Cross Beg where the bodies were found today,' Beck added. 'He owns it.'

'Does he? You raided it last evening, saw it on Pulse. A brothel, that right?'

'That's right,' Beck said. 'Although I have no direct evidence linking him to any murders.'

'That's a little more than a bit of background,' the superintendent said then, tugging on his perfect tie knot. 'How did you know about all this?' He nodded towards the custody area. 'I mean, what we found, in the industrial estate.'

Beck leant against the wall. 'I didn't.'

The superintendent waited, but Beck said nothing further.

'That's not an answer, Inspector.'

'It's the only one I've got. Sorry. I saw Bastic take off. In his car. From Cross Beg. We followed, like I said. I had an... instinct. That's the best I can do.'

The superintendent's hand fell away now, his arms hanging by his sides. 'I don't do instinct... What's your name by the way. Peck? As in Gregory?'

'No sir, Beck, as in... Well, I don't know.'

'Well, Beck, in any case, you've opened something here, so I suppose I should thank you. It looks like a chop shop. We'd heard rumours of something like it, but rumours only... until today that is. Also, add kidnap and assault charges possibly in there too...'

'Chop shop?'

The superintendent smiled. 'Yes.'

'What have you learned?'

The superintendent folded his arms. 'Need-to-know basis only, until we get this sorted, see what's what... Now, what are we going to charge all these lovely people with?'

'Um,' Beck said. 'What do you mean, "need-to-know basis"?'

'Exactly what I said. I don't reveal details of my active investigations. Not to anyone. Nothing personal. It wouldn't be prudent to do otherwise, not the way I see things. I don't know you, Inspector, is what I'm saying.'

Beck smiled, shook his head. 'Oh, you don't trust me. That's what you're saying. I can understand that. So that's your investigation, is it? Heading, motor fraud, subheading I hazard to guess the cloning of high-powered UTs with those wrecks we saw earlier.'

'What makes you think that's the way it is?'

'I've come across similar in my time. That's the pattern.'

'Really?'

'Superintendent, need I remind you we're on the same side here? Anyway, I won't be so circumspect. I'm investigating three murders. Plus a prostitution ring. Plus what I believe to be a case of human trafficking. Plus, a possible missing person. All related, I'm convinced, I just don't know how. Not yet. I don't really care about motor fraud.'

The superintendent brushed an imaginary speck of dust from his shirt. And Beck got the idea that the only side the superintendent was on was his own.

'I would suggest,' the superintendent said, 'that everyone be held in custody for the minimum twenty-four hours as part of your Cross Beg murder investigation. Here, at Mill Street. That should tie things down nicely until we see what's what.'

'Really? But like I said...'

'I heard you, Inspector. Yes, yes. Three murders. I got it. This is regional HQ. It's more prudent they be detained here anyway. Until you've worked out what's what. Like I said.'

'I get the impression,' Beck replied, 'Mr Bastic will have his solicitor round here in double-quick time.'

'He can be round here double quick all he wants. Bastic stays. They all stay. We'll charge them, motor fraud to begin with, and keep them in custody. I can reveal this much to you: that motor of his, the Mercedes, will need to have all its identification plates and numbers in order and in the correct sequence. Because we'll be pulling it apart. He's a cocky bastard, don't you think?'

'I want to speak to Bastic,' Beck said.

'I thought you would. And I think I know what it is you're going to ask him.'

'You do?'

'Yes, of course. You're going to barter for information, using the information that I want. "Tell me what's going on and I'll see what I can do with this car-cloning business" sort of thing. It's not going to work, Inspector Beck, because I'm giving nothing away. Clear? Anyway, relax, Bastic is going nowhere. As I say, you'll have time to tie things down.'

Beck was beginning to see why whizz-kid here had made it up the career ladder quicker than a monkey with a scorched arse. He paused, then: 'You won't let me speak with him?'

The superintendent spread his arms wide. 'Tell you what, why don't we meet halfway…?'

Beck waited.

'I'll be interviewing him myself. Personally. Later. Just as soon as they've gone over that car. If it is a clone, and I suspect it is, he'll find it impossible to wriggle out of this little fix. He's getting prison time. That, in my opinion, will be the time to leverage any additional information from him that you want.'

Beck shook his head. *Leverage.* Jesus.

'I'll remind you a murder investigation *leverages* everything else into second place… Three victims now. So, tell you what, I'll meet *you* halfway. I want to speak to the foreign national, the one with the scar on his cheek. And I want a vehicle, namely a motorised camper van parked up at the Galway Industrial Estate, seized and forensically examined. Also, I want interpreter services – his English is not so hot. Bulgarian is the language. And I want it all in the next ten minutes.'

The superintendent didn't bat an eyelid.

'No problem,' he said.

CHAPTER THIRTY-SEVEN

'Name,' Beck barked.

The man was seated, slumped low in his chair, arms folded, knees flapping back and forth. Tall and athletic, with a shaved head, he was dressed in a red zip-up jacket, black T-shirt underneath, blue jeans and brown leather boots with the laces undone. He turned his head this way and that, dark eyes scanning the room, but didn't answer. On his right cheek, Beck saw, was a long scar in the shape of a scimitar.

It was a small interview room and directly behind Beck and Claire was the door. The superintendent had insisted on having one of his men present, so a uniform stood in a corner of the room.

Beck pressed the loudspeaker on the desk telephone, placed it at the edge of the desk between himself and the man.

'Hello, interpreter, are you there?' He leant towards the telephone.

'Yes, I am here.'

'Will you please ask the prisoner his name? Thank you.'

The interpreter spoke quickly. A moment later the answer came: '*First I wish to know why I have been arrested.*'

'Your name please.'

'*My name is Lukac Crofkaz.*'

'Tell him he's lying. His real name is Antoz, his second name, I believe, Domi. Tell him Sergey Domi is dead. Ask him why he is lying to me. Did he kill those people?'

Antoz's eyes widened as the questions were fired at him, and he became very still. His knees no longer flapped. Instead, he stared at Beck.

'He says: *What people? Kill what people?*'

'Has he killed them?' Beck said. 'Is that it? If he didn't, why won't he give his real name?'

The interpreter said this to the man, who suddenly sat forward, speaking rapidly.

'*Okay, okay, my name is Antoz Domi. I have killed no one. Tell the policeman this. And what is this about? Did you say my uncle is dead?*'

'Yes. One of three people in Cross Beg within the last forty-eight hours or so, the others an unidentified female and an elderly farmer. All beaten to death.'

As the interpreter spoke, Beck watched Antoz, noted the way he looked to the phone, his eyes widening, as he grew pale.

'*I never killed anybody. Why have they arrested me? I will not speak until I am told the reason for my arrest.*'

'Tell him,' Beck said, 'that keys found in his possession fit a camper van believed to have been observed at the scene of one murder. A comparative analysis of the tyre tracks is underway as I speak. Tell him the house, Six Cedar Grove, and that camper van, were both being used as brothels. That is enough. Tell him that.'

The interpreter told him this.

Antoz buried his face in his hands.

'Oh shit,' he said in heavily accented English. 'Oh shit.' He took his hands from his face and looked at them, like a very frightened boy. 'I tell everything,' he said. 'Everything.'

He fell silent for a moment, then continued, through the interpreter: '*I am of the mountains, and life is harsh there. All the young men of my village have left. We follow each other. We are of different clans, but we are all of the same blood. We seek a better life, but people do not trust us, look down on us, will not give us work. All we seek is a better life, a chance.*' He paused, looked at Claire and

Beck, then continued. '*Yes, we all dabble in a bit of this and a bit of that. We must survive after all. But I have never killed anybody, and I have had nothing to do with brothels. Yes, of course, there are girls, but they are businesswomen. I just drive the van, nothing more. I drive. The men we visit are old, they are desperate and pathetic. I hear the girls say some want to only watch, nothing more. Their eyes caress them, and spit forms at the corners of their mouths. Some have strange fits, dropping to their knees in frantic prayer, shouting for forgiveness, shouting for the girls to leave and to never come back... but always, always, always, they are the first to await our return the following week.*

'*The house in Cross Beg, I do not live there. I live in the van, I prefer it. I feel safer, because we have many enemies, my uncle and I. They would kill us without a second thought. Perhaps these are the men you should be looking for. Not me. For I have killed nobody, certainly not my own uncle. If I did, I would be banished from the mountains; a curse would follow me and whatever children I have forever more. I would never find peace, only torment, for eternity.*'

'I swear,' he said, speaking in that heavily accented English again. 'That is the truth.'

'Where were you last night?' Beck asked.

The man hesitated, scrambling for an answer.

Beck had seen it all before, and it was always the same: calculating.

'*I was away. Sergey has a temper. He was angry and I was afraid. I was driving until he cooled down.*'

'Why were you in Galway then? With Bastic? About to be cut into little pieces? Ask him that, interpreter.'

Antoz laughed when he was asked, but it was a brittle, nervous laugh.

'*Cut into little pieces? No. No. It was a misunderstanding, that is all.*'

'Tell him I get the distinct impression Mr Bastic knew nothing of this camper van. So again, ask him, why has he come to Galway? I want to know. And why in that van?'

The interpreter said this to Antoz, who shrugged his shoulders.

'The van,' he said in English. 'I live in the van. I already tell you this.'

'What a lovely fairy tale,' Beck said. 'That's alright interpreter, you don't need to tell him that. Tell this man he'll be spending time in a cell until we can work out exactly what part he played in all this. And that I don't know what to believe about what he's just told us.'

As Beck and Claire left the interview room, he shouted in English after them.

'Antoz has killed nobody. Nobody!'

Beck thought: *You would say that though, wouldn't you?*

CHAPTER THIRTY-EIGHT

A glowing sign, 'The Road House', shone through the falling snow at the side of the road up ahead.

'Pull in,' Beck said. 'We need to eat.'

Beck waited for Claire's objection, but none came. She merely nodded. A moment later they were turning into the car park, maybe a dozen or so other vehicles scattered about.

They went into the pub. It was a large open space interspersed with thick brick pillars, bric-a-brac lining the walls, a flagstone floor and rough-hewn wooden tables and a roaring fire at one end: traditional. On the walls were fixed old metal signs, and from the ceiling Mason jars and wicker baskets hung, also a couple of oil lamps and a bodhrán. Claire sat at a table. A few other tables were occupied and a handful of men sat drinking in small knots along the counter. A sign proclaimed: FOOD MUST BE ORDERED FROM THE BAR AFTER 5 P.M.

Beck stood at the counter and ordered thick vegetable soup and homemade brown bread for Claire, a tuna roll for himself.

'I'll bring it down, okay?' the barman said.

Beck gave a slight nod of his head, an indication that he wanted something else. The barman approached.

'A pint of Guinness too.'

The barman reached under the counter for a glass.

'I'll bring it down with the food, too, sir. Okay?'

'And a double whiskey,' Beck added, the pitch of his voice unconsciously elevating, insistent, desperate even, as he added, 'I'll take that now.'

The barman was about to place the pint glass against the draught tap. He hesitated, glancing at Beck, then replaced the glass back under the counter. He turned and picked up a tumbler from a stack, brought it to the optic and pressed it twice, turned and placed it before Beck.

Beck picked it up and drank back the contents.

'Thank you,' he said.

He went to the table and sat opposite Claire. She was texting on her mobile phone. She placed the phone onto the table and leant forward.

'The *Connaughtman* is running a news feature. Lucy just told me the title of it.'

'Which is?'

'Battered to death.'

'Not very original, but short and brutally sweet. About sums it up.'

Claire tapped a finger absentmindedly on the tabletop. 'She was worried it might be a bit too blunt. It's a local paper, after all.'

Beck laughed.

Claire's eyes narrowed. 'Something funny?'

Beck said nothing.

'Soup and brown bread,' the barman said, standing by the table, hovering the plates and a pint of Guinness on a tray above them.

'Me,' Claire said. 'Thank you.'

The barman placed the contents of the tray onto the table top and left. Beck lifted the pint of Guinness and took a long draught from it.

'I knew something wasn't right with you,' Claire said, taking a spoonful of soup and blowing on it. 'And I don't need an exam book to tell me that.' She glanced at the Guinness.

He told himself he didn't have to answer. That this was his business.

'Are you drinking or working?' Claire asked then.

And Beck knew it was her business. Because he was working, and drinking, both at the same time. And officially he couldn't do both.

'Just trust me,' he said. 'Will you do that?'

But he knew he didn't fully trust himself.

Claire swallowed some soup. 'Tell you what,' she said. 'You can do whatever you want. You're a big boy. Drink yourself to death if you like. Sad but true. What can I do? But if anyone asks, I didn't see you doing it.' She smiled. 'No offence.'

'No offence,' Beck said, and took a bite of tuna roll.

She wouldn't find that response in her sergeant's exam test booklet either, he knew. He took a sip of Guinness, washing down his food. They ate in silence. When he finished he pushed his plate aside, leant forward.

'I would,' he said slowly, 'like to tell you. If that's okay?'

She looked at him, nodded once. 'Yes. That's okay.' She fell silent, waiting.

Beck took a deep breath, and began. 'My father was a policeman. But you know that already, because I told you. My mother was a music teacher, piano... but I told you that too, right?'

Claire shook her head.

'No? Well, that's what she was. I don't think it was anything formal. I don't remember any certificates or diplomas on the living room wall. I don't know anything about it, in fact, how she learned to play, or where, I mean, although I wish now that I'd asked, except we had a piano and she played it very well and gave lessons. It may sound very middle-class, but we weren't well off – the piano was bought second hand. My father's wages weren't much. A policeman didn't get paid a great deal thirty or so odd years ago. Okay, I'm getting a little bit off the subject here.'

'I don't think that's getting off the subject,' Claire said.

'Don't you? Okay then. We lived in a red-brick house in Newglass...'

'Didn't you say you were from Dublin?'

'No. I never did. I worked in Dublin. Can't you tell by my accent?'

'Your accent is completely neutral.'

'My accent is completely neutral, is it? I'll take that as a compliment. I spent my entire career in Dublin before I came here, to Cross Beg. I like the city. As you know. It suits me. But I'm from Newglass, in County Mayo, next stop New York as they say. Anyway, my first recollection – or one of them – is going with my father through the town searching for my mother. I'm not certain what age I was, maybe ten. I don't remember much of my early childhood, which is good I suppose in a way, because it means it didn't affect me, or at least, it didn't imprint my consciousness. Bad memories usually do, much more than the good, in my opinion. I was too young to understand, is what I'm trying to say, but that was all about to change. I don't know where my sister was that day – Helen, remember, I told you about her. She's in Australia, been there for years.'

'Is she married?'

'Yes, with two children. She's a nurse, at Sydney Children's Hospital. Andy, her husband – he's Australian by the way – is a secondary school science teacher. Good people. Where was I...? I was with my father, he was dragging me behind him through the town. I knew he was looking for my mother, although he didn't say so. We went to a house, a big house, in the posh part of Newglass, where all the knobs lived. It was covered in ivy and there was a huge car parked outside. He knocked on the door but no one answered. He knocked and knocked until eventually the door did open. A small man was standing there. He was bald, with shiny teeth and tanned skin, I remember. My father asked him where my mother was and he told him, this man, that my mother was with him, in the house.

'Well, that always stayed with me. It never left. I remember it like it was yesterday. I wanted my mother to come to us, not to be with this man. I didn't understand what it was all about, of course, but I wanted my mother, and this man had her. So I started crying, and my father started shouting at the man and then the door closed in our faces. My father walked away and I went after him and followed him home. Nothing was ever the same again. Nothing.

'The small bald man was Ambrose Donegan, a local business-man. He owned a factory, was rich and had a big flashy car and house.'

'Wasn't he married?' Claire asked.

'No, he wasn't,' Beck replied. 'Although he did marry, much later, and to a much younger woman. The attraction was his voice, I think. He was a great tenor, and my mother loved music.'

'Was your father musical?'

'Nooo. He actually disliked music. She and Donegan were having an affair. For years they'd been having an affair. And I know now that this was when my father finally heard about it, or allowed himself to hear about it. Because the whole town knew. I didn't know that then, but I know it now, everyone knew about it.

'Anyway, I came home from school one day and...' Beck's voice faltered. Claire was about to say something. 'No,' he said, 'it's okay. I'm fine. I came home from school one day. It was a week or so before Christmas. Their bedroom, my mother and father's that is – I think they were still sharing the same bed – had a double window. It was like a small double door, or a French window, with a small ledge outside. My mother always kept it locked, because it was dangerous of course, with two young children in the house. She had the key, only her, no one else.

'I went into the kitchen and I could see my father lying on the ground outside in the yard.' Beck's eyes began to moisten. 'My father. He'd fallen out the window. Jesus, his head was... Well, I suppose Eddie Kavanagh reminded me of it. Brought it all back. There was something almost the same. I thought I had dealt with it long ago. But I can't get it out of my head. It's like it's there, in front of me, all the time. Eddie Kavanagh, my father, side by side, both the same... I think I'm going crazy at times with it. I see it everywhere. The only time I don't see it is when... when I drink.'

'You mother, Beck. What about her?' Claire asked softly.

'My mother? She died soon after. Got a clot in her brain. Six months later in fact. We, Helen and I, were taken into care. There were relatives of course, but my father's two brothers both lived in America, and my mother's sister, Auntie Ruth, lived in Scotland. So, I was sent to St Gabriel's... I don't know what you'd call it, a half boarding school, half industrial school, "for orphans and troubled children" is how it was described, but the truth was, the most troubled of all were the religious brothers who ran the place. They were only young fellas themselves, looking back, early twenties most of them, sexually repressed it's safe to say, and deviant in their ways... Oh, Christ, I don't want to talk about that...' Beck fell silent. After a moment he went on. 'Helen had a tough time too, in Dublin, at an equivalent institution for girls. They were worked harder than the boys. In St Gabriel's, we were put to growing vegetables, for the kitchens. There were plenty of us, so it wasn't that hard – a couple of hours a day was all. But with the girls it was different. Because there was money to be made from their labour. They were put to work in the convent laundry. It had contracts with all the big hotels and offices in the city, and they were sent out cleaning big houses too, and making clothes, uniforms, for the government. The nuns ran their own little business empire. The girls were slaves of a sort, and those of single mothers, who were in the majority, were treated harsher than the others, the ones who at least had parents. The Brothers didn't care so much about that sort of thing, about the status of your mother, but the nuns did.' Beck sat back in his chair. 'That's the gist of it,' he added. 'For now. Okay?'

He wiped a napkin across his eyes. 'Now, let's go. I need to get out of here.'

CHAPTER THIRTY-NINE

There was a TV news crew and a handful of reporters outside the station when they got back. The roadway in front was taken up by marked and unmarked cars, some double-parked. Claire found a space a little down the street and pulled in. Beck saw someone walking along the pavement towards them in the wing mirror, a woman. She caught his eyes and gave a discreet wave. Beck instantly knew Claire's wife Lucy Grimes was adopting a best-friends approach. Her wave was discreet because she didn't want the other reporters standing further back to notice. Claire lowered her window and Lucy went round and leant in. In the weak light it looked as if her head was suspended in thin air.

'We've been told there's a briefing,' Lucy said, 'and afterwards, Superintendent Wilde is going to give a press conference.'

Lucy glanced at Beck. She was smiling, but it was a smile that was strained. Who were they fooling? Neither liked the other.

'Nothing you want to say, you two?' she added.

Claire glanced at Beck.

'You might,' he said, and Lucy's eyes became a mixture of contempt and curiosity, 'want to speak to Mill Street. A Superintendent Browne. Ask him about an incident at the Galway Industrial Estate earlier today, something to do with car cloning. Now, you didn't hear that from me.'

'Hey, Luce, something we should know?' A small mousy man was standing behind her. 'I mean, we're all looking out for one another, ya, aren't we?'

'See you later, babes,' Lucy whispered to Claire, and stood back from the car, turned to Mousy. 'Ya, Murphy, right.' She raised a hand, folding all but the middle finger, which she displayed prominently as she passed him by.

'Why'd you tell her that?' Claire asked. 'I thought you didn't like her.'

'Maybe you're right,' he said. 'But I think I like Superintendent Browne even less.'

CHAPTER FORTY

Three killings in as many days was the murder-investigation equivalent of the kind of blazing inferno that would draw in scores of firefighters and engines, and now officers had been drawn in from almost every district within the division. But while additional fire tenders and manpower always assisted in extinguishing a blaze, additional police officers in an investigation like this could sometimes get in the way.

Beck was considering this as he surveyed the room, pleased with his analogy. While he often considered briefings a pain in the arse, on this occasion he felt it was warranted because, if nothing else, he needed to stitch things together.

The plain clothes and uniforms were talking amongst themselves, as if at a social gathering, the occasional loud guffaw and laughter sounding about the room. Still, Beck needed this gathering, and the timing was good, because he felt he was riding a wave, balanced perfectly, skimming the curling white tops, focused, in the zone. But surfers never stayed upright for very long – he knew that too.

'Quiet,' Superintendent Wilde said, clapping his hands twice. 'Your attention. Please.'

Silence rolled through the room and people shifted, turning to face Wilde and Beck standing together on one side of the whiteboard, SOC Inspector Mahony on the other. Wilde twisted the top of a marker pen back and forth in his hands. The whiteboard was half filled with Wilde's scrawl, a series of asterisks and lines of cursive writing, a couple of vertical lines separating different sections with headings, names, dates, locations... Wilde reminded Beck of a performer with a full backing orchestra but who still insisted on bringing along his own guitar. The whiteboard was the equivalent of a prop.

There was a small rectangle of space left on the whiteboard. Wilde wrote in tiny writing into it, 'Sergey Domi. Un-ID'd female. Missing un-ID'd female'. He stood back then, as if admiring it, before going through the details of the case, details everybody was already familiar with, turning occasionally to the room to face his audience, before going back to looking at the whiteboard. Finally, Superintendent Wilde wrote 'blunt force trauma' and the whiteboard was full.

'It appears a female may be missing,' Wilde told the room. 'But we're not certain. We only have a witness statement, nothing concrete, but it's a fact that one girl who was there last night when we called was not there this morning. A rudimentary description of her is available on Pulse. Make sure you go look at it. The immediate area around Cedar Grove, all fields, outhouses, etcetera, are being searched. We found what appeared to be prints in the field behind the house, but these were indistinct smudges more than anything due to the rough, soggy nature of the terrain. We're continuing to see if we can pick these up anywhere else, but nothing so far. Our killer appears to know the area well. No tyre marks have been found, so likely he got in and out on foot.' He paused. 'The extent of violence used was, well, there's only one word to sum it up: shocking. That poor girl's face was pummelled into an unrecognisable mess. More violence was used against her than the male. Which I consider significant, indicating a pent-up rage towards women, on top of an already existing substantial rage. But we'll deal with that later.' He paused, stroking his chin, pensive. 'The pathologist,' he continued, 'has indicated our killer is probably tall, because some of the deep lacerations to the face of the male found at Six Cedar Grove are consistent with an implement being swung in an upward trajectory. He was likely initially stuck while standing, because he was found outside, so hadn't been lying down. It also seems likely he answered the door and walked out of the house. The pathologist compared the injuries with those of Edward Kavanagh – on their own not enough to form an opinion. Edward Kavanagh was struck straight on, but the killer might have been standing on higher ground, we don't know. Consequently the pathologist couldn't draw an inference to his killer's height. But now, we believe the killer of the male victim at Cedar Grove was several inches taller than him, and that being the case, the pathologist is of the opinion he is approximately 5 foot 11, or the same height as Edward Kavanagh. The pathologist also believes our killer is someone young, possibly athletic… Inspector Beck?'

'Yes?'

'That man, what's his name… Antoz?'

'Yes. Antoz Domi,' Beck said.

'How tall is he?'

'Similar to Eddie Kavanagh, as it happens.'

'Hmm,' Wilde said, seemingly content with his contribution. He fell silent, glanced to Beck.

As Beck began to speak, outlining events, Superintendent Wilde stroked his chin again. He hadn't heard of the events in Galway until just before the briefing. Beck continued with his verbal sketch, working things out for himself as he went along, giving context, tying strands together. This could only be done the way he was doing it now – by talking in front of a room full of other investigators.

'But,' he finished, 'Antoz is not the key link to Cedar Grove. Charles Bastic is. I believe he's the so-called Boss Man. It's he who controls Six Cedar Grove, although not, however, the mobile brothel. My instinct is he knew nothing about it. It was Sergey and Antoz's side earner. I can't prove it, I can't prove any of it, not yet, but that's what I believe.'

'You managed to follow Bastic all the way to Galway?' Wilde said then. 'How exactly?'

Beck nodded. 'With a little help from another emergency agency.'

'What agency? What type of help?'

'The coastguard, sir. A helicopter.'

Wilde's brow furrowed and his eyebrows shot up.

Beck raised his eyebrows in turn.

'I see,' Wilde muttered. 'No one informed me.'

'It was a very fluid situation, boss.'

'I'm sure it was… And Bastic is being detained in Mill Street as well, you say? He needs to be here. This investigation trumps every-bloody-thing else.'

Beck nodded.

'So, why didn't you bring him? Here I mean. To Cross Beg.'

'Superintendent Browne wanted him in Mill Street, that's why. If I can put it like this, he's got major trust issues.'

'Superintendent Browne, our commissioner-in-waiting. Leave that to me.' Wilde folded his arms. 'You are serious, aren't you, Beck, a helicopter? For real?'

'I am.'

'And you can do that?'

Beck was about to answer, but Wilde said, 'You know what? I don't think I want to know.' He paused. 'Bastic – been after him for years. Can't believe it looks like, at last, we have the bastard.'

Beck could see Wilde's clenched fists at the end of two long, hanging arms. Nothing worse, Beck knew, than for a policeman to have a personal vendetta. And he should know.

'Considering the amount of violence used,' Wilde added, 'it is surprising that we haven't come across this person before. Therefore, he is indeed likely to be young, starting out in his career as it were. If that wasn't the case, surely we'd have come across him before. I mean, he didn't just pop out of thin air. We need to curtail his career.'

'Or he's from a different jurisdiction.' Garda Dempsey said.

Wilde nodded, looking across to the other side of the whiteboard, where the SOCO stood. 'Inspector Mahony.'

The SOC officer coughed once and nodded his small, bony head. 'I'm very sorry, but I don't have a lot. However, we still have some tests to run in the lab. I was bringing samples to Dublin for further analysis when we were called back here. We didn't expect two more homicides – no one expected that. One thing...' He glanced at Superintendent Wilde. 'It is uncertain if more violence was expended on the female victim. Because she was slightly built so, while that might appear to be the case, injuries to her would inevitably be more substantial. Just to clarify that point.'

Wilde looked towards a window, and back again. Beck knew he didn't like having his views questioned in front of lower ranks.

'Preliminary results from our first scene,' Mahony went on. 'That of the murder of Edward Kavanagh...'

'Yes. Yes. We know that's the first murder scene,' Wilde sounded grumpy.

'Okay.' Inspector Mahony looked about the room. 'We lifted some prints from the fencing stake, the murder weapon.' Heads nodded. 'But the presentations are partially obscured, the preservative oil in the wood leeched when the wood was cut...'

'Can you just get on with it?' a voice piped up.

'So,' he went on, 'we treated it overnight and got results. Two sets of prints actually, one the murder victim's, and the other... well, possibly his too.'

Again, he paused.

'What does that mean?' Garda Frank Costello called from the back of the room. 'The killer's got four hands? An Indian deity, something like that? Is that what you're saying?'

But no one laughed. Even if it was funny, people didn't laugh at any of Costello's jokes.

'Maybe,' Mahony said. 'But one set of prints came from garden gloves, the type with those distinctive... well, welts I'd call them, you know, on the fingers, for grip.'

'So,' said the same voice that had piped up earlier. 'This doesn't assist us any in identifying the killer, does it? What have you got that'll help us do that? Specifically.'

'Who is that?' Mahony peered down the room.

'Me.'

'Who's me?'

'Sergeant Erskine. Mill Street.'

And Beck thought: *Aha.*

'Thank you for your contribution,' Beck said. 'And what is your role at Mill Street? If I may ask.'

The sergeant had jet-black hair and was sitting straight-backed, hands on knees, formal.

'With respect,' he said. 'I don't see of what relevance that is.'

'With respect,' Beck said. 'Just answer the question.'

'Operations. General.'

Beck considered. 'Specifically. Superintendent's office. Correct?'

The sergeant gave a slight pout: *so what?*

'Yes,' he said.

'Thank you,' Beck said. 'Just so as we know.' He turned back to Inspector Mahony.

And just then, Beck felt it, the wave-changing momentum, like a rip current pulling him in a different direction. He suddenly thought of Dr Gumbell. More than anything, Beck realised that a career working alongside the curmudgeonly, opinionated and definitely alcoholic state pathologist had given him – he searched for a word – an... expectation. That was it. Gumbell, in a table of forensic scientists, was premier league. Applying the same standard to his stand-in, Dr Keane, had been a lapse of judgement.

The rip current pulled against him, and Beck could feel the wave begin to break behind him, threatening to take him under.

He heard Superintendent Wilde's voice, as if he were speaking on a very bad phone line... 'The surviving female taken from the property is currently recovering in hospital. We need to speak to her, but won't be able to do so until tomorrow at the earliest.'

Beck suddenly felt like he would faint, so he mumbled that he had to take a call, walked slowly towards the door of the Ops Room, feeling as if he were walking into a steadily narrowing tunnel that threatened to squeeze him to death. But he walked on, narrowing his eyes, seeing only fragments of wall and floor, chairs and finally the door. He pulled on the handle and opened it, stepped out into the corridor, stumbled along to the end, pushed through and went into the car park, turned his face into the cold wind, leant down and picked up a handful of brittle snow, rubbed it into his face.

'Beck.'

He looked up. Framed in the light of the doorway was Claire.

'What's happening with you?' she said.

He didn't answer. There was no answer to that.

CHAPTER FORTY-ONE

Beck opened the door, and Max rushed to greet him, jumping up and leaning against him with his two front paws. Beck embraced the dog and Max nuzzled against him, then sat on the floor, raising a paw, and touched Beck's leg.

'It's okay, boy. I'm home. You hungry?' He patted the dog and turned his head, listening. There was no other sound in the house. He went into the kitchen, Max trailing behind. Beck took a tin of dog food from a bag on the table, opened it, scooped the entire contents into a bowl and placed it on the floor for Max, who began to wolf it down immediately. Beck went to the back door and opened it, left it that way for Max to go outside if he needed to.

He turned his thoughts to Natalia. Already the aroma of perfume and Indian food had been usurped by the familiar dank, musty smell of the house. He noticed a note on the worktop by the sink, resting against the electric kettle. He knew without reading it that Natalia had gone, and considered the smell, or stench, had always been there, but because he'd nothing to compare it to, he simply hadn't noticed. But now he had something to compare it to. He realised too that a part of him had hoped that Natalia might have changed her mind, or at least have remained a little while longer. But she had not. He picked up the note and began to read:

> My dear Finnegan. I've left, as you can see, but I did tell you, so it shouldn't come as any great surprise. It just wasn't what I'd expected, that's all, you and me, playing

house together. But I should have known, because when it comes to you, nothing is as expected, is it?

I suppose I'm hurt, Beck, that's what I'm saying, and I know, in your way, you are too.

There's a lot more I could say. But I won't. I don't want to say anything I'll regret. What I will say is I love you, Finnegan. I don't know fully what type of love it is, or what form it takes. But it's love, I have no doubt. But more than anything, sometimes I want to shake you. I really do. I want to shake you and make you realise how truly wonderful you are, how loving and understanding you can be. When you let your guard down, that is. But you don't do that nearly enough. And I need more than that.

Goodbye, Beck.

Natalia.

P.S. Don't try and contact me. Don't make this any harder than it already is. Please.

It came back then, the thought he had earlier pushed to one side – why this woman fascinated him. He knew the answer, he felt, he'd always known the answer, he just hadn't wanted to admit it, that was all. But he did now. It was because Natalia reminded him of his mother.

Jesus.

Beck dropped the note onto the worktop, went to the table and sat heavily into a chair, feeling both relief and regret at the same time, withdrew from his pocket the naggin of whiskey that still had a little left in it. The waves had carried him to shore now, and dumped him there. His head was beginning to hurt again and the rest of the world seemed like shit. It was always the same… He grasped the bottle and drank it down, loving the burning sensation at the back of his throat, fooling himself that his headache had already begun to ease, and that colour was being restored to the world.

He told himself again: *Just enough. No more. No less. God damn it, just enough!*

He placed the empty bottle onto the table and stared at it, reached into his pocket for his phone, scrolled through his numbers, found the one he wanted, was about to press call when the telephone rang instead, the station number flashing across the screen. He answered.

'Yes.'

'Boss.'

Beck recognised the voice but couldn't put a name to it.

'We've been looking through the CCTV from the whor... I mean, Six Cedar Grove...'

'Yes.'

'We spotted someone familiar.'

Beck felt a nerve tingle in his belly. 'Who, for Christ's sake?'

'Jamie. McLoughlin. Our postman.'

Claire was waiting for him in the foyer when he got back to the station. She had just left to go home when he'd rang, and had turned around and come straight back.

'A little discretion is called for,' Beck said. 'I've told Superintendent Wilde we'll look after this.'

'Very thoughtful,' Claire said, but couldn't conceal the scepticism in her voice. 'It's not...'

'Procedure,' he finished for her. 'You're right. So, how would you play this?'

'Well...' Claire began, thinking. 'He's a suspect. And, until we eliminate him from our enquiries, what we should do is arrest him for questioning, or request that he attend voluntarily at the station. Simple. He should be brought in, for sure. That's the correct—'

'I know, I know,' Beck said. 'Anyway, I've rung ahead. It's Christmas, he's working late.' He checked his watch. It was almost nine thirty. 'Until midnight in fact. He'll meet us outside the rear of the post office in five minutes, at half past. It's quicker this way, believe me, and, when someone thinks you've done them a favour, they usually give you something in return. He may have nothing to do with this, Claire, remember that, and hauling people in can piss them off.'

'You've spoken to him already?'

Beck nodded.

'And if he's not there? What then?'

'Then,' Beck said, 'I've played this all wrong, haven't I?'

It was two minutes after half past nine, and they sat in Claire's Renault Clio on Brendan Street, at the back of the post office. They had agreed to save time by travelling in her car. Beck craved a cigarette. He was about to give in to it and get out of the car when he spotted Jamie McLoughlin emerging through the metal door in the wall on the opposite side of the road. He spotted them immediately, walked quickly across the road and got into the rear of the Clio. He was in his work uniform, shirt open at the neck, no jacket, sweating.

'I really appreciate this,' he said, and Beck instantly noted the nervous agitation in his voice. 'I really do.'

Beck glanced to Claire, and she caught the look.

'As a man,' Beck said, 'who has made many mistakes in his life, I believe there are two sides to every story. You know where I'm coming from in all this? So tell me where you're coming from. Don't mess me about now, like a good man. The truth... As you know, I'm doing you a favour.'

'Yes, yes, of course. I won't mess you about. Because if this got out, Christ, if this got out, I mean...'

Beck sat at an angle, peering back at McLoughlin, who was in the centre of the rear seat. He could see the postman's eyes turning to take in Claire.

'We're waiting,' Beck said.

The postman made a clucking sound, the sound of a tongue in a very dry mouth. Beck reached into a pocket and withdrew his lozenges.

'They're strong,' Beck said, holding out the pack.

'Thank you.' He took one, and, a moment later: 'You probably know I'm married. Christ, like I say, if this gets out... Miriam always told me if I messed about, even just once, that was it, she'd leave me. And I believe her. I have two kids. Look, I've been stupid. Please, if I get out of this, I'll never do anything like it again.'

Self-preservation, always the primary factor. Beck thought to capitalise on it.

'No guarantees,' he said.

'Aren't there?' The postman's voice rose an octave. 'I mean, you said to me we could keep this to ourselves, didn't you?'

'Of course,' Beck said. 'Yes, we can. But that is so long as this stays under my control, if you follow me, which will only happen if everything you tell me stacks up, and I feel certain you're telling me the truth...'

'I will tell you the truth, I swear it.' There was desperation in his voice now.

'Good, then you should have nothing to worry about. You were in that house for sexual services, weren't you?'

The postman paused.

'Don't waste my time,' Beck said. 'There's nothing you've done that will shock us.'

'Yes,' the postman said, dropping his head onto his chest.

'How many children have you got?' It was Claire.

'Two.' The voice was a whisper.

'Things good at home?' she asked.

He nodded. 'Yes. Not perfect. But nothing is perfect, right? But overall, yes. I love my wife… Oh, Christ… Please, if this gets out, if this gets out… It can't get out. Tell me it won't get out. Please. Tell me. She'll leave me. Miriam will take the two kids with her. I can't live without them, I can't…'

'Steady on there, Jamie. Relax. I want to know where you were last night and—'

'I've been working every night this week. Overtime. It's Christmas.'

'How's that possible?' Beck said. 'You were delivering post in the morning, when Eddie Kavanagh's body was found. Surely if you were working—'

'My overtime shift at the sorting office starts at midnight, until 6 a.m. – that's when the regular shift starts. Six hours, double bubble. I then work my regular shift until midday. A total of twelve hours. A twelve-hour shift is very doable.'

'Then how come you're working now? You just said your hours are midnight to 6 a.m.'

'I swapped. Just for today. It's my… wedding anniversary tomorrow, so I'm not working tonight.'

Beck shook his head. 'The time on CCTV shows you at Cedar Grove just after 11 p.m. on Sunday night. How long were you there?'

'Three quarters of an hour, give or take. Like I said, my shift starts at midnight.'

'So you went there before your shift, yes?' Claire said.

'Yes.'

'Okay, and then you were at work, in the post office? We'll check.'

'Yes,' McLoughlin said. 'I was. You can check both my clocking-in card and the CCTV. The whole place is covered in cameras.'

Beck thought about that. 'You're working until midnight now, are you?'

'Yes.'

'You get a copy of your clocking-in details, and the CCTV, for the last three nights to Detective Garda Somers by morning. I don't care how you do it. Otherwise I'll be looking for a warrant, and I don't think you want that.'

'No. No. I don't. Thank you. You'll have it. I promise.'

'Good,' Beck said. 'Now go back to work.'

McLoughlin opened the door, hesitated before getting out. 'I'll never do anything like this again, never. I promise. I love my wife and kids so much, really.'

'You tell your wife that lately?' Claire asked.

McLoughlin was silent.

'Because,' Beck said, 'the love of a good woman is hard to find and easy to lose...' He glanced in the rear-view mirror, caught McLoughlin's eye. 'Whatever reason brought you to Cedar Grove can be sorted out, if you see what I mean?'

The postman nodded. 'I see what you mean. Of course, it can be sorted... and it will be sorted.'

'Off you go.'

The postman got out and closed the door. Beck watched him head back into the post office.

'I know,' he said to Claire. 'It's not bloody procedure.'

CHAPTER FORTY-TWO

The dial tone gave a hollow echo, signifying the person was out of the country. Beck was sitting at his kitchen table. Max lay at his feet.

The phone was answered after the fifth ring. 'Beck, what do you want?'

'Nice to hear from you too.'

'I'm about to go down to dinner. What is it?'

And Beck knew, by the subtleties of intonation, the intake of breath, Gumbell was as sober as a... well, as sober as a state pathologist.

'Are you giving a speech?' Beck asked.

Gumbell paused. 'How did you know?'

Beck grinned. 'I know you too well.'

'You're drinking, aren't you?'

'I prefer to call it coasting, having the sun on my face.'

'Ha, ha, ha, and bloody ha ha, again. Oh how the mighty have fallen...'

'I don't know,' Beck said. 'You asked why I called. I don't know why I called. Not exactly.'

'I seem to remember short shrift from you when the roles were reversed recently. I rang you in a condition of inebriation. Remember what you told me? You told me—'

'Go to sleep. That's what I told you. You were smoking in bed and talking about drinking more. I seem to remember you thanked me... granted, it was some time afterwards when you did.'

'As you will thank me too, I have no doubt. Now, goodn—'

'Steady on,' Beck announced. 'I told you. I'm coasting. But I want your advice. Do you understand me?'

Gumbell took a slow breath. 'Yes, I understand you.'

'Then give me a minute. Three murders. In forty-eight hours. Blunt force trauma in each. Use of excessive violence. Your boy Keane is here doing the cutting and stitching, on all...'

'And...'

'And,' Beck said. 'And bloody and... He's not giving me any nuances, any lightness and shade.'

Gumbell was quiet. Then said softly, 'I could take this as a compliment'.

Beck smiled. He had considered Gumbell impervious to praise, but realised now he was not.

Beck made a low humming sound.

'You only make that sound when you're pissed,' Gumbell said. 'It's irritating... So, what is Keane saying to you?'

'He's saying,' Beck began, 'that our killer is possibly young, athletic, tall, and—'

'Wait, wait, wait,' Gumbell said. 'Stop right there. I deal in strict science, unlike your philosophical mumbo jumbo at times, Beck...'

'Well, it works for me...'

'Shut up, Beck. I look at the body as a biological organ... Don't yawn, let me finish. It, the body, is predisposed to illness and, of course, death. It is designed that way, a slow deterioration of the cells assuring at some stage – sooner or later – the ending of life, and ultimately the continuation of the species by leaving enough bloody room for the rest of us to follow on behind.' There was a rustling sound, and a small explosion in Beck's ear. Gumbell had coughed. 'You've been round the block, Beck. You know young doctors like to give the impression they know everything, when in reality they know little except how to drink and get inside nurses' knickers... And Keane told you what? That it was someone young, did he?'

'It was a mutual conclusion. Like I said, the—'

'And you believed him? My God, Beck, you want to buy shares in Donegal sand, exporting the finest grade shingle to Dubai? A sure earner. How could he or anyone else possibly know that? There's a chap in Bali, apparently still fishes with a hook and line, dives to a hundred feet on one gulp of air, stays down for up to four minutes. As fit as the proverbial fiddle and as strong as a bull. He's ninety-four years old, for God's sake.'

Flick, Beck considered, the sound of something being turned completely onto its head, as he thought of a size twelve boot kicking him in the arse.

'Thank you,' Beck said. 'I won't detain you any longer. Enjoy your dinner.'

He hung up before Gumbell could speak, sat there tapping his phone against his chin, lost in thought, as he whispered, 'Now, why didn't I think of that?'

A sound drew his attention. He turned. Max had moved to the door, was sitting looking at him. Beck checked the time, then heaved himself up from the chair with a sigh.

'Come on, boy. You need a walk.'

Max wagged his tail once, in total agreement.

CHAPTER FORTY-THREE

The dog appeared nervous of the dark at first. They made their way to the town park. Although the park lights would be off, Beck knew it would be bright enough from the street lamps outside and from across the river for them to move around. Beck had no lead, but Max stayed close. When they reached the park, Max appeared reassured, and began to wander from Beck a little, as if testing his confidence, until suddenly he bolted, running back and forth across the wide green area at its centre, his speed increasing each time to a frantic pace. Back and forth he went, until eventually, he plopped down, exhausted, on the grass by the wrought-iron railing next to the river, his tongue hanging out, panting furiously. Beck noticed for the first time that Max's muzzle was partly grey. He was not a young dog. Beck could see the water flowing past in the darkness, could feel the power of it, could hear it, as if it were breathing. Despite the hour, he was restless.

'Come on, Max,' he said, clicking his tongue on the roof of his mouth. They made their way home. As they passed Crabby's supermarket, Beck rushed in just as it was closing for business, leaving Max waiting obediently by the door.

'I need some dog biscuits, boy,' he said, going through the doors, but he knew this was merely an excuse.

Once back at the house, Beck opened the packet of dog biscuits, placed a couple in the feeding bowl, emptied the water bowl next to it and refilled it with fresh water. But Max was already asleep on the couch. Beck left the house again.

As he made his way along the street once more, it started to snow again, and he felt as if he were inside a snow globe, looking out at a great black universe that was the sky. He glanced at his watch: 11.15 p.m. He tried to remember what time he had spoken with Gumbell. Was it moments ago, or had it been hours?

A clinking sound came from inside his pockets. He put his hand in and took out a miniature bottle from the Whiskeys of the World collection. He'd bought it in Crabby's earlier. He peered at the bottle, like a prop from a doll's house: Canadian Club. He opened it and drank back the contents – it was enough, just about, he considered, to fill two shot glasses. Which suited him fine. Just enough. No more. No less. Just enough. Provided he continued being capable of making that distinction, of course.

He mounted the steps to the station and pushed through the door, normally open but closed now against the cold and snow. He crossed the foyer to the security door and was about to press the keypad when he realised he'd forgotten the code. He turned. The public office counter was deserted. He approached and pressed the button. It was next to a sign that said:

If unattended please press once. ONCE ONLY.

The windows inside the station were all closed, and Beck could detect a smell, of sweat and old socks. When no one answered, he pressed the button again, for longer this time.

A sergeant emerged from behind a partition. Beck didn't recognise him. There were dark patches under his eyes and his shirt was crumpled. He observed Beck with a mixture of apathy and suspicion. Mission statements and public service reminders were forgotten about as he snapped, 'What? Can't you read the sign? Press once, for God's sake.'

And Beck remembered a holiday in New York one time, and a cop's response when he'd asked directions to somewhere or other before walking off: '*I ain't no tour guide, mister.*'

The sergeant began to approach the counter but stopped some feet short. Number one in the unofficial policeman's rule book: always maintain a safe distance until you know what it is you're dealing with.

'You're already pissing me off,' the sergeant said. 'What is it?'

'A triple murder,' Beck said. 'Is that enough?'

And Beck could see the tired, red-rimmed eyes stirring to life.

'You've been drinking,' the sergeant said, more a statement than a question.

'Yes. But I'm off duty.'

'Off duty?'

Beck took out his wallet from a pocket, opened it and slapped it on the counter, displaying his ID.

The sergeant stepped over now, peered down at it. 'Beck. I've heard about you. Why couldn't you just say? Jesus Christ.'

'And you?'

'Cahill, from Ballinasloe. They sent me over 'cause someone called in sick.'

Cahill stretched and pressed a button. A buzzer sounded and Beck walked down to the security door.

'If I had said who I was,' Beck said, pulling it open, 'then I'd never have known how charming you could be.'

The last time he had been in the dank police basement was months before. He hadn't known it even existed until Claire Somers had brought him here, when they needed to search through old files as part of an investigation into a murder and child kidnap. As with back then, he wondered now if the past might provide answers to questions posed in the present. He'd had a thought. It might be nothing, of course. But he didn't think it was.

He walked along the narrow hallway to the end, flicked the ancient light switch just inside a door. In here was contained a chronicle of crime stretching back to 1922, to the foundation of the State itself. The oldest files – along with documents such as State land deeds, official correspondence and intelligence reports from the Civil War – were stored on sagging metal shelves dusted in the chalky powder that was the dried residue of mould seeping in from the damp walls, which had crystallized over time. The air smelt of dust and damp and time itself. The files and other documents were slowly being digitised and transferred to the Pulse system. At this rate, some of the oldest might be lost, disintegrating into thin air, by the time the IT specialists reached them.

There was a table in the centre of the room, stacked with more files. Beck pulled the file from the top of the stack closest to him. On the front, written in faded marker pen, was the year: 1953. He replaced it, flicked through some of those beneath it, discovered they were not in chronological order, but all were from the 1950s. He moved to the next stack – 1961 was on top – and began going through it. The year he was looking for, 1966, was near the bottom, and he pulled the file out. He opened it and began going through the contents, quickly deciding they held a common theme, a homage to sloppy reporting and to partial and missing facts. A sign of the times from back then, perhaps, but also a smokescreen, a hall of mirrors concealing the lazy work practices of the era. There were lots of missing property reports (robberies and thefts), wives scalded and lacerated and bruised (domestics), drunken males tussling and falling and ending up with serious wounds (assaults), but a paucity of proper, recorded crime.

Footsteps sounded from along Main Street, light filtering through the air vents high on the wall from the street lamps outside. The footsteps receded and the only sound was his breath-ing as he continued turning the damp sheets of paper. Beck hadn't quite known what he was searching for, but now, he knew what he had found.

He looked at the report before him, glossed over its contents, gaining a view, a perspective, a verdict of what it was about. He moved on, noting the handwriting, smudged with the passing of time, the words in a black heavy scrawl. He knew this one was different. He held the piece of paper with its motif of a harp, the emblem of Ireland, in the centre at the top. The old gothic script about it had once been used by government departments, reflecting, he considered, the dour austerity of the time. Reading the contents, he felt his heart kick inside his ribcage. Because he knew everything had to come from something. That was why he was here, in the oldest portion of the old station, beneath the veneer of modernity. But he hadn't expected this.

He uttered two words: 'Good God.'

CHAPTER FORTY-FOUR

Beck returned home. He slept for merely a couple of hours before he woke again. And during those hours the alcohol had not been enough to douse the dreams completely, merely enough to ensure they smouldered rather than sparked into flame.

Beck shook his head and opened his eyes, felt a stab of pain in his head. His throat was dry and he swallowed with difficulty. There was a sound, distant, like wind rustling through leaves. Slowly he stirred, sat up, fumbled in the pocket of his jacket that lay on the floor next to the bed and took from it the last remaining bottle. He emptied it in one swallow. The small, pretty, colourful Whiskeys of the World box was on the floor, an ignominious end to an item advertised as the perfect gift for the discerning special someone in your life.

He lay back, waiting for the edges to soften. He checked the time: 6:45 a.m. He could remain here, staring into the darkness… or he could… A thought began to formulate. He became aware then of a gentle sound next to him. He peered over his shoulder and saw Max lying on the duvet. He smiled as the dog opened his eyes and stared at him, and Beck could swear the animal could see right into his very soul.

'Stay there, Max, it's early. I'm going out for a little while.'

The dog made to get up, but Beck reached out and nudged him back down gently, patted his head. 'Sssh, Max, you stay, good boy.'

A sighing sound came from the dog as he closed his eyes again.

'Good boy,' Beck said, and left the bed.

Max opened one eye and watched him leave the room.

CHAPTER FORTY-FIVE

This was the sensation that drove him. This was a feeling that he both circumvented and craved all at the same time. This was a feeling that was fleeting, insistent, but demanding always to be fed. This was a feeling that could ultimately kill him too. If he allowed it to, that is, if he didn't grasp the reins, pull up the careering beast before it was too late. And yet, despite this, he kept coming back for more. It was no different to heroin, cocaine or amphetamines. Amphetamines might cause your teeth to rot and your face to age with the speed of a movie on fast forward, but alcohol always aroused a certain sympathy – '*Ah, the poor fella, sure he likes a drop.*'

Beck thought of his father lying on the ground, blood seeping from his head, and his mother rushing to him, covering his eyes with her hands. How could he have forgotten? Everything stirred back into life by the murder of an elderly farmer.

Sunday afternoon, three months or thereabouts after his father's passing, now officially labelled an accidental death. He had gone to the matinee in the Astoria Cinema. The entire auditorium, mostly boys like himself, whooped and stamped their feet as the posse rode through the badlands of New Mexico, until Ned, the elderly usher, came down and shone his torch in their faces, told them he knew all their mothers and their fathers and if they didn't behave he'd throw them all out and tell their parents. But once he'd gone they'd started up again. And on the way home, they'd jumped on each other's backs shouting 'Giddy up there Bessie' or hidden behind walls, shooting with pointed fingers at the Indians attacking the wagon train. 'I shot ya, lie down, you're dead' and 'No I'm not, your bullet hit me sheriff's badge so it did, I'm not dead.'

And there were the times at the Crowleys' house, when Mrs Crowley would tell him, 'It's time to go home now, Finnegan. Dominic and Andy are going to bed. Will your mother not be wondering where you are?' And he would take his time, not going back to the house until darkness had settled, walking the streets of the town. When he got home, Helen would be in the kitchen, drinking from a cup of tea, old before her time. They wouldn't speak. There was nothing to speak of. He would get his supper, always bread and thick-cut ham, and take it up to his room. Nothing was ever the same after Daddy died. He could hear his mother, stumbling about in the night. She was never the same again after Daddy died either. Mr Donegan visited frequently for a time, but then suddenly stopped completely. And then, six months or so after his father had died, his mother went too. A cerebral thrombosis, sudden, swift, in the middle of the night. Just like that. Gone.

He walked through the deserted town, layered in snow, cold and pristine. It seemed, yet again, like he was the only living soul in the whole world. Or in Cross Beg, certainly. He thought of his father's old cowboy books, and an image played over in his mind, vague, transitory, fleeting. He tried to catch it, but it was too quick, slithering away again before he could.

But he felt certain it was trying to tell him something.

The busiest time for the Hibernian Hotel, being the only hotel in the town of Cross Beg itself, was midweek. Its twenty rooms were usually taken up by travelling salespeople and other general business types. And now, Beck also knew, by a nun, one Sister Agnes Kavanagh. He sat in a leather armchair in the foyer, from where he had a view into the restaurant, bustling now for the most part with men in suits eager to get a start on the day. He summoned a passing waitress.

'Could you get me a drink?'

She was in her late twenties, Beck guessed, a wedding ring on her left hand; probably juggled the job with raising a young family. 'Coffee, is it?' she said.

'Yes, with a double brandy in it. Please.'

Her eyes ran over Beck, taking him in now. Her expression seemed to say, *I still have to get my kids to school, for God's sake. I don't need this!*

'Are you a resident?'

'I'm on a case,' Beck said, rummaging in his pocket, taking out his ID, holding it up. 'It's important.'

The waitress was silent. Beck considered she was thinking she wasn't being paid enough for this. But she nodded vaguely, neither a nod of acquiescence or otherwise, and walked away.

Beck crossed his legs and uncrossed them, ran a hand over his stubbled face. He was jittery, his mind a dark cauldron of half-formed thoughts.

He knew it was Eddie's sister the moment he saw her. A small stumpy woman, in a long blue skirt, white blouse and blue cardigan. Her hair was thick and white, gathered behind her head in a bun. He stood.

'Sister Kavanagh,' he called. He held his breath; something was at the back of his throat. He swallowed it back down.

She was at the restaurant door now and turned. 'Yes?'

Beck stood slowly, very slowly, indicated the chair next to his. 'Could I have a word?'

She hesitated.

'I'm a police officer.'

She crossed the foyer and stood before him. 'A police officer? About my brother Eddie?'

Beck nodded, sitting down. She occupied the chair he had indicated, tottering on the edge, facing him.

'If you don't mind my saying,' she said, 'you don't look very well.'

Beck was about to answer when the waitress reappeared. She placed a steaming cup before him.

'Can I get you anything?' he asked the sister.

'I'm fine. I'm having my breakfast soon. Thank you.'

Beck passed a twenty euro note to the waitress. 'That's fine,' he said.

The waitress smiled and left.

'That's an expensive coffee,' the nun commented, watching as Beck began to drink. He gulped at the contents, and when he placed the cup back on the table, it was almost empty.

The nun's expression changed, glancing to it, then to him, a subtle shift, understanding settling in.

'You're not staying with your brother?' Beck asked.

'There's only one bedroom in that house. No. Anyway, I have much to do... I am keeping busy. If I stop it will all become too much, and will consume me. I am surviving simply on the power of prayer at the moment. I have to ask, are you any closer to finding the person responsible for this heinous crime?'

'Perhaps,' Beck said. 'Now, I won't keep you very long. Firstly, I'd like to sympathise with you on your tragic loss.'

'Thank you.'

'Did you keep in touch with Eddie very much, if I may ask?'

'Not as much as I should have, or would have liked to, in light of what's happened. I regret that now... I've read the reports.' The sister looked away.

'Reports?' Beck said.

'Yes... of the mur— I can't bring myself to say it.'

'I understand,' Beck said.

'It seems he was beat— I can't even say the words. It's so shocking.'

Beck was silent, pondering, feeling the alcohol seep into his system, a lightness spreading through his body. He sat back in his chair, resting his hands on the armrests.

'You find that shocking,' he said. 'Unfortunately, it's my stock-in-trade, even in a town such as this.'

She looked at him now, and he could see the resemblance to Tommy Kavanagh: the same forehead, the same deep-set eyes.

'But he is dead,' she said. 'He will be judged, don't you understand? That's my point. The way he died – murdered, pulled brutally from this life, with no time for penance. I worry about it.'

'Is that all that concerns you?'

She shook her head. 'Of course not. But his judgement, it's worth more than life itself. I'm talking about eternal salvation.'

'We will agree to differ. I want to ask you something.'

'Like I say, I didn't keep in touch with Eddie as much as I would have liked. Nor Tommy. So I don't know a great deal.' She clinched her hands in her lap. 'What a dreadful business.'

'It's not about Eddie, Sister Agnes... Well, it is, in a roundabout way. It's about Emily Tuffy.'

The nun's eyes narrowed as she peered at him. 'Who?'

'Emily Tuffy. Your late brother, Eddie, he and she were, one time...'

'Oh, Mimi. That's what everyone called her. Yes, they went out together one time. He was broken-hearted when she left.'

'When she left?'

'Yes, she went to America... never came back. What has Mimi Tuffy got to do with any of this?'

'Maybe nothing,' Beck said.

Sister Agnes stood suddenly. 'Isn't this all very unorthodox? Coming in here to talk to me like this, at' – she glanced at her watch – 'eight o'clock in the morning, looking like you've just crawled out of a dumpster... and, I have to say, stinking of drink.'

'Who exactly told you?' Beck said. 'That she'd gone to America.'

'What?' The word was sharp, like the crack of a whip. 'I don't know... I can't remember. She just went. Like thousands of others. We all knew it.'

'What about her family?'

'What family? She didn't have a family. Mimi was raised by the Sisters of Charity in Galway, poor child. She was an orphan. Her mother wasn't married and died in childbirth. You wouldn't believe how common that was back then. The sisters reared a lot of such children, and I don't believe they were, or indeed are, shown the gratitude they deserve. Understandable she would want to go to America. Most did. Or England. Or Australia.'

'Wasn't she adopted?'

'No. She was raised in the orphanage, until she was eighteen. Many were.'

Beck fell silent. He thought about that. An orphanage, where earthly concerns were secondary in the pursuit of the salvation of the soul, both for the mother who had given birth out of wedlock, and for the child itself, born under the shame of sin, then raised for the greater good of the Mother Church. Although in Beck's case it was different. He had been born in wedlock, but all else was similar.

'Now,' he said, 'my question. I discovered something. Late last night in fact. At the garda station, going through old files. Does the name Sister Assumpta McNeely mean anything to you?'

Sister Agnes paused. 'Sister Assumpta,' she said, surprise in her tone. 'What about…? Did you know her?'

'Did you?' Beck said. 'Do you?'

'Of course. A saint, I have no doubt. She's been dead many years now. She was a second mother to those girls. She helped me on my path too, because through her good work I found the inspiration I needed, the courage to devote my life to the service of the Lord. The whole country knew of her good work. I gave up my weekends to go and help in the orphanage in Galway. How did *you* know her?'

'I didn't.'

'Then…?'

'She signed the letter.'

'What letter?' Her tone was sharp again.

'Reporting Emily Tuffy missing. It seems that girl may never have left the country and gone to America at all. I have it here, let me read it for you. It's very short.'

Beck withdrew the neatly folded sheet of yellowed old paper from his jacket, opened it with care, adjusted the distance at which he held it so he could view it properly.

'*Dear Sir,*' he began, and looked up. He added, 'This is to the officer commanding Cross Beg garda station at the time, by the way.'

The sister nodded.

'*I write in connection with an issue which is causing me grave concern. A girl, Emily Tuffy, raised by the Sisters of Charity in Galway, was due to visit me last Saturday, 18 February. She never showed up. Whilst this is highly unusual, I chose to overlook her nonappearance in the certain belief that she would contact me in due course with an utterly plausible and contrite explanation. She never did. When I contacted her place of employment, McKay's newsagents, of Plunkett Hill, Cross Beg, I was informed that she had not shown up for work over the preceding number of days. Subsequently, numerous people have told me that Emily, or Mimi as she is better known, has left and travelled to America! Well, needless to say, I am quite shocked by this. Mimi never intimated anything of this nature to me – that she was thinking of emigrating to America – and I was always of the opinion that there was a close bond between us. My mind has been considering all possibilities since. Was she, heaven forbid, pregnant? Did she leave out of shame? Is that why she did not inform me? I cannot think of any other plausible explanation and cannot stop thinking of her. So, I would be most grateful indeed if you could look into the matter. Mimi, as I say, was employed at McKay's newsagents, Plunkett Hill, Cross Beg, and lived in a small bedsit above the shop. I know she was a popular girl and had many friends, the names and addresses of whom I can forward should you so require. I look forward to hearing from you at your earliest convenience with your thoughts on how to proceed this matter. Yours...'*

Sister Agnes blessed herself. 'Holy Mother,' she said.

Beck wanted her to say something more, anything, to shine a light onto what he hadn't been certain of to begin with.

He waited, wishing he could have another 'coffee', could feel—

'Sister Assumpta must have had grave concerns,' Sister Agnes said. 'She wasn't one to overreact.' Her eyes glazed over. 'She enjoyed the attention, you know...'

'Who, Sister Assumpta?'

'No! Mimi Tuffy, of course. Eddie wasn't the only one who liked her. So did Tommy, and...' She paused, her voice softening as she added, 'Dermot Healy, too.' She continued, her voice normal once again, 'It drove a wedge between them, between Eddie, Tommy, and Dermot Healy. They'd always been friendly up to then, but they fell out. Eddie and Tommy even stopped talking completely for a while.'

'My impression,' Beck said, 'was that Eddie and Tommy were quite close. Does that mean they never spoke much to begin with?'

Sister Agnes sighed. 'Two brothers like that. Living in the same house. Grown men, I'll remind you. The house that Tommy lives in now was a bit of a ruin back then, but it still had a roof, and he'd go there often just for his sanity, I think. Thank God for it. There was a lot of that back then, bachelor siblings living together. It's not healthy. The truth is...' The sister paused. 'Mimi only had eyes for Eddie. Dermot Healy couldn't accept it, he just took to drink, poor man, for a while at least.' Again, that look in her eye. 'I always considered Dermot would have made a good husband and father.' She looked at her hands. 'Alas. It was not to be.' Glancing to Beck, she added, 'My brother, Tommy, well, he moved on. He seemed to get over her lack of interest very quickly. He's pragmatic, I'll give him that. Usually the animal that can't find a mate leaves for pastures new. But neither Dermot Healy, nor my brother Eddie, did. It saddens me that neither of those men got to have families of their own, to raise children in the love of a Christian, God-fearing family. They would have been exemplary fathers, I have no doubt, and, Heaven knows, the country, the world indeed, needs much more of that. Wouldn't you agree?'

Beck got the impression she felt sorry for herself too. Was this why she had chosen to become a nun? Because she'd no other choices? Because she was too scared to leave? And had she a thing for Dermot Healy herself, he wondered?

She stiffened now, staring at something behind him, her eyes moving, tracking whatever it was. 'My goodness. A dog. It just came in the door of the hotel.'

'Really?' Beck said. He turned and saw Max cross the foyer and come and stand beside him. He patted Max. 'In any case, I'll leave now, take this animal with me… Unless you want him? Don't you recognise him?'

Sister Agnes looked utterly confused. Beck patted Max once more and stood. 'He's your brother Eddie's dog, Max. I'm looking after him, until we can find a suitable home.'

She smiled. 'What a very Christian gesture. Thank you.'

'And thank you, Sister,' Beck said. 'Your assistance is greatly appreciated.'

Sister Agnes looked from Beck to the dog. Befuddled was the word to best describe her expression.

Beck stood on the street corner outside, his hands in his pockets, shuffling from one foot to the other, trying to keep warm. Max stood still beside him. Claire Somers should have been here by now. She'd said when he'd rang that she was almost in Cross Beg, a couple of minutes away at most, that's all. He should have stayed in the comfort of the hotel, had some more 'coffee', this time in a bloody mug. His body was processing the alcohol quicker now, his liver attuned to the slow, steady supply of poison, responding with great efficiency to ridding itself of the toxins. The biting wind went through the thin fabric of his jacket and into his very bones. His body was tired, he knew that, and he had not eaten. He closed his eyes, trying to clear his mind, if only for a moment.

'Beck!'

He snapped them open again, noting the car in front, Claire Somers behind the wheel. He crossed the pavement and opened the rear door.

'Jesus,' she said. 'The state of you.'

Max jumped in.

'You can't put that animal in here.'

'We'll drop off Max on the way to the station.'

Max lay down on the back seat as Claire shook her head, put the car in gear and pulled away from the kerb.

Beck's phone rang.

He answered, and listened.

With the phone still pressed to his ear, his voice urgent, he said, 'Tommy Kavanagh's place. Now.'

CHAPTER FORTY-SIX

'All things must come to an end. And so too must life. So, it will end now because I have decided it will be so, but, more than anything, because I have suffered enough, and I cannot stand by and watch any longer. I cannot endure. It is I who has had to carry the secrets, it is I who has lived a life like a solitary animal, when all I sought was a little companionship, a pleasant voice, an occasional embrace... None of these were ever mine. I have led an empty and lonely life. Until now that is. But now, through death, I will start anew.'

The barrel of the shotgun was too long to comfortably place between the floor and his jaw. It would not be possible for him to rest his head against it. I will have to hold it myself, *he decided.* There is no other way.

'Holy Mary, Mother of God, the Lord is with Thee...'
BOOM!

CHAPTER FORTY-SEVEN

What Beck noticed first was the absence of smoke curling from the chimney. Tommy Kavanagh's door was closed, and he could see the curtains were drawn. When they reached the door they realised it wasn't fully shut. He pushed gently and it opened, and as they entered, in the murky half-light filtering through into the big room, everything appeared as normal.

Then, a sound.

Beck listened. It was like a low growl. He turned, looking back to the door, but could see nothing. And it came once more, louder this time, from somewhere below. Beck cast his eyes downward. And there was Tommy Kavanagh, sprawled on the floor by the table, his head propped back against its leg, lost to the shadows. Beck took two long strides and reached him, bent down, as Claire flicked on the light. The old man clutched at his forehead, staring at Beck, blood seeping from between his fingers.

'What happened?' Beck asked, pulling the old man's hands away from his head gently. He could see the wound, small and nasty, but apparently not too deep. 'Have you any other injuries?'

'No. The bastard just caught me there.'

'Who?' Claire asked.

Tommy Kavanagh raised himself onto an elbow, extended a hand towards Beck.

'Here,' he said. 'Give us a hand up.'

'No,' Beck said. 'Stay where you are. We'll get you a pillow. I'll call an ambulance.'

'No you feckin' won't. The bastard didn't get me proper, I'm telling you. Now, help me up, for the love of God.'

Beck sighed, grasped Tommy's hand and pulled, dragging him up from the floor.

'What happened?' Beck asked again.

The old man walked slowly across the room. He went to the sink and ran a tap, bent down and placed his head into it. He raised a finger: *I'll be with you in a minute.* He straightened and held a dishcloth to his head, looked at both detectives.

'I should have known. I should have known.'

'Should have known…?' Claire said.

'I heard a knock at the door. And when I opened it he was just standing there.' Tommy Kavanagh ran a hand over his face. 'Ah, he got me good. I should have known. He wouldn't have done this to me years ago, I can tell you. I would have…'

'What happened, Mr Kavanagh?' Beck said. 'Tell us that.'

'Can't you see what happened? Dermot Healy. He did this. I should have closed the door right in his face. He had blood on him. He told me *he'd* been attacked…' The old man stared into space.

'He'd been attacked?' Beck said. 'What happened to *him?*'

'How the hell should I know?' Kavanagh said. 'I didn't get time to find out.'

'So why did he attack you?' Claire asked.

'He demanded my shotgun, and I wouldn't give it to him.'

'But he got it, did he?' Beck said.

Kavanagh nodded.

'Shit,' Beck muttered.

'What could I do?' Kavanagh's voice became a low whimper. 'I was taken by surprise. I told you. He clipped me one on the forehead.' The old man gingerly ran a finger around the wound. 'He hit me on the head with something. If he hadn't taken me by surprise, I…'

'Yes, yes,' Claire said. 'And what time was this?'

Tommy Kavanagh walked slowly to a chair and sat down. 'An hour ago maybe,' he said. 'I think… I don't know. I was out cold. When I came round I rang you.'

'Where is he now?' Claire asked.

'How should I know that?'

'But he doesn't have a car?' Beck said.

'No, he doesn't… Look, can I be left in peace? My brother's funeral is later today. I need to lie down. Then I'll be fine. Please. This is a nightmare, surely to God. A nightmare.'

'My advice,' Beck said, 'is that you get yourself looked at. But I can't force you to do that… Are you sure you won't change your mind? We'll bring you straight over to the hospital?'

The old man clenched a fist and banged it on the table. 'I'm sure, I tell you. God in heaven. Will you all just leave me in peace? I've had enough, I tell you, enough. Is it too much to ask to just be left in peace?' He paused, then added, his voice low. 'Ah sure, I know you mean the best. But please. Go now. I'll be fine. I have Eddie to bury. That's what I have to do.'

Beck glanced to Claire. 'Fine, Tommy,' he said. 'But you have my number, if you need—'

'I know, thank you. Now go.'

When they pulled up outside Dermot Healy's front gate, Beck felt it again: something was not right. It was open too, the gate, and so was the front door. But no one seemed to be about. They got out of the car and approached. The snow was a smooth gloss devoid of any prints, as was the garden path and the path running along the front of the house.

'Hello?' Beck called into the doorway. 'Anyone home?'

The only sound was the raucous chatter of magpies, from somewhere off in the distance, as if replying to Beck.

He stepped into the house, stood there again, listening. He beckoned with a nod for Claire to follow and they moved slowly along the hall, checking the room next to it: empty. They went into the living room, where they had not been invited before – there was nothing but a frayed sofa and an armchair in it, and a glass-fronted dresser with a couple of framed photographs inside. The kitchen was the same as it had been previously, cold and empty. There was a closed door leading off it. Dermot Healy's bedroom, Beck guessed. They crossed the room and Beck knocked on the door a couple of times.

'Dermot Healy, are you in there? It's the guards.'

There was no reply.

Beck reached for the handle and opened the door. They stood, taking in the scene. Blankets were piled on the floor by the bed, a length of metal pipe lying on a corner of the mattress, smeared with blood and what looked to be particles of flesh and other bodily matter stuck about the top of it.

Claire took a sharp intake of breath. 'Jesus. What happened here?'

Beck stared at the pipe. Was that the Cedar Grove murder weapon? 'Don't touch anything,' he said. 'Leave it for the technicians. Come on.'

They stood outside amid the further raucous chattering of magpies. The sound appeared to be coming from the rear of the house. Beck led the way along the path and down the side into the back garden. A flurry of black and white wings took to the air from a stack of old tyres in the wild grass. They walked to it, and as he approached Beck could see a body on the other side, slumped back against it, a shotgun on the ground. He stepped round the tyres and looked.

Two thirds of Dermot Healy's head was gone, leaving behind a seeping vestibule of tissue and exposed muscle and veins, like rubber tubing, along with one remarkably intact but empty eye socket. The other eye stared out from a portion of grey flesh pockmarked by stray buckshot, and all was contained beneath the weirdly smooth head, ocular in shape, tufts of hair on either side. It reminded Beck of a coconut. He stared. Pushing through the images was a superimposition, a floating flickering image of his father, reappearing yet again, as if making up for lost time. It seemed in fact that he could almost reach out and touch it. *Hello, Father.*

Beck stared at the wreck of Dermot Healy's face, as if trying to exorcise himself of the images of a lifetime, to finally rid himself of it all, to finally find peace. He began to shake.

He realised, in a way, that he envied Dermot Healy. *And yet I don't want to die!*

He felt something soft and warm on his shoulders, and with it a pleasant aroma, sweet and welcoming, as Claire pulled him into her, holding him close, and he began to cry.

CHAPTER FORTY-EIGHT

They found the note as they were removing the body. It was wedged between the stock of the shotgun and Dermot Healy's thigh. As before, a local SOC unit from Ballinasloe had arrived first. Superintendent Wilde considered this team would be sufficient. The SOCO was of the opinion Dermot Healy had likely placed the note in a prominent position, weighed down by something, a small stone maybe, but in a death spasm it had ended up where it had. Because suicide notes, by definition, the last communication from a tortured mind, were not meant to be difficult to find. When they had placed the body into a body bag, the SOCO handed the clear plastic evidence bag containing the note to Beck, the words written in large block writing:

> *I'm sorry for everything. But it has to end. God will judge me, I know, but so too will my victims. I will meet them on the other side. But I beseech you, the living, to not judge me harshly. I couldn't go on is the simple truth. I am sorry for what I have done. Dear God, please forgive me.*

Beck stared at the note.

'Have you dusted this?' he asked, his tone measured.

The SOCO shook his head. He was wearing gloves, but nothing else, no suit or covers.

'I want it dusted,' Beck said.

'No problem.' The reply was delivered with the false cheeriness that bordered on condescension. Beck wondered at the attitude, also the choice of words. If it wasn't a problem, why hadn't he done it already?

The answer, Beck knew, was that they'd already made their minds up. The case may demand the customary procedures – forensic examination, autopsy – but already it was being wrapped up, tied with a double knot and a bow placed on top: suicide. Just as history was an interpretation, different academics offering different theses on the same topic, so too was suicide often an interpretation. Vile deeds sometimes masqueraded as such, Beck knew. Did the same apply here? An interpretation, Beck considered. Or the easiest option.

He returned the evidence bag to the SOCO. Something was scratching at Beck, way down deep. But he couldn't reach it. Not yet.

CHAPTER FORTY-NINE

'I would consider it conclusive.' Superintendent Wilde was searching through a desk drawer. It was a couple of hours later and they were back at the station. 'And the man admitted to the murders, did he not... in the note?'

Beck sucked on a lozenge, tasting the mixture of menthol, peppermint oil and stale alcohol. Claire had just informed him that Jamie McLoughlin had forwarded his clocking-in details and the CCTV footage from the post office. There were no surprises in either. The man had clocked in on time and was present at his workstation at all times with the exception of short meal and comfort breaks.

Beck felt nauseous, and the periphery of his vision was frayed. He mentally struck a pen through Jamie McLoughlin's name. He felt an urge to shake his head, to try and adjust the reception, but he could not.

Wilde found what he was looking for: a small, black Dictaphone.

'Here it is,' he said, holding it out for inspection, turning it over in his hand. 'You don't look so well,' he said. 'Anything I should know about?'

'Are you saying...' Beck began, ignoring Wilde's question, but the superintendent suddenly got to his feet, leant forward onto the desk.

'I know where you want to go with this.' There was an uncharacteristic hard crust to his tone. 'Don't. Okay? Understand? I know you've been drinking too. Just in case you think I don't. I'm not stupid. This is a suicide, Beck. Okay? Got that?'

Beck took a breath and... smiled.

Wilde observed him.

'I'm not in the mood,' Wilde said. 'This is finished. I have everything I need to put this to bed. Galway has Bastic. And I have this.'

'Galway has Bastic? You said he and—'

'I presume they have,' Wilde replied. 'No information is information. Browne has the lid down. Hard. On both of them. That Antoz chap. Turns out there's a European arrest warrant for him. An assault in Paris, from a couple of years ago... I never liked him. Browne I mean. He's younger than you, you know, and already a superintendent. That sergeant at briefing yesterday, what was his name...?'

'Erskine.'

'Yes. He's been reporting back, making no secret of the fact either. Anyway, I consider this case, until evidence to the contrary emerges, as solved. I'd be happy to present what I have to any jury and let them decide, if I have to. But in this case it will be a coroner. Suicide, Beck, leave it at that, it's enough. And we got Squeaky Ward back where he belongs' – Wilde smiled – 'wearing his best frillies. Come on, lighten up. Dermot Healy is our killer. He may have been old, but age is a number, right?'

'That's it, is it? And all Antoz answers to is a European arrest warrant? Nothing else? He could be our killer. And, by the way, we never found out what he was doing with Bastic either.'

Wilde looked at the Dictaphone. 'And we probably never will,' he said. 'That's Galway's problem. Not mine. I don't care.'

'But...'

'But nothing,' Wilde snapped. 'Nothing links him to any murder scene except one piece of circumstantial evidence: the motorhome. And no blood residue was found in that vehicle, either. We have no proof that he was even the person who was driving it during those times. And his prints are not on any murder weapon, remember.'

'The missing girl?' Beck said.

'Missing girl! What missing girl? We searched, an expensive wild goose chase as far as I'm concerned. And, of course, we don't have any report of any missing girl to begin with...'

Beck went to speak again.

'I know what you're on about,' Wilde said. 'Look, we don't know how many girls were in that house. So how do we know if one is missing? We don't.'

'That depends,' Beck said, but he didn't really have an answer for that. 'But—'

'But, again. But what? There weren't any other prints, in the snow, from the back of the house, anywhere. Nothing.'

'So? It would be easy to wipe them. And personally speaking, if I were to shoot myself—'

'Thought of it, have you?'

'I wouldn't choose a shotgun...'

'It's better than hanging,' Wilde said. 'If you get me.'

Beck knew Wilde was selecting words to suit his own narrative.

'And I certainly,' Beck added, 'wouldn't shoot myself in the face. Not after I'd just gone to the trouble of leaving a note. If I cared enough to do that, I'm not going to turn around and shoot myself in the face. I'm just not. What I'm saying is it doesn't fit the...' He searched for a word, thought of the sergeant's exam test booklet. 'Suicidal profile.'

'He may not have meant to shoot himself in the face. Did you ever think of that? The gun could have slipped. Anything. But the act, choosing the means, might have been a statement in itself. You know how it is. Males prefer the more violent acts, because they're angry. You know that.'

'Thing is,' Beck said. 'Dermot Healy wasn't angry, not that I could see. A bit depressed maybe, but then again, who isn't? Boss, you need to consider this more carefully, that's what I'm saying…'

'Don't you talk to me like that.' A vein was starting to pulsate in Wilde's neck, his face turning red.

Beck was silent.

'Bloody philosopher. Don't get my goat up, Beck. Sometimes things are what they are. Why can't you accept that? It's the reason I have this' – he tapped the extra diamond-shaped epaulette on his shoulder – 'and you don't.'

No it's not, Beck thought. He got to his feet.

'Where're you going?'

The room momentarily lurched. Beck turned, ostensibly to push his chair out of the way, but in reality holding on to it for dear life.

'I,' he said, 'have a funeral to attend.'

He straightened, took a breath and walked to the door. It was all crap, every bit of it.

CHAPTER FIFTY

The driver had kept the engine running, presumably, Beck thought, to keep warm. The driver was ignoring health and safety regulations by smoking in a workplace, which is what the hearse was. But the driver was safe enough – after all, who was going to complain? Certainly not the passenger in the rear. Beyond the iron rails set between rows of limestone pillars forming the church perimeter, the swollen river had risen to within feet of its walls. The water tumbled and churned on its way to the sea, crashing against the arches of the town's two bridges, moving at the pace of a brisk walk, millions and millions of gallons tumbling along. And above it all was the sky, a continuous mass of grey and black, shifting, restless, brooding.

Inside the cathedral, the small gathering of mourners was scattered amongst the three front pews of the central aisle. The coffin sat on a bier in front of the altar, surrounded by candles in gleaming holders, a framed photograph of Eddie Kavanagh inside the wreath on top.

Beck thought of the girl whose face had been beaten to a pulp. Where would her funeral service be held? Who would attend? Anybody? He thought too of Dermot Healy. Was he really capable of all this? The question Beck was actually asking was: *Could I have gotten this so wrong?*

The voice of the lone priest sounded then, echoing through the ornate interior, a measured, practised, echoing cadence, carrying Beck's thoughts with it. There were no acolytes, clergy, hymns or organ player for Eddie Kavanagh. He would leave this earth without fuss and with little notice, just as he had entered it.

Beck took from his pocket the naggin of Jameson he had bought on the way over. He coughed to disguise the sound of the breaking seal. He looked behind him, to the rows of empty pews that stretched to the vestibule and the exit doors, large lancet windows on either side. He drank enough and put the bottle back into his pocket. He could see Tommy Kavanagh sitting at the end of the first pew, next to his sister. A half dozen or so family members – all elderly – sat next to them. Beck knew they were family members because the first pew was traditionally reserved for them. He had attended many funerals of murder victims, and found the families usually appreciated it. His motive, however, was never strictly to offer condolences – although that was part of it – but more to observe. Beck had learned that killers themselves were often among the mourners.

He closed his eyes and heard the words of the priest drift around him and float upward into the high vaults: 'Eddie, as he was known, was a warm, friendly man full of God's goodness. I know he would not object to me describing him as a simple man, but more than anything, Eddie was a good man, a gracious man, a man with a huge heart and he did not, did not, deserve to be taken from us in such a brutal, callous way…'

Beck's mind wandered. Maybe it was the acoustics, the tinny sound struggling to fill such a vast space, but it brought to his mind the old Astoria Cinema. The tall brooding figure, the Virginian, riding his horse Joe D along the track to the Shiloh Ranch; *The Virginian*, a tale of love and revenge, violence and hate.

Yes, something was scratching at Beck again, way down deep, and he couldn't quite reach it.

He stood, stepped out into the aisle, genuflected and quietly walked out of the church. He lit a cigarette, had a long draw and took his phone from his pocket. It was then he realised he didn't have the number. He cursed. He dialled the station instead, told the duty sergeant what he wanted, and after a long pause he was connected.

'Yes.'

'Hello. Can I speak to the SOCO who attended the suicide in Cross Beg earlier today.'

'That'd be me.'

'This is Detective Inspector Beck. I spoke with you, remember?'

'I remember.'

'You dust that note for prints yet? The one found with the body.'

'Of course.'

'And?'

'And nothing. No match. On the system, that is. I wasn't expecting any. But the prints on the note did match those found on the metal pipe at the house. I compared them with those of the deceased, Dermot Healy. A match. As I was expecting.'

Silence.

'That's it? No other prints?'

'None.'

'Thank you,' Beck said, and hung up.

He took a last pull on his cigarette and dropped it to the ground, stubbed it out beneath his shoe, thinking. The Virginian never had a name, but some believed he was Jeff Davis.

He churned this over in his mind.

The mourners were emerging from the cathedral. They formed a loose circle around the hearse as Eddie Kavanagh's coffin was placed inside it. The loose circle then coalesced into a line of people that began to file past Eddie Kavanagh's family, shaking their hands. Beck joined the short queue. When he reached the nun he took both her hands in his and squeezed gently, said he was sorry for her loss, to which she gave a slight smile, told him it was thoughtful of him to have come. He moved on to Tommy, whose hand, despite the weather, was hot and clammy.

'Sorry for your loss, Tommy.'

Tommy nodded. 'Thank you for coming.' He added in a whisper, 'Just get the bastard who did this, okay?'

Tommy's shoes had been polished to a gleaming glint, Beck noted, and in the lapel of his black suit was a small, white flower.

'In memory of his love of nature,' Tommy said, when he noticed Beck staring.

'Of course,' Beck muttered, and walked away.

But Beck didn't believe a word of it.

He was thinking: *How did I miss this?*

CHAPTER FIFTY-ONE

The snow began falling again. Heavy persistent snow, as if the weather gods had finally made a decision. Gone were the intermittent flurries – now the snow was a heavy flickering curtain of white that cascaded to earth, blanketing Cross Beg. Eddie Kavanagh's body had been consigned to the ground, and the small band of mourners had retired to the Hibernian Hotel where Sister Agnes and Tommy had arranged for tea and sandwiches to be provided. It was not quite a wake in the traditional sense, but on an evening such as this, the mourners were anxious to return to their homes before conditions became too hazardous for travel. Already, Cross Beg was practically deserted, its citizens hunkering down behind closed doors and, judging by the smoke coming from a multitude of chimneys, before blazing fires. The smoke over the rooftops was revealed in the light of the street lamps, before fading into the night sky.

CHAPTER FIFTY-TWO

He opened the photo album. He had been looking at it lately, again and again, ever since he had taken it from Eddie Kavanagh's house. As he did so he ran his hand over the leatherette cover, felt the stencilled outline of flowers, the gold-coloured, rust-specked metal staples along the edges. He lay the page flat on the table, the excitement like an electrical pulse through his body. There she was, staring back at him, on a summer's day some time back in 1962, the sun shining from behind her, casting her body as a dark outline beneath the fabric of the dress, alluring, mysterious, exhilarating.

He remembered the day he had first set eyes on Emily Tuffy. He had gone to the newsagents to buy a pen to write a letter to America. He had half a notion of emigrating to New York, to stay with an uncle he had there. But he knew now he was only fooling himself. He didn't have the courage. She was behind the counter. He was very shy, and he had a habit of not looking people in the eye. Her hand rested on the pen as she slid it across to him. She didn't take it away again. Not immediately. So he looked up. Without thinking. And he felt something then that he had never felt before and had never felt since. There was someone in this world for everybody he believed, but most never met them. And he met that person the day he looked into Emily Tuffy's eyes. But Emily Tuffy never looked at him.

CHAPTER FIFTY-THREE

Beck cut a forlorn, even strange, figure, hunched as he was against the snow, walking along by the edge of the road. It was getting dark, and he moved like a shadow. As the minutes passed, and the night ever deepened, he appeared to disappear more and more into the black. He did not have a hat on, and occasionally he shook the snow from his hair. Despite the weather, he moved quickly, in that way of people who have a purpose, a mind focused far off on something else. As was his. He no longer craved a drink, or thought of his father, or his mother, or religious brothers in black capes. He was at peace, in a way. Because there was only one thought on his mind. And it was a question: *Could I be correct?*

He realised too that he would not trust his theory with anyone but Claire, but where the hell was she? He had tried ringing. No answer. He had left a text instead.

Beck continued on. When he saw Mullaney's pub come into view a little way ahead, he was surprised. He had thought it would have taken him longer to get here. He continued, his only certainty being that he wasn't certain. If he was wrong about this, then he was wrong about Dermot Healy too. *I would consider it conclusive,* Wilde had said. Beck shook snow from his head again. As he turned off the road before Mullaney's, he cursed. He had forgotten to bring a torch. He was also unarmed, which was inevitable. Wilde knew he'd been drinking, so would never sanction a firearm being issued to him. *I haven't fully thought this through,* Beck considered.

He walked on.

*

The flakes swirled around the figure kneeling on the gravel by the old cart's wheel, hands joined together in prayer. The front door to the house was open, snow cascading across the rectangle of light spilling out into the night. Tommy Kavanagh got to his feet, blessing himself. He turned and walked with surprising speed towards the house. Beck considered he had never seen him move so quickly before. It was the speed of a man years younger. He made his way inside, and the door closed behind him. Through the curtained window on each side of the door, light glowed, presenting an image of simple, wholesome cosiness.

As pretty as a postcard.

Beck stood hidden within the bushes. After the door closed, he stepped out, skirting along the edge of the cobblestone yard. He approached the house, went to the first window. The curtains had been securely pulled together at the centre, but they were too small to cover the entire space, leaving a slight gap along the edges. But there was enough for Beck to see the table laid out with a couple of plates of food – brown- and white-bread sandwiches mostly, from what he could discern. In the centre was a cake. It had two tiers, in reality one sponge cake placed on top of the other, and what looked like empty spools of thread taking the place of dowels. He watched Tommy fill two small glasses from a bottle of sherry and step around the table and behind the curtain, partially out of view. He held out one of the glasses to someone whom Beck could not see. Tommy half turned then, and Beck watched his profile, saw him smile, raising the glass to his lips and taking a sip, running his free hand over his oiled and perfectly combed hair. And Beck could see a tear form in the corner of his eye and begin to trickle slowly down his cheek. Beck held his breath, listening, as Tommy's lips moved, but could not hear what was being said. Tommy placed his glass down on the table, and suddenly he clenched his fists and shouted. Beck had no difficulty hearing the words: 'I want you to feel. I want you to feel. God damn it. I want you to feel. FOR ME!'

What the hell? Beck thought.

But then Tommy smiled, unclenching his hands, and stretched out one as if to stroke somebody, his expression one of tenderness and madness all at the same time. The only sound was the soft *tac tac tac* of the snow falling to earth.

And then Beck heard it, a shrill, muffled sound, like piano keys in the higher register inside a closed room. He knew what it was. His phone, ringing, from somewhere within the depths of a pocket.

Shit!

He stared as Tommy Kavanagh immediately placed an index finger to his lips. He'd heard it too. Kavanagh indicated to the person with him to be silent, as he turned his head slowly towards the window, nostrils crinkling, as if sniffing the air. He looked directly at Beck, but Beck knew it would be almost impossible for Kavanagh to see him.

Beck looked away, frantically fumbling about in the fabric of his clothes, searching for the damned phone. He felt the outline in his trouser pocket, and stabbed a middle and index finger against it, again and again, until eventually... silence. When he looked up, in through the window, Tommy Kavanagh was gone.

Beck hesitated, wrong-footed, scrambling to work out the best way to deal with this. If Kavanagh came out, he'd likely do so through the back door, come round the path at the side. Did he have another gun in there? Still, Beck hesitated. And still, no sign of Kavanagh.

Damn it!

Beck turned, walked to the gable wall – the one furthest from the path – and went through the wild grass and overgrowth to the back of the property. The curtains on the windows here were not drawn, and the light through them showed him the way. Beck had a clear view inside. It was empty.

He blinked, carefully made his way to the back door and turned the handle. It was not locked and, without stopping to think, he stepped inside. He could feel the wave of heat from the Jubilee range wash over him. There was a smell: perfume. Where the hell had he – *they?* – gone. He crossed to the table, stood looking about. He made a decision. He moved towards the door again, reaching for his phone, about to ring the station. He had delayed far too long already in doing this.

'You,' the voice said.

Beck's head shot up, just in time to see Tommy Kavanagh emerge from the high, narrow cupboard by the sink. He almost smiled. *You cunning bastard. I never thought of that either.*

'What're you doing here?' the old man asked, his tone polite, matter-of-fact.

Beck saw that the bedroom door was open. Kavanagh followed his gaze.

'You're the smart one?' His voice hardening. 'Yes indeed, you're the smart one. Top of the class. Even if you're a lush, you're the one who's here, aren't you? Not anyone else.' Kavanagh smiled.

'There's not much to smile about,' Beck said. 'Is there now, Tommy?'

Kavanagh ran his left hand over his oily hair. Beck noted he held his right arm stiff by his side. He could see why. It held a long, black, metal poker. Again, Kavanagh followed his gaze.

'Sharp, aren't you?' Kavanagh said. 'Now. I don't have a lot of time.'

'Don't you, Tommy? Why's that?'

'Sit down there, at the table.' He pointed with the poker. 'Don't have me ask you again. Sit. Before I clock you one.'

Kavanagh took a step forward and raised the poker in a smooth, sudden movement. Beck instinctively stepped back, raised his arms to fend off the blow. None came, and Kavanagh gave a crackly laugh. 'Sit,' he said.

Beck went to the table, pulled out a chair and sat down.

Kavanagh smiled again and approached. He pulled out the chair next to Beck but did not sit down. He stood in the space where it had been, went to place the poker onto the table, but at the last moment swung it in an upward movement.

Crack!

Beck cried out in pain as the blood spurted from his head.

'Don't make a mess,' Tommy Kavanagh said, reaching for a towel from somewhere and throwing it to him. Beck, dazed, grabbed it and pressed it to his head. The wound stung. His vision was blurred and he shook his head to try and clear it. It didn't work. He closed his eyes, opened them again. Still the same.

'Christ,' he muttered.

'Tell me,' Kavanagh said. 'Did you ever think an auld fella like me could do all that I did, did you now?'

'All what, Tommy? You mean…?'

Beck shook his head again, his vision beginning to settle.

'Of course I mean all that, you know what I mean, don't go all coy on me. What am I trying to hide at my age, anyway? Nothing. What will they do to me? Lock me up until the end of my days? Do I care? All I wanted was a little love. Is that too much to ask?'

Beck felt uncomfortably warm. He could hear the sizzling sound of the fire burning behind the stove door in the Jubilee range.

'Would you like to meet my new wife?'

Beck forgot about the stinging wound to his forehead. 'What did you just say?'

'My wife,' Kavanagh repeated. 'Let me go get her.'

He crossed the kitchen and disappeared into the bedroom, but came back out again, his arm stretched behind him, lost in the doorway, where he paused.

'Come on,' tugging gently.

She emerged. The girl from the brothel. The one who'd called herself Britney. The blonde one. Pale, sickly looking. Her eyes, Beck immediately noticed, were no longer rolling about. She wore an old dress, white one time he guessed, now faded to yellow, some of the sequins across the front missing, loose threads hanging from the lace cuffs.

Beck's mouth opened as he stared.

She wore a wedding dress.

Kavanagh smiled at the girl, but her face was an inscrutable blank mask. She stared, unblinking. Petrified, Beck thought. Tommy Kavanagh's own smile partially faded, becoming a twisted caricature. His bony hand curled tighter round the girl's wrist, tighter and tighter until she opened her mouth and screamed.

Tommy shouted what Beck had heard him shout before: 'I want you to feel. I want you to feel. God damn it. I want you to feel. FOR ME!'

'That's enough now, Tommy. Let her go. Good man.'

Tommy froze. He stared at Beck.

'Would you mind letting her go?' Beck said. 'If it's love you're after, you're going about it the wrong way.'

'I may be old,' Kavanagh said, 'but I know how to do this. I have holy water and I have asked Him to bless our union and He agreed. In hindsight I can see now that everything has happened for a reason, even if I could not before.'

'You have a habit, Tommy,' Beck said. 'Don't you? That poor girl at Cedar Grove. What was that about? Jeez, her face…'

Kavanagh's face darkened. 'She was the same! She couldn't fool me. "I love you, baby," she'd say. The bitch! Did she take me for a fool? How many broken hearts must a man endure? I could see it in her eyes. I knew she did not want to be with me, even if, as you know, I paid my money the same as anyone else…' He turned to the girl again, his voice high and shrill. 'Please, please, my love, I must be honest, I paid for love, for tenderness, all that should be given freely by those we love and cherish, and who love us in return… but she did not love me.'

Kavanagh cocked his head to the side, looked at Beck. 'On your own, are you?' he said, his voice lowering, conspiratorial.

Beck said nothing.

'I'll take that as confirmation then that you are. By the way, it's always been easy for me to spot an alkie. After all, I watched my own father for long enough.'

He took his hand from the girl, went to the press above the sink, reached in and emerged clutching a full bottle of whiskey. He unscrewed the cap, approached Beck, but kept a safe distance, glancing to the girl. He reached forward and placed the bottle next to him. 'It's good when you know what a person wants. And you want this, don't you? Drink up.'

Beck looked at the bottle. 'I don't think so,' he said.

'Then you'll have something to eat, surely?' Tommy said, gesturing. 'Some cake. I have plenty of cake. I'm just a little short on guests, that's all.'

'Tommy?'

The old man angled his head as he looked at Beck. 'Yes?'

'This is ridiculous. You know that, don't you?'

Tommy Kavanagh pursed his lips. 'I don't see it like that at all.' He slapped the poker across the palm of his hand.

'Even,' Beck said, 'if you do somehow manage to get away with this, it'll only be a matter of time before it comes to an end, before you're caught. It's inevitable.'

'Really?'

'Yes. Really.'

Tommy Kavanagh shook his head. 'I don't see it like that at all. I told you. Now, will you drink up? I won't ask you again.'

'How do you see it, then? Surely you can tell me that?'

Tommy stared at Beck from his old, craggy face, and his eyes were on fire. 'I should have done this the first time.'

'The first time? You mean… Mimi?'

'You're good. Yes, of course.'

Again, no sound but the sizzling from the Jubilee.

'And anyway…'

'What happened to her? Mimi?' Beck pressed.

'I believe there is no sin where there is good intention,' Kavanagh said. 'Ah, what are you looking at me like that for? If I have taken life it has only been with the best of intentions. I should have died back when Mimi did. We would have been together ever since.'

The inscrutable landscape of words was beginning to make sense now, a tangible understanding settling in.

'I saw you kneeling out there,' Beck said. 'You were praying. I was watching. Tell me, why that exact spot, Tommy?'

The old man stepped over to the table, used the poker to push the bottle towards Beck.

'Drink up. Drink up, damn it. NOW!'

Beck got to his feet. 'I've heard enough bullshit from you…'

Beck didn't see it coming. His brain was stodgy, his perspective and vision altered, his sense of distance askew. Kavanagh seemed further away than he actually was. So when the poker slammed into his stomach it came as a complete surprise. He gasped for air, winded, and slumped back into his chair.

'Don't test my patience.'

Beck held his stomach, waiting for his breath to settle.

There was a rustling sound, and Kavanagh's head snapped back towards the girl. If she had been planning something, she appeared to have had second thoughts, folding her arms and dropping her head.

Beck reached for the bottle and removed the cap. He raised it to his lips and took a long swallow.

'There's a good boy,' Kavanagh said. 'You drink the whole lot of that now, don't waste a drop. It's no problem to you, is it? And I have a few of these to help you along.' He took from his pocket a small bottle of tablets, placed it onto the table.

'I get it,' Beck said. 'You're a cunning old bastard. Kill me and have it look like suicide. Ah, Tommy, you're devious alright. That's what happened to Dermot Healy, isn't it?'

Kavanagh said nothing, just stared at Beck.

'Yes,' he said then. 'He had to die, because when I killed him, I killed the old me too. I prayed as I did it, "Holy Mary, Mother of God"... And I told him the reason why, that it was because I had suffered enough. That it was I who had to carry the secrets, who had to live a life like a solitary animal, when all I sought was a little companionship, a pleasant voice, an occasional embrace.' He looked to the girl. 'Now I am free to live. And to love.'

'But Eddie was your brother. Your *brother*.'

The old man bit his lip. 'Mimi wanted him. I never forgave him for that, or her. And he wanted Britney too.' He looked at her. 'My beautiful wife. I saw the engagement ring on his dresser. He'd locked it away all those years ago, after Mimi left. It was too much for me. That he wanted her too.' He clenched his fists. 'Too much I say. Too much! I couldn't take any more.'

'Mimi is buried out there, isn't she?' Beck said softly. 'Underneath the old cart wheel. Where I saw you praying earlier.'

Kavanagh glared. 'What gives you the right to spoil this for me? How dare you. I took care. I took great care. Nothing of me was ever left behind. I read the papers, you know. You mightn't think so, but I do. I know what gets people caught. Not me, not little old Tommy Kavanagh. I'm too clever. What harm is in poor

auld me? They never got me beforetimes, and they'll never get me
now either. I'm too clever for you all.'

They never got me beforetimes either.

'Jesus,' Beck said. 'You've done it before, haven't you? There
are others, along with Mimi Tuffy, I mean. From the past. Aren't
there? Tell me.'

Kavanagh took a step closer and raised the poker. 'No. You tell
me. What brought you to my door? TELL ME!'

'You did. Yourself. Because you're not as clever as you think.
You're like all the others I've ever dealt with.' Beck thought of
the Scarecrow, leaning over his desk in the classroom, and of Mr
Donegan, and his mother, the way his mother smiled sometimes
at his father, her secret... 'You thought you were clever, did you?
Well, you're not. Mimi Tuffy had gone to Medicine Bow, had
she? That's what you told me. Remember? How clever is that? She
married a man named Davis, you said. Well, that would be Jeff
Davis, wouldn't it? That was your little joke, wasn't it? Way too
clever. Way too clever by far. It's always the way with the... lunatics.
I much prefer that word to psychopaths myself.'

Kavanagh raised the poker higher. Beck suddenly didn't care.

'And when you told me – remember? – that Mimi Tuffy had
disappeared to America. Well, I thought that a very odd word to
use. I've never heard it said someone who'd emigrated to America
had disappeared... But that aside, did you think you were the only
one to have read *The Virginian*? Beck pointed towards the front
door. 'I saw it, over there, on your shelf. It brings back memories.
Of the movie, and the book, but it's the book that has all the detail.
I should have realised earlier, because it's obvious really, if you'd
read the book. And I'd read the book!'

'What?' Kavanagh said, holding the poker aloft, frozen. 'That?
No. There's more to it than that. Has to be.'

'Not really. What were the odds? And it's not unusual. I could
list off a host of high-profile murder investigations solved by

nothing more than an ill-placed comment, a remark, a coincidence, nothing more, because someone thought they were too clever. But I have to ask, when you say you should have died with Mimi back then—'

'What of it?'

'Were you jealous of your brother?'

Kavanagh's face darkened again, but he lowered the poker, held it in front of him. 'I hated the bastard. If it wasn't for him, I could have had Mimi. I know I could.'

'So why wait all these years to do what you did?'

'You ask too many questions.' And, turning towards Britney: 'I want another chance, that's all, at happiness.'

Beck glanced at the girl too. That's all she was, a *girl*.

'You're a dirty old man, Tommy, that's what you are.'

'No,' Tommy shot back. 'I'm a lonely old man. Loneliness can drive a man crazy.' He began raising the poker again.

'What are you going to do with her? Will you both live here? Happily ever after, is that it? How's that's going to work?'

'You ask too many questions. That's what you do. Now, take another drink, a good long one this time. Go on, I've wasted enough time on you.' Using the poker, he nudged the bottle closer to Beck. 'Go on. Or you'll feel this again.'

Beck reached for the bottle, but hesitated, his hand hovering over the neck. Kavanagh moved so quickly he had no time to react. The poker sliced through the air and struck his shoulder. Beck felt something give, and squealed in pain.

'Aaaagghh!' He grasped his shoulder but the pain was too intense, so he released it again. 'You bastard, Kavanagh. You absolute bastard.'

'Tut tut,' Kavanagh said. 'Take a handful of those pills as well. You'll soon feel nothing. Go on. Now!' He banged the poker down onto the table.

Beck grabbed the bottle and drank.

'Now,' Kavanagh said. 'The tablets. Take some of those too.'

Beck shook some tablets from the container with one hand and began popping them into his mouth.

'Now, more liquor. Take more. Come on. Come on.'

'Josef Fritzl, ever hear of him?' Beck said. 'Kept his own daughter as a sex slave, in the basement of his house. For years. She had seven children by him. Something like that you have in mind here?'

'Drink that feckin' bottle down. And those pills. NOW!'

'Okay, Tommy. Okay. One question: how you going to get away with this? Just curious. If I'm going to die, why not tell me?'

'Come on. Come on. Drink up. I'll tell you as you go.'

Beck began to drink again.

'You walked out here, didn't you?' Kavanagh said. 'You're an alkie. A lush. Call it what you will. You've been hitting it hard lately, that's what I heard. You would have been seen walking the road. Had to be. You fell. In the snow. That little wound to your head there. And your shoulder. That's how you got those. They'll find your body in a ditch, or maybe a bog hole, whichever is the easiest for me. Who wouldn't believe it? Who? They've believed everything else up to now, haven't they? Death by misadventure, that's what they'll call it.'

'Oh yes,' Beck said, the whiskey dulling his senses now, making him woozy, slurring his words. 'That's exactly what they'll call it.'

'You're doing nicely there,' Kavanagh said, tapping the poker on the shoulder he had just struck.

Beck winced.

'Keep it going,' Kavanagh said. 'Keep it going. And here, a few more of these...'

Beck felt stubby fingers pulling back a corner of his mouth, pushing in more tablets. He took another long swallow from the bottle — it was two-thirds empty now — and washed the tablets down.

'Drink all of it,' Kavanagh demanded. 'All of it.'

Beck laughed suddenly, a high-pitched rolling drunken sound. 'Drink. Feck.'

He raised the bottle to his lips. He knew what awaited him now – oblivion and death. He hesitated.

Kavanagh seemed to sense what he was thinking. He struck him again, on his forehead now, pressing the poker into the wound caused by the first blow. Beck screamed in pain.

'Drink.'

Beck raised the bottle. There was no going back now.

CHAPTER FIFTY-FOUR

Death, a vast empty expanse of nothingness – no dreams, no memories, nothing. An eternity. On and on. Infinity. Beck floated. If this was death, he liked it. Yes, he liked it very much. Way off in the distance, he could see it, a flicker of white light. It excited him. Because he knew what it was. It was the light he'd heard so much about, that he didn't believe existed. But now he knew it did. For there it was. The white light, guiding him home. *I am home, Lord. I am home.* It started to glow brighter, stronger, larger, dissolving the black universe about it as he drew nearer. Nearer to heaven. He truly could feel the power of the Creator now. Yes indeed, he could feel the power. He was crossing over from this life to the next. And then he felt it, the hand of God upon him, strangely on his eyelid, pulling it up, and His voice, from way off. It sounded strangely effeminate…

'Beck. Beck. Come on, Beck. Open your bloody eyes.'

'I am home, Lord' he slurred. 'I am home.'

'Beck!'

The light retreated, dimmed, compacting into a floating orb.

'Beck!' The voice again. 'Beck!'

And he was staring into the face of God, and he realised it looked vaguely familiar. He heard the voice again. But it was different this time. It was his own.

'Claire? Is that you?'

'Of course it's me.'

He turned his head. What appeared to be black spindly outlines were all around. He could see they were the branches of bushes. He looked down. His head appeared to be floating above the ground, and his arms were spread on either side of it.

He moaned. He was dreaming. Had to be. But just then he felt a searing pain in his left shoulder, another, less intense, across his head, and knew this was not a dream. No, this was real. Something began to push up from the back of his throat, unstoppable, and he began to retch once, twice, and started to vomit.

'No, Beck. You'll choke. Hold it. Get out of there first. Stop. Do not vomit. You could die... seriously. You've already been sick, I can see it dried around your collar.'

Out of there? Out of where?

He swallowed, pushing the contents of his belly back down. His nose stung, bile seeping out. And then he felt the stab of pain again, from his shoulder, and everything came back to him.

He looked down as a shape moved by, paused, turned, a long black face now above his, looking down. Max.

Beck swallowed again and gulped in air.

'He found you.' The voice of Claire, behind him, her hands going under his shoulders, and before he could say anything she began tugging. 'You're in a hole, a bog hole in the marsh. In time, it'll just suck you in.'

The pain tore through him. He dug his teeth into his lips. It was all he could do to stop himself from screaming. A tremor shimmered from his stomach up into his mouth, an acidy bile clawing at the back of his throat. He swallowed again, but he could not hold it much longer. He felt the pain as Claire pulled again, and he used his feet to push himself, his boots sodden and heavy, and dug and clawed at the ground with his fingers, raising himself a couple of inches – enough to allow him to use his good elbow as an anchor to lever himself up that little bit more. He did not stop, not once, because if he did he knew the pain would consume him and he would slide down again, and so he continued, the pain a white-hot cauldron that he knew he had no choice but to push through. He splayed his feet and hands, Claire pulling from behind, and slowly he managed to pull his upper body free, before collapsing forward, waiting for his pulse to settle before beginning again, the pain in his shoulder a numbing, ceaseless agony. And then he felt it, his chest contracting, once, twice… He just had time to prop himself up and turn his head as a geyser of vomit erupted from his mouth. He vomited for a long time, convulsions that racked his body until there was nothing left but yellow bile.

'There must be twenty in there,' Claire said.

He was panting, thirsty, weak.

'Feck it,' he called. In one swift movement, he grabbed his shoulder, pushed with all his might against it, the pain erupting to new levels until *CLICK!* And then he lay there panting, the pain hollowed out, intense, but bearable now.

'Twenty what?' he mumbled.

'Pills,' she said. 'Thankfully mostly not dissolved.'

He ran a hand over his clothes, wet and slimy, grabbed at a thick branch in front of him and hauled himself the final few feet from the bog hole. He felt something next to him, warm, soft. He touched it. It was Max, who began licking his hand.

'How did he get here?'

'I went to your house. After I got your text. Just in case. I let myself in. I had a feeling it would do no harm to take him with me. He found you. Led me straight here. I thought he was just coming back to his old house. But it was you he was looking for. What about those pills?'

Beck patted the dog. 'Kavanagh gave them to me. Along with a bottle of whiskey. I should be dead. How long have I been out? Where the hell am I anyway?'

'It's almost dawn.'

Hours then, Beck thought. He factored in that what had helped him were his tolerance levels built up over the last couple of days.

'We're behind the road, near Mullaney's,' Claire said. 'Aren't you drunk? Cold?'

'I suppose I am drunk. I don't feel it though.'

'You could be hypothermic. Don't you feel the cold? We need to get out of here.'

Beck sat up. 'You ring this in?'

'Yes.'

'And… where are they?'

'That night sergeant, from Ballinasloe, the one who's standing in – what's his name? Cahill. He said he met you the other night, said you were probably sleeping it off somewhere, to do nothing about it until morning. That you'd be home by then.'

Beck got to his feet, slowly. He was unsteady.

'We'll stop at the station on the way back,' Claire said.

'He has a girl. Britney. No. It's down to us.'

'No. I'll call it in. They can't ignore it now. We wait.'

But Beck was already walking away.

'Come on,' he said over his shoulder. 'Turn on that torch.'

'What about the dog?' She put the phone to her ear.

Beck stopped. 'Bring him.'

'He'll bark.'

'He won't. He's a sheepdog. Believe me, he knows.'

CHAPTER FIFTY-FIVE

It was 6.10 a.m. The house was in darkness, completely still. They paused where Beck had paused the night before, in the bushes along the edge by the cobblestones. A trail of pain pressed in from his shoulder and up into his head above the eyebrows. He did his best to ignore it. He ignored too the fatigue clawing through him, and his stiff damp clothes. He had to continue.

'I need to get into that house.'

Claire said nothing.

'Claire?'

'No. We wait. Listen to me. We wait.'

Beck took a step forward. 'Don't you see?' he whispered. 'It might already be too late. No. I can't wait. I can't.'

He strained his eyes against the darkness. He could discern shapes and outlines against the white of the snow. Claire muttered something behind him, and he heard the word 'procedure' repeated again. But as he made his way forward, she followed. He led the way round to the back of the house, pressed his face against the window. The curtains were still not drawn. All lights were off. He held a finger in the air, indicating for Claire to not make a sound. He listened. He had the feeling that Kavanagh was no longer here, but at the same time not far off. Hearing nothing, he went to the door, tried the handle: locked.

'The torch,' he said. 'Give it to me.'

Claire handed it to him. 'You're not going to turn it on, are you?'

He rolled up the bottom half of his jacket, leant towards the door and pressed the fabric against one of the small glass panels in it. He took the end of the torch and tapped it against the glass through his coat, once, twice, until there was a plopping sound, followed by the tinkling of the broken glass falling onto the floor inside.

Beck dropped his chin onto his chest. He felt dizzy again. A stab of pain went from his shoulder into his head. He took a deep breath, swallowing down some more bile. He used the sleeve of his jacket to knock out the remaining shards of glass, placed his hand in, fumbling about until he located the door latch, then opened the door.

'Claire. Please. Forget bloody procedure.' He stepped into the house. 'Move lightly. And keep your voice down.'

'He's in here?' she asked.

'I don't know,' Beck said.

His eyes, adjusted to the darkness, picked out the items of furniture ahead of him as he moved. He went straight to the cupboard and pulled open the door. Everything had been removed – there were no shelves, crockery, nothing was in here. He stared into the darkness, his eyes shifting from top to bottom. He bent down, felt along the floor, unsure of what he was looking for. There was a narrow space along the edge at the bottom of the cupboard, enough for him to place an index finger into. He pulled, and the floor shifted. Using his finger as a hook, he began to hoist.

'Give me a hand.'

Claire knelt down and together they lifted it out. It was a square of plywood. They stood back. In the near darkness it was just about possible to see a sliver, a perfect rectangular shape in the floor of the cupboard, a light seeping through from underneath. Beck bent down again, ran his hand over the surface of the floor. In the centre was something cold, metal: a handle, lying flat within a groove in the wood. The plywood had been placed on top to conceal this light, Beck guessed. He lifted the handle and pulled gently, just enough to see if what he suspected was a trapdoor would open. It did. He put the trapdoor down again, went onto his knees and pressed his ear against the wood: silence.

Claire beckoned to him. She began walking towards the open door, went outside and turned, beckoning again, frantically this time: *Come here. Now!*

Beck stood and followed.

'That's enough,' she said when he reached her. 'We withdraw and wait. Procedure. Yes, call it what you will. We don't know what's down there, Beck. Be realistic.'

'I have a good idea what's down there.' He turned to go back. 'I've wasted enough time already.'

'Beck.'

'Keep your bloody voice down. Go back if you want. And get some help.'

He walked towards the house. At the threshold of the door he hesitated. Of course, Claire was right. He shouldn't go in. He wasn't well enough for a start. His judgement was impaired to say the least. He knew he was dehydrated, probably needed stitches in his head, and his shoulder... Well, he didn't know about that. It had most likely been dislocated, which he'd fixed, probably. He knew all this. Beck took a breath, and stepped in anyway. He crossed the room to the cupboard, stopped, listening, before bending down and gripping the trapdoor handle. He knew once he lifted it, there would be no going back. He lifted it.

No going back.

The space ran between two walls of crude wood panelling at the bottom of one half of a metal stepladder strapped to the wall by lengths of rope. The space was just high and wide enough for Beck to stand in unimpeded. He could see nails protruding from the wood and bent flat into it. A single light bulb hung from the ceiling, casting a dull glow. Beck took a step and the floor creaked, the noise unusually loud in the confined space. He held his breath, and continued. At the end of the space, or corridor, were flickering curls of yellow coming from what seemed to be a doorway. There was a scent in the air, a pleasant scent, of lavender maybe, and a surprising warmth too for a place that appeared naturally inclined to be nothing other than cold and dank.

He walked along the creaking floorboards as quickly and softly as he could. But Beck knew there was a recklessness to his movements, fuelled by a rage – a rage from his past, towards himself, but mostly now towards Tommy Kavanagh. When he came to the wavering light at the end he stopped, waiting, listening, then took a step forward, into the flickering curls of yellow, and looked. He stared at the wall opposite, a rough wall of brown earth, covered – or held back – by welded mesh. The other walls were of wood. As he entered, he saw his shadow join those already dancing on the walls, darting shadows, moving up and down. He looked about at the dozens of glow-worms that were the candles spread all around this space. There was a fire too, a small open fire set in a hearth in a metal surround built into a wooden wall.

There were no windows, and in the dim room he could just about make out a bed and a table, a washbasin and towel. The open door was sturdy, of thick wood with a big, old-fashioned key in the heavy metal lock.

Before Beck turned, in the shifting light, he took in the items hanging on the walls: necklaces, rings, bracelets and a couple of women's watches, a brooch and a hat pin... He froze. There were also photographs. Beck took a step closer. Four photographs in all, pinned to the wall. One he recognised: Mimi Tuffy. He quickly discerned a pattern. Each group of items was separated from the other and had a photograph above. It had to be that the items belonged to the person in each photograph. Why else would they be arranged in this way? And he knew, just *knew,* each woman was dead, and this was their memorial.

A movement caught his eye, and he saw her, huddled at the head of the bed, her outline almost indistinguishable from the shadows. It was the girl, Britney.

She stared at him, and beyond him. Beck moved down by the side of the bed towards her and, at the end, against the wall, turned. He knew Kavanagh was there, so was not surprised. But he was surprised he no longer had the poker. Instead, he had a large, black handgun.

'Mementos,' Kavanagh said, flicking the barrel towards the wall. 'Reminders, if you like. Of the others. It's important to have reminders, don't you think? No matter. You've made me very angry now. Are you alone? How did you get out of that hole? Come on, tell me quickly. I should have killed you properly before I put you in there.'

He looked Beck over, and in the flickering light Beck thought the scene reminiscent of a horror movie.

Beck glanced to the side, saw the girl raise her eyes and look at him.

'I came back for her,' he said. 'You see, I know what it's like. To be alone, at someone else's mercy.'

'Call me old-fashioned,' Kavanagh said, 'but I'm the man of this house – let's get that clear first. Do you understand? Do you? Look at me.'

Beck looked into Kavanagh's eyes. He was quite mad. No doubt.

'Yes, yes, a man must be master of his home. His household. It's when his authority is questioned, and then, ultimately of course, is disregarded, that inevitably, the system breaks down. I won't allow this to happen. Do you understand me? You will not question me. Ever again. Not once. You will do exactly as I say. You will do it without question.'

Beck realised now he was no longer talking to him. He was looking towards the girl, Britney. She nodded, glanced at Beck, then back to Kavanagh.

'Don't look at him!' Kavanagh roared. 'You are mine now. My wife. You will never look at another man again. You are mine! You hear?' And his voice just as quickly softened. 'Now, take off your clothes.' Then, he pointed the handgun at Beck. 'If you look at my wife while she undresses, I will kill you.' He gave a high-pitched laugh, utterly insane. 'It is the custom, in the bedroom, the husband must be the first to see the body of his wife before she can see it herself in the reflection of a mirror. If he does not, then she will be unfaithful. So I must see her first, before she sees herself.' He looked at Beck. 'And not you! You have come between a man and wife. This is our wedding night, and you are here in our bedroom, keeping me from my wife.' He looked to Britney, his eyes lingering. 'Good.' he said, as if to himself. 'You will wait for me.' And to Beck, his voice a low, deep, rumble: 'Get out.'

Kavanagh stood to the side and nodded towards the doorway. Beck knew if he was to have a chance of overpowering Kavanagh, it would be as he passed him now. But Kavanagh stepped back, well back, and pointed the handgun. Beck could hear the loud click of the hammer being pulled back. He did not move, because he knew this was probably his only opportunity to find out. Beck was desperate to know, too stubborn a cop to let it go, but also because he knew what it was like *not* to know, as he had not known what had happened to his father. And so, if Beck took it to his grave, which seemed likely, he had to ask...

'Who are they? The girls on the wall. Not that it makes a difference now, because I'll soon be joining them, so you can tell me, can't you?'

There was a long pause, then Kavanagh's face contorted in a twisted smile. 'I'm smart,' he said, his voice changing in pitch, like a general talking of his victories on the battlefield. 'Smarter than you are, of course, and you seem to be the best of all the dimwits, but that's not saying much. And if you doubt me, the proof is in the pudding: you're where you are, and I'm where I am. You know about Mimi Tuffy, so I won't waste my time on it...'

'Won't you? Because I don't know. Tell me...'

Kavanagh's eyes narrowed, and his lips raised in a half-smile. Suddenly, he began to cry. 'I loved her. I couldn't let anyone else have her, you see. I loved her *so* much, it still hurts. I built this for her, this basement. It could have worked out, it could have been beautiful... Aw, Mimi, why didn't you love me back? None of this would have happened.'

Kavanagh stepped forward. 'I'll tell you,' he said, and Beck felt an urge to pounce, to take a chance, but he knew Kavanagh's finger could press the trigger much faster, so he waited, and Kavanagh began to speak.

'The second girl, after Mimi, was Dolores Keating, the old vet Tom Rice's secretary. You won't have heard of him, that's years ago now. Stuck-up bitch, I can still see her looking down her nose at me while I was standing in my wellington boots with my coat tied together by a piece of twine. He was knocking her off, you know, Rice, the randy old goat. Twelve children he had with his wife, but that wasn't enough, oh no. He was riding every women who'd let him. And plenty did. He couldn't get enough of them. And there was me, I couldn't even get one. And she had the cheek to look down her nose at *me*!

'So I waited one evening. I didn't know what I was going to do, only that I was going to do something. It was easier than I expected. I couldn't believe it. I bundled her into the back of my auld Anglia van. I didn't even tie her up, just had the doors open and pretended I was taking something out, and when she was passing – like clockwork, six o'clock every evening she left that office – I just pushed her, and in she went. Jeez, it was that easy.

'I kept her for weeks, I did, but they were searching for her, so I had to finish her off. I buried her body and threw her stuff off the cliffs. Her clothing was found washed up on the rocks days later. They ruled that she fell from the path while out for a walk, even though they never found a body, of course. She was always walking, that one. Still, I was surprised no one asked questions. I didn't intend for it to continue after that. So I went quiet, for a couple of years. But you know, I missed it. And I could feel it, you know, building in me, slowly, slowly, slowly, the pressure, always building and building, like a steam engine until I was about to blow. I had to do it again, had no choice really. But I resisted for as long as I could. I prayed to be delivered from this... maelstrom. I know that word, see, I *am* smart.

'I spoke to my sister, Agnes, told her I had great confusion in my life – didn't tell her what, exactly – and what she said I took as a sign. She said if my intentions were good, then nothing else mattered, that sometimes those with the best intentions were often the least understood. That was enough, that changed everything, because my intentions *were* good. And I knew then, in a way, I had been given dispensation. This was the Lord's work. And wh—'

'But,' Beck interrupted. 'What of Mimi Tuffy? Tell me, please.'

'You know what happened to her!' Kavanagh roared. 'She's underneath the cart wheel. Why must you goad me? Why...?' He raised the handgun, advanced on Beck. Beck stiffened, ready for the blow. But it never came.

Kavanagh stopped.

'The other two,' he said, with a slight nod of the head, that same tone back again, a general gloating about his victories. 'Tracy King and Larissa Nugent. They *thought* they were smart. Prick teasers, the both of them, short skirts and bleached-blonde hair... unless you were a certain type of man, of course. If you were one of the bigwigs, then it was a different story. They'd drop their knickers then alright. But for the likes of me, jeez, your tongue would be hanging out at the sight of them two. I knew what they were at, like bait in their get-ups, bright and shiny, to catch the big fish... I used to see them outside the Lilac, that big old building out the Ballinasloe road there, with the roof falling in on it. One of the best dance halls in the country it was in its day, till it closed in 1974. Every Saturday night, the only place to be… I was outside one night after the dance – Rick Speer had been playing, one of the biggest showband stars at the time – looking at the couples heading up the side of it to where there were no lights and they could go courting. And jasus I wanted to be one of them, but I wasn't. And then I saw them, Tracy King and Larissa Nugent, linking each other, giggling, heading for the busway at the end of the car park. Those two weren't courting anyone, they were biding their time, waiting to land the big fish… I didn't have to throw them in the back of the van, they practically ran after me all the way to it.

'You know how I did it? I went down and stood by the bushes where no one could see me. You could go through them bushes to the road outside, where my van was parked. The car park was often full so we'd have to park outside. Pitch dark it was out there. I gave them a bit of a fright, because they didn't see me. No one could see me where I was standing. I tried to have a bit of banter with them, but they were having none of it, were walking on past until I said that Rick Speer was my first cousin and said that he'd be calling to my house on his way back to Dublin for a cup of tea. Made up the whole spiel as I went along, about how he was my Aunt Maud's son, how I often went up to see him in his big house in Dublin with the gold taps, where I would meet all the other great showband stars of the day. I could see their eyes lighting up, but then I thought I'd better shut me mouth because I didn't know who Speer's mother was, but they might.

'Ah, like moths to the flame they were, moths to the flame, never even questioned that I might be lying. No one lied back then, especially in a small town. It was a sin, you'd have to tell the priest in confession. Good Catholics we were, never told lies.

But I did. Of course, I would have preferred not to have taken the two of them, thought that might be a bit of a handful, but I knew they wouldn't come with me if they were on their own, that would be way too much to expect. But together... oh, they came along alright, practically skipped their way into me van. And you know what? The two of them together was easier than I thought. They had each other, see, so one comforted the other, and they began to plot after a couple of days, about how to escape, because I could hear everything, see? I used to stand outside and listen. I'd say things like "I'm awful sorry for what I've done, I'll go to hell for this, I'll let you go tomorrow if you promise not to say anything about this and to be nice to me this one last time." I strung them along like that for a couple of weeks. And those bitches, well... It couldn't end well, could it?'

Kavanagh shook his head. 'I thought I'd gone too far though. Dolores Keating was one thing, but how was I going to get out of this, two girls now gone...' He pointed the handgun, flicked the barrel towards the doorway. 'But I don't want to talk any more. Move.'

Beck remained motionless. 'Tell me. I'm not moving.'

Kavanagh observed, said nothing for a moment, as if debating, then shrugged. 'Makes no difference now,' he said. 'I did nothing, that's what.'

'Nothing?'

'You heard me. Their disappearance became a mystery. You hear about this sort of thing all the time, people disappearing off the face of the earth. It was easier back then, because there was no CCTV, there was nothing. But people have forgotten about it, they always do. Bet you never heard of it, did you?'

'What did you do with them?' Beck ignored Kavanagh's question.

'What did I do with them, you ask.' Kavanagh gave another twisted smile. 'Well, wouldn't you like to know? I can't give away all me secrets, now can I? Where's the power in that? Eh? Now MOVE! I won't tell you a second time.'

'Okay. Okay. One more question, was there anybody else? Was there?'

Kavanagh gave Beck a long, hard stare, the kind of stare that told Beck he was wondering if it wasn't time to get this over with. Right now. Beck glanced at Kavanagh's finger – it was still resting on the trigger guard.

'You policemen are nosey bastards, aren't you? I tried a couple of times to do it again, but sloppy, half-hearted attempts. There were a couple of times when I almost pulled it off. One girl was hitch-hiking, but she didn't like the look of me and wouldn't get in the car; another I tried to grab off the street one night but she kicked me in the balls and ran off... Anyway, I didn't really care. Because I had the memories. That's what was real, that's what mattered, especially of Mimi. All I had to do was play them over and over again in my head. You see, everything lived on' – he tapped a finger to his head – 'in here.' His eyes became distant. 'Until Britney, that is. Isn't she the most beautiful creature you have ever seen? And now she's mine. All mine. And Eddie wanted to take her away from me. Well...' His voice softened. 'I couldn't let that happen, now could I?' There was a silence, and then he shouted, 'Move! Do not say another word. Move! Now! This is way past closing time.'

Beck did as he was told now. He walked across the room and passed into the narrow space outside. Kavanagh pushed him towards the stepladder. Beck felt a sudden pain in his back and realised that Kavanagh had shoved the tip of the barrel into it.

'Up,' he growled. Beck climbed, slowly, awkwardly, knowing it was impossible to do anything else.

Beck had a feeling, clung to it, that when he re-emerged, blue beacons and headlights would be illuminating the house, voices would sound, calling for Kavanagh to surrender, telling him that the house was surrounded. Like in the movies. But there was nothing. It was as dark and silent as before. Beck knew for certain: he was alone.

As Kavanagh followed him up into the room, he turned on the light, and Beck squinted against the sensory onslaught. He felt the barrel of the gun on his back again. He saw Kavanagh scoop out a plastic bag from a bunch hanging from a hook on the door. He put it into a pocket. There was only one reason Beck could think of why he would want that.

'Walk,' Kavanagh said. 'Out. Straight ahead.'

Beck didn't move.

The gun slammed into him, and Beck arched his back, the pain slicing through him. Kavanagh pushed Beck through the doorway. The snow and grass made a brushing, crinkling sound against his boots, and there was a dullness in his shoulder, as if the limb was missing. The pain in his back was receding, and he could feel his heart cantering in his chest, and there was lightness to his head. He thought he might pass out. But he followed Kavanagh's instructions, walking along secret pathways through dense shrubbery, by the edge of a field through moss and reeds where footprints would not be retained. Kavanagh, he had no doubt, was of this landscape – every craggy inch of it was known intimately to him. He had the intelligence of a predator, the cunning of a fox. No wonder he had never been apprehended.

As they rounded a thicket of bushes, Beck knew what Kavanagh had in mind. They were returning to the same bog hole, which Kavanagh would put him into again, then place the plastic bag over his head, and suffocate him. When Beck was dead, he would remove it, stuff his mouth full of muck and soil. Death by misadventure. There was no doubt.

'This isn't going to work, Tommy,' Beck said, because he could think of nothing else.

'Oh, *Tommy*, is it? Cosy chat, like. *Tommy*, indeed. Keep walking. We're almost there.'

'There was someone with me, I think you should know that. My partner, Detective Garda Somers. She knows. They'll find the basement, Tommy. It won't be long until they get here. You won't get away with it. Can't get away with it. Give it up now, Tommy.'

There was a cackling sound. The old man was laughing.

'Ah, you would say that, wouldn't you? Hurry on there so, and I'll go back and clean the place up before they get here. Get rid of the evidence, like. Thank you for the – what do they call it? Heads-up, that's the saying, isn't it?'

'You won't have enough time.'

'Stop talking. Move! Or I'll finish you here.'

But they were almost there. Beck recognised the spindly branches, and he could make it out now, the black circle in the snow that was the hole he had frantically crawled out of earlier. He felt it, his panic beginning to rise.

Christ, he really was alone.

He stopped, and turned, facing Kavanagh, took a step towards him. He knew he didn't have a chance, but also that he had to do something, no matter how futile. His strength was almost gone, his body weak, buffeted by too many storms. What he was really trying to do, he knew, was hang onto his dignity. He thought of his Uncle Paddy, a Lancaster rear-gunner flying nightly raids over the German industrial heartland during the Second World War. He could hear his voice now, as if he were standing beside him. *We all have to die. There's no way out. So when it's your turn, for God's sake, make sure you die with dignity.*

'Fuck you, Kavanagh,' Beck spat. 'Fuck you.'

Kavanagh did nothing, not until Beck had taken another step and was almost upon him. With that surprising speed of his that far belied his years, his free hand shot out and Beck felt it on his chest like a sledgehammer, sending him reeling backwards. He landed on his arse, right next to the bog hole. He hadn't the strength to get back up again.

'Shimmy a little to the left, Mr Hero, and you're almost there. I'm going to wait right here and make sure that bog hole gobbles you up. A few inches, and down you go. MOVE!'

Beck could see the new day beginning to press through the darkness, dawn arriving. Kavanagh stepped forward, behind Beck. Beck braced himself for a push, a kick to his back. It had to come.

In the bushes ahead of him was a gap, highlighted in the grey light of the new day. And from it darted a shadow, an outline, taking to the air, a long graceful flowing movement, and then down to earth again, low and sleek, but only for a fraction of a second, before it rose up again. Beck could feel the cold wash of air on his skin as it darted by his face. It did not make a sound. Beck turned, just in time to see Kavanagh raise the handgun and pull the trigger, the blast shaking the air, a sound so loud it was out of all proportion for the small handgun that had made it. But Kavanagh was not trained in the use of handguns and had not made allowances for trajectory or the speed of his target. Even if he had been trained, he probably would not have had time anyway. Because Max was moving so quickly, and when he let off the shot, it was already too late.

Kavanagh roared as Max clamped his jaws onto his lower leg, sharp incisors and canines tearing and ripping through his flesh, and staying there.

Tommy Kavanagh howled, bringing up his other leg, and just as he was about to kick the dog… *Clop!* And again, *clop, clop, clop.*

Beck had not noticed, preoccupied as he was by watching Max attack, but Claire had come up behind Kavanagh, began striking him with her baton – *clop, clop, clop* – disregarding procedure in the use of reasonable force. She had given in to what the sergeant's exam test booklet had warned her against: emotion and adrenalin.

She stood above Kavanagh, panting, the baton held ready to strike again if needed. Max finally released his leg, but did not move, his hackles up, lips curled over his teeth, baying.

Beck plopped onto his back, staring at the sky.

In the distance, they could hear the sound of sirens. Beck thought: *About bloody time.*

CHAPTER FIFTY-SIX

It was later that evening. Beck sat on the sofa in his cold living room. On the table next to him was a bottle of Spanish brandy.

But he hesitated.

In the aftermath of all that had happened, he did not experience the normal sense of anticlimax. Apart from a dull throb to his shoulder and also his head, he felt nothing. Nothing at all. And that was the problem. He had not come down.

At the hospital they had closed his head wound with fifteen stitches, hooked him to a vitamin and saline drip. A couple of hours later, he'd felt remarkably better. And now, here he was, alone, in the silence of this house. He had spoken to his sister in Australia, who had sounded restless, harried. The combination of motherhood, a full-time career and family life. It could do that. But he also knew that was not the reason. Because she had also sounded... scared.

It was the time of year. Because he knew for her it was the same, and neither knew how to speak about it. And so they didn't, they acted as normal, when all was not. It was never mentioned, the calamity, that had afflicted both of them, and still did. Never discussed. Not once. Ever a festering wound. But he'd decided to change all that. He'd said, 'I can still see him. On the ground, blood all about his head. She had the key to the door in her hand.'

There was silence on the line, an empty vacuum that stretched all the way to Australia, and all the way back in time, to that day.

'It was her,' Helen said. 'She pushed him.'

Beck felt as if he had been stung. Not by what Helen said, but that she had said it at all. It was a curious feeling to have something voiced that had never been mentioned before.

'Did she tell you that?' he asked.

'No. I just know. A feeling.'

Beck was silent. 'Christ,' he said. 'She had the key in her hand. I saw it.'

'Finnegan, remember, it wasn't easy for her. They should never have gotten married them two, you know what he was like.'

'Yes. I know.'

'I've dealt with it, Finnegan. I've done a lot of work. On myself I mean. I've never told you this, but I've been in counselling for years because of this. It saved my life. Look, you won't want to hear this, but I'm going to say it anyway: there's no solution to be found for any of this in a bottle. You and alcohol, Finnegan, your struggle, it doesn't help.'

For a moment Beck felt it, a rage, a desperate need to deflect what she had said, to throw it back, have it find its target in her vulnerability: *Been on the weighing scales lately?* He opened his mouth, an anger stirring, but then, catching himself, said softly, 'I know.'

'Finnegan. I've got to go. But we need to talk more about this. Promise we will.'

'I promise. Goodbye, Helen.'

Since speaking with her, he had been sitting here, alone, in the living room, looking at the bottle. He reached for it now, determined, wrapped his hand around the neck, about to open it.

It was then he felt a sensation on his arm, and he turned. Max was leaning against him, on his hind legs, resting one paw on his arm. He hadn't heard him come in. The paw was pink beneath the claws, black fur with flashes of white on it. Max's face was inches from his, the look uncanny, all-seeing, an old soul.

Max made a sound. It was hardly audible to Beck, but it may have been an ultrasonic scream to Max. Beck squeezed his hand tighter around the neck of the bottle, about to turn the cap, and the sound from Max grew louder, his paw pressing harder into him now.

Beck replaced the bottle onto the table.

'It's okay, Max.' He stroked the dog. 'It's okay.'

Max jumped onto the sofa beside him, curling in against him, as if seeking protection from something and offering it at the same time. Beck could feel the warmth of the animal's body, the gentle regular pattern of his breathing against him. He closed his eyes, and like that, both of them, animal and man, fell asleep.

He awoke a little later, groggy, disorientated. Max opened his eyes and sat up, his head in front of Beck's. They looked at one another.

'Come on, Max, my legs are numb.' Beck shifted, and the dog jumped onto the floor.

Beck knew that sometimes the unconscious mind was more powerful than the conscious, and this offered an explanation as to why people routinely did things they'd never intended. So now, instead of picking the bottle up, Beck picked up his mobile phone. He had not consciously intended to. In any case, he scrolled through the numbers and found the one he wanted. It was answered almost immediately.

'Hello, Beck.'

'You said I could call, if I ever needed to talk. When we met in Frazzali's, remember?'

'I remember.'

Beck took a deep breath.

'Well, I need to talk.'

CHAPTER FIFTY-SEVEN

One Week Later

FROM: ci.egan@dublincastle.com: Chief Inspector Norman Egan, Head of Criminal Intelligence

TO: department.heads@dublincastle.com

SUBJECT: Private & Confidential

With immediate effect, in return for a supply of information on organised crime in the Galway region, Charles Bastic will be immune from criminal prosecution for all matters outstanding. Further immunity at discretion of C.I. Egan.

Major focused operation code named Operation Clean Streets to follow.

All department heads in receipt of this email to read and then delete, including the embedded file.

Information on illicit drug distribution in the Western Region has been provided.

Authorisation for forward notification to be referred to the Commissioner's office.

This initiative is under the direct command of Superintendent David Browne, Mill Street Galway.

CHAPTER FIFTY-EIGHT

Four Weeks Later

Her Honour, Judge Clementine O'Rourke, peered over her half-rim glasses from the bench at Galway Circuit Criminal Court to Tommy Kavanagh, sitting in the dock flanked by two burly prison officers. She was silent for a long time, which was unusual for her. But then again, this was an unusual case. Apart from a single cough and a rustle of robes, there were no other sounds in the courtroom.

The sunlight streaming through the large windows behind the judge's bench had been unusually intense, and the grey blinds had been pulled down, diffusing the light and creating an atmosphere of separateness from the world outside. Despite the policy of the court services to create a less intimidating environment with soft tones in wood and fittings, and judges and legal representatives no longer being required to wear wigs, the old stone building still oozed the intimidating power for which it was designed and built. Like many official buildings, it had been constructed in the 1800s – in 1815 – a grey stone Graeco-Roman structure with an imposing Doric portico.

Tommy Kavanagh was oblivious to it all. If he was intimidated, he wasn't showing it. He sat in the dock, staring ahead. If anything, he seemed bored.

'Will the defendant stand?' the judge said. She spoke with the authority of someone who brooked no defiance.

But Tommy Kavanagh did not move.

'The defendant will stand! Why isn't he standing? Get him to his feet.'

An officer nudged him.

'Stand!' the judge commanded.

Kavanagh looked at the judge and got to his feet in a slow, lazy movement. The judge held his gaze.

'You stand accused of the murder of your brother, Eddie Kavanagh, also your neighbour, Dermot Healy, so too Petri Duboitz and one Sergey Domi. Furthermore the kidnap and murder of Emily Tuffy, Dolores Keating, Tracy King and Larissa Nugent. You are also accused of the kidnap of one Liliya Abadzhiev who, along with Ivet Savov and the late Petri Duboitz, was believed to be a trafficked sex slave. You are also accused of the attempted murder of a police officer, and paying for the procurement of sexual services.

'I have read the various psychiatric reports on you, and I note the general consensus: highly intelligent, deviant, cunning and immoral, and without a shred of remorse... Quite interestingly, it says without any definable mental illness either. *Definable*. So there is no exoneration, merely no diagnosis.

'Now, what have you to say for yourself? Do you offer anything by way of explanation, or apology, for your vile deeds?'

A loud wailing suddenly sounded from the public gallery. Sister Agnes jumped to her feet, hands clasped before her, as if in prayer.

'Please, Tommy, pleeeease, for the love of God...'

Tommy turned his gaze towards his sister. For a moment he seemed to falter, his lips drooping, head falling just a little. But then he turned away, no longer smiling, or smirking, straight-backed, staring ahead, seemingly impervious to all around him. Sister Agnes looked down, and quietly resumed her seat.

The judge turned her gaze to Beck, sitting at the prosecution bench. He was wearing his dress uniform, freshly pressed, the leather and buckle of his Sam Browne belt both gleaming.

'On behalf of this court,' Judge O'Rourke said, 'let me pay tribute to the work of Detective Inspector Finnegan Beck, whose unwavering commitment and dogged determination ensured that Mr Thomas Kavanagh did not escape justice. Thank you, Inspector Beck, on behalf of all of us.' She turned her attention to the public gallery. 'What this case has also made apparent is that where complacency rules, crime is nurtured. Whilst murder and kidnap are its apex, we also see here how public apathy and indifference allowed a sordid prostitution ring centred on young, trafficked females – one of whom is now dead – to flourish. I ask you, in a small Irish town, how was this possible?'

People shifted in their seats, looking away.

'A dark chapter, a very dark chapter indeed, has finally been closed in the history of Cross Beg. Let us think for a moment of all the victims, and determine that they never be forgotten. And let us never forget the vile wickedness of the person who stands before us today and the boundless evil in his heart. But also this.' She returned her gaze to Kavanagh. 'The accused has refused to admit his guilt, and has refused to assist the authorities in identifying the whereabouts of the remains of his victims. This court has no doubt, secure in both the testimony of Inspector Beck and the evidence discovered in what I can only call that dungeon of horrors, that Thomas Kavanagh is solely responsible. I shudder to think of how his victims met their final ends. His refusal to co-operate is a cruel and heartless attempt at exercising control over this court and its proceedings, and so too, even now, over his victims.'

The judge turned to the prosecution desk. 'Inspector Beck, what of the two surviving victims? What has become of them?'

Beck stood, and cleared his throat. 'Your Honour. The girls are now in the care of officials from the Irish Refugee Protection Programme. Ivet Savov, who was found alive at Cedar Grove, had overdosed on an illegal substance, the circumstances of which remain unclear. However, she has made a full recovery and both women are now drug free. Both are being provided with proper social care and support and efforts are ongoing to contact their families.'

Beck fell silent. He wanted this information to resonate with the court. He wanted them to understand that these anonymous girls were real, and even though they were from the other side of the world and alien to them, they were of the same flesh and blood, with talents, hopes, dreams, which was why they had fled their homeland in the first place.

Judge O'Rourke did not speak for some time, by so doing adding her own resonance to his words.

'Thank you, Inspector,' she said then.

Beck sat down, and the judge looked to Kavanagh.

'The jury finds you guilty on all counts for the crimes for which you stand accused. On each you are hereby sentenced to life in prison without any possibility of parole. It is there you will spend the rest of your natural life, and where you will die.'

Kavanagh jumped to his feet. 'All I wanted was love,' he roared. 'If I had gotten what I sought, none of this would have happened. It's not my fault. It's the bitches. They didn't love me...'

'Take the prisoner away,' the judge shouted over him.

The two prison guards manhandled him from the dock, and it took all of their efforts. It was not until they had taken him through the doors at the bottom of the stairs by the dock that order was restored.

Kavanagh was gone.

CHAPTER FIFTY-NINE

One loop of the town. Completed in entirety that morning without stopping. It was evening now and Beck sat in his living room, Max curled on the floor by his feet. While the majority of the population had gorged over Christmas, Beck had led an ascetic existence, exercising, eating well and simply, cutting down on cigarettes. He felt healthy, detoxed.

Max whimpered and wagged his tail, dreaming. Beck smiled. In the short time he'd had him, Beck had come to love the old dog.

His phone rang. Since Beck had returned to AA meetings, Vicky had rung every evening.

But it wasn't Vicky.

Silence…

He listened, the phone pressed to his ear, trying to decipher sounds. But there were none. He was about to speak, but stopped. He knew it was Natalia. *Be honest with yourself,* he thought. He played this statement over in his mind. He thought of his father, who had never been honest with himself, and his mother, who was never honest with anybody. *Forget them, it's about you. YOU.*

He hung up, got to his feet. It was time to make the meeting.

EPILOGUE

The wooden bench had appeared literally overnight, bolted onto a bed of freshly laid concrete in a clearing to the side of the old Lilac Ballroom, close to a small lake with views of the mountains and hills off in the distance. The council wanted it removed, because they had not given permission, but because, too, of what they said were the negative connotations it held that some, tourists particularly, might find upsetting. But there was nothing they could do, because the land was private, even if exact ownership was proving difficult to establish. The reaction of the public, however, was universally favourable. They considered it a fitting memorial. Because a memorial it was. Fixed to the bench was a brass plaque listing the victims of Tommy Kavanagh, with the exception of Sergey Domi. At the bottom was a simple inscription: *Through death may they find peace. Please pray for them.*

Sister Agnes, with assistance from her Order, the Sisters of Mercy, had considered the bench the least she could do.

A LETTER FROM MICHAEL

Firstly, may I start, as I did last time, by saying a huge thank you to you, the reader, for choosing to invest your time in *Her Last Goodnight*. If you did enjoy it, and want to keep up to date with all my latest releases, just sign up at the following link. Your email address will never be shared and you can unsubscribe at any time.

www.bookouture.com/michael-scanlon

I began this book with a vague sense of the story I wanted to tell, so allowed myself to be led by it rather than the other way round. Modernity has made the world a much smaller place and technology has allowed people to interact with each other more than ever before – I know a lady in her eighties who is as adroit on her mobile phone and tablet as any savvy teenager, but she is the exception rather than the rule. Loneliness and isolation are very real issues for many people living in isolated areas of Ireland today. A long time ago I read a story about a person convicted of a murder which had occurred decades before. The person killed was thought to have disappeared. People assumed he had just upped and left. But a hole in a peat bog, or bog hole as it is called, eventually gave up its secret. This made me wonder if there were any other bodies out there, somewhere, undiscovered, of people who had just 'upped and left'. It's a chilling consideration and one used to form part of the plot in this book.

I hope you loved *Her Last Goodnight* and if you did I would be very grateful if you could write a review. I'd love to hear what you think, and it makes such a difference helping new readers to discover one of my books for the first time.

I would love to hear from you too, and I am on Twitter if you'd like to reach out! Also I now have a Facebook author page – quite a feat for a technophobe like me. Why not visit? You'll find me at @MichaelScanlonAuthor.

Many thanks,
Michael

@MScanlonAuthor

@MichaelScanlonAuthor

ACKNOWLEDGEMENTS

I would like to thank those closest to me: my wife, Eileen, and daughter, Sarah, also my good friends Andrew Maloney and Noreen Quinn. I would, once again, like to thank my wonderful editor, Isobel Akenhead, for all her hard work. I once asked her what her job entailed, and she replied that it was like being a set designer, except instead of working with props, she worked with words. When she gets a first draft from me, she sets about making it the best it possibly can be, moving things about, taking things away, suggesting additions, softening the lighting here, turning it up there. The end result is always infinitely better than what she first received. Also, a heartfelt thanks to copy editor Rachel Rowlands and proofreader Natasha Hodgson. As always I would like to acknowledge the entire Bookouture team, those savvy, techie people who have made the company such a success. And the bloggers and book reviews and the Bookouture author family. Thank you to all.

Printed in Great Britain
by Amazon